v-1,5

HOT SEAL
REDEMPTION

HOT SEAL Team - Book 5

LYNN RAYE HARRIS

The Hostile Operations Team® and Lynn Raye Harris® are trademarks of H.O.T. Publishing, LLC.

Printed in the United States of America

First Printing, 2018

For rights inquires, visit www.LynnRayeHarris.com

HOT SEAL Redemption
Copyright © 2018 by Lynn Raye Harris
Cover Design Copyright © 2018 Croco Designs

ISBN: 978-1-941002-33-9

Chapter 1

"I know you're in there, you rat bastard!" Bailey yelled, pounding on the door as she did so. She shot a glance at little Anastasia in her stroller—the baby was still asleep, though probably not for long. But Bailey needed to reach Alex Kamarov worse than she needed Ana to sleep, so she kept pounding.

Dirty bastard. Knocked Kayla up and left her to have the baby by herself. Not that Bailey had known the first thing about it since her sister had taken off around six months ago with only a brief note.

Going to California with Melanie. I'll call.

Kayla had not called, and Bailey had fretted the entire time. But postcards came every once in a while, and Kayla's Facebook page sported the occasional photo. Maybe Bailey should have been more worried, but she was used to Kayla taking off. Her sister would be gone for a few weeks or a few months, but she always came back again. Usually when the money ran out and she had nothing left.

But this time she'd returned with a surprise. A

bouncing-baby surprise. Bailey had opened the door just a week ago to Kayla and Ana. Kayla hadn't wanted to tell her at first who the father was, but Bailey insisted. After a couple of days of pushing, she got a name.

Alex Kamarov was a Navy SEAL Kayla had met while waitressing at Buddy's Bar & Grill. Bailey had only been in there a handful of times, mostly when Kayla was still working, and she knew the place was overrun with tall, muscled military types. They were also the type who often came to the Pink Palace and hooted the evening away. Bailey shuddered. To think one of them had touched her sister. Knocked her up and let her deal with it alone, damn him. It pissed Bailey off more than she could say.

Bailey had argued with Kayla about the baby, but for some reason Kayla wouldn't hear of asking Alex for money. Three days after her revelation, Kayla left again, this time leaving a note that said she didn't have time for a baby and didn't want to be a mother. She knew Bailey would know what to do with little Ana.

Yeah, Bailey knew what to do all right. After she'd gotten over Kayla's figurative roundhouse kick to the gut, which she still didn't understand because she'd have sworn Kayla adored the kid the way she'd fussed over her, Bailey had piled the baby into her old Volkswagen, praying the whole time that today wasn't the day it gave up the ghost for good, and puttered over to the house she'd found when she'd started searching for Alex Kamarov. She hoped he still lived here.

Ana made a noise and Bailey started to tap rather than pound. It had taken forever to get the kid to sleep, and Bailey didn't want to have to start over again.

"I know you're in there, you rat bastard," she

repeated as she tapped on the door repeatedly. "Answer the goddamn door!"

She lifted her hand to hit the door again, but it opened and she stumbled, colliding with a hard body. Bailey scrambled backward, trying to right herself without falling. The man—very tall, very broad, very sexy, with no shirt and a pair of boxers, not to mention a head of dark hair standing up as if he'd just gotten out of bed—squinted into the light.

Holy mother of—

"Are you Alex Kamarov?"

"Yeah. Why?"

His voice was gravelly with sleep, but it still managed to drip down her spine like honey. *No, stop. He's a bad man. A man who takes advantage of young women and leaves them high and dry.*

"Because you need to step up and stop shirking your responsibilities, that's why."

"Lady, I don't know who you are or what you're talking about."

Fury rolled through her. She reached for the stroller and turned it so he could see little Ana, who was thankfully still asleep.

"I'm talking about your baby, Alex. *Your baby.*"

His leaf-green eyes narrowed. She resolutely did *not* focus on the happy trail of dark hair leading down his abdomen and disappearing beneath the boxers. *Eyes, Bailey. Look at the eyes.*

They were pissed-off eyes. Sexy eyes.

"You expect me to believe that's my kid? I don't even know you, lady. You could be anybody, making shit up for reasons of your own."

Holy ab muscles, she wanted to punch him. What

kind of man knocked a woman up and didn't even care? "How dare you? I am *not* making this up. Anastasia is *yours.*"

She wasn't expecting the sudden grin that broke out on his face. It wasn't immediate, but when it happened, it was not at all what she'd thought it would be. She'd expected an explosion, not a response that intimated she'd just told him a great joke.

"Sorry, babe," he drawled, "but you're going to have to prove it."

Bailey stiffened. How could she make this man step up and do the right thing? There were tests, sure, but would he take one?

As if Ana sensed the turmoil in the air, she let out a wail. Panic flooded Bailey. She didn't know what to do when Ana cried. Hell, she barely understood the diapering process, and here she was, full-time caregiver. The kid was cute but overwhelming as hell.

Bailey picked the baby up and pressed a kiss to her forehead. Yeah, she was out of her depth, but it wasn't Ana's fault. "Hush, little angel. Hush. Auntie Bailey's got you. Shh."

Alex Kamarov suddenly held the door open. "Why don't you come inside until she stops crying?"

Uncertainty rushed through her, twisting her belly into a knot. He was big. So big... "I-I don't know..."

"Look, if I'm the father—and I'm not saying I am— you don't expect I won't ever want to see the kid, do you? Which means bringing her here to my house. So come inside and figure out what she wants."

"What she wants?"

"Diaper. Food." He cocked his head to the side. "You ever take care of a baby?"

She thought about lying, but she was too exhausted. Besides, what did it matter? "I'm learning."

He held out his hands. "Give her to me."

Bailey blinked, tightening her grip protectively. "You? What do you know?"

He arched an eyebrow, his arrogance palpable. "I'm the oldest of six. I know a thing or two. Now hand her over and come inside. Or stand out here and let her scream. Your choice, Bailey."

Her name. He'd said her name. She didn't like the way her heart fluttered or the way she wanted to obey his command. But if she didn't take this to the next step, how could she expect him to agree to any tests, much less accept responsibility? God knew she needed the help. She was barely getting by as it was. A little cooperation couldn't hurt.

Bailey handed him the baby, eyeing him warily. He took Ana with sure hands, tucked her into the crook of his arm, and started rocking her back and forth while singing a song… in a language that wasn't English.

He went through the door and Bailey rushed in behind him, her heart pounding as she imagined what might go wrong. What if he slammed the door on her and kept Ana? She couldn't let that happen. He turned to look at her.

"You have a bottle?"

"Uh, yes."

"Can I have it?"

She went back onto the porch and pushed the stroller inside. Then she grabbed the diaper bag Kayla had left her and took out one of the bottles with infant formula. Kayla had said she couldn't breastfeed because her milk didn't come in. She'd been so skinny that Bailey had believed her, though now she wondered if Kayla had simply been setting it up so she could leave. Because she sure hadn't hung around for long before disappearing.

Bailey handed Alex the bottle. He took it and gently inserted it into Ana's mouth. The baby latched on and ceased crying instantly. Bailey didn't like the shard of jealousy that stabbed into her. How many times had she tried to give Ana a bottle when she was crying and it didn't work?

Too many.

"How did you know?" she asked.

Alex Kamarov looked up from his contemplation of Ana and lifted an eyebrow. "Because her diaper wasn't wet or stinky, so that was choice number two."

"Choice number three?"

"Gas, probably. I'd have thought about that if the bottle didn't work."

Bailey rubbed her hands down her arms and took in her surroundings. It was a small house, but the furniture looked welcoming and the room was clean. It didn't look like a bachelor pad. In fact, it looked almost unlived in. Like a crash pad rather than a home.

She knew all about crash pads. Growing up, she and Kayla had been dragged by her parents from trailer park to trailer park until they finally landed in one so awful that nobody seemed to care if the rent was late. Bailey had sworn she was getting out of there as soon as possible. The minute she turned sixteen, she'd done it—and she'd taken twelve-year-old Kayla with her. Their mom was dead of a drug overdose by then, and their dad was so high he didn't care.

She walked around the room now, looking at her

surroundings but not touching anything. A wave of tiredness washed over her. She'd had long nights and longer days lately. She had to work tonight, but she still hadn't arranged any childcare. If she brought Ana to the club, the girls would love it but Deke would have a shit fit. He didn't permit the girls to bring children to the nightclub.

Especially not the kind of nightclub he ran. Bailey closed her eyes and told herself, the same as she had every day for the past few months, that it was temporary. Stripping earned more money than waitressing, and if she wanted to go to college and make a better life, she had to choose what would get her the most money the fastest.

Except that stripping wasn't as lucrative as she'd hoped. After rent and bills, her take-home was healthy but still not enough to cover tuition. Her goal now was to save as much as possible and take out loans for the rest. Hence the cheap car and the cheap apartment.

"Why don't you sit down, Bailey?" His voice was soothing, his words welcome.

She started to sink onto a couch and then stopped, stiffening. "I'm fine."

"You aren't fine." He cradled little Ana, who sucked her bottle and acted like a perfect angel. "You're dead on your feet."

"Babies do that to a person."

His grin was lethal. Arrowed right down into her toes and back up again, ricocheting off the neglected regions that hadn't seen any action in, oh, about a year now. Since she started at the Pink Palace. She didn't meet nice guys in her job. The ones she met turned her off so, yeah, that was that. She didn't know if she'd ever have a normal relationship again. She'd seen far too much of the dark side of men's behavior.

"Yep, sure can. So sit down. Tell me why you think this little girl is mine."

"You aren't supposed to be nice about it," she grumbled. But she sat. Leaned her head back on the chair. Closed her eyes for a second. Just a second, and then she'd open them again and tell him what Kayla had told her about their meeting and the night they spent together.

The sliver of jealousy she felt at the thought of this man stripping her sister naked was uncharacteristic. Really, it was just because she hadn't had sex in so long. That was it. Not because he was stunning. And even if he *was* stunning, he was still a prick for letting Kayla have Ana on her own. She couldn't forget that, even if his couch was soft and the room was warm…

"I'm not nice, Bailey," he said softly, his voice dripping down her spine. "But I'm not an asshole either."

"Prove it."

Chapter 2

Alexei didn't have to prove anything. And even if he wanted to, the point was moot. Bailey was asleep. She slumped to the side, a curtain of lavender hair sliding over her face and blocking it from his view.

Why the fuck he'd invited her inside was still not clear to him. Other than the fact the baby had been crying and she clearly didn't have a clue what to do. She'd been desperate and tired, and he'd been reminded of his mother in a way. Of the look she'd gotten on her face when the younger twins started to cry and the elder twins followed suit. He'd been the only help she'd had when his brother was still too young to participate, and he'd learned how to feed, diaper, and rock before he'd been old enough to grow hair on his chest.

Alexei frowned down at the baby in his arms. Her little eyelids fluttered as she sucked the bottle. She had a shock of dark hair, but she was still so young. Not much more than a few weeks old. It was hard to see features at that age.

Still, she wasn't his.

He didn't fuck without a condom (which he provided). And he didn't come inside a woman's body either. A woman would have to be awfully fucking fertile to have his baby since he wrapped up and pulled out before he came.

No, she definitely couldn't be his. But whoever the woman on his couch was, she thought he was the father of this kid. So who was the baby's mother, and why wasn't she here?

The baby finished the bottle, and Alexei found a towel so he could burp her. She spit up on his shoulder, predictably, and then he checked her diaper. Yep, she'd pissed herself. He rummaged through the bag and found a fresh diaper, changed the baby, and then rocked her to sleep. He tucked her into the stroller with her blanket and straightened, sighing.

Jesus, not what he'd expected to do this morning. He scrubbed a hand through his hair, yawned, and scratched his chest absently. The woman on his couch was out. Stone-cold out. He recognized the signs of someone who'd had more than she could take.

He went over and peered down at her, studying her. Her lavender hair still covered her face. She wore a fatigue jacket and jeans with sneakers. Nothing fancy, but somehow it was intriguing. He wanted to know what was under that jacket, though he'd gotten a peek at full breasts encased in a navy tank top.

She snored softly. Alexei frowned down at her. He should wake her and make her take the baby and get the fuck out, but he knew he wasn't going to do it. Instead, he reached for her—softly—and arranged her on the couch so she was lying down. She didn't even wake as he grabbed a blanket and spread it over her.

So he had a woman and a baby in his house, and he didn't know who either of them were. He looked at them both for a good long minute and then headed for the shower. He didn't spend much time, in case the baby woke, showering and toweling off in record time. Not hard to do considering he was a sniper and could spend days downrange not showering at all. Showers were a luxury, no matter if they were quick or leisurely.

Alexei finished dressing—jeans, a T-shirt, socks, hiking boots—and headed back to the living room. Bailey was still asleep on the couch. Ana was asleep in her stroller. Alexei sighed in relief, then frowned at himself for the response. What the hell? This woman and kid were in *his* house, infringing on *his* space, and he didn't really know who the hell they were. So why did he care?

The answer was that he didn't care. He was just being a decent human being. For now. It's what his mother would want him to do. He could be decent and helpful and still be rid of this woman by late afternoon.

He muttered a curse to himself—in Russian, of course, because that's all he'd spoken until he started watching American cartoons as a toddler—then headed for the kitchen and fixed coffee. While it brewed, he poured some cereal into a bowl, added milk, and ate it standing up while he waited for the coffee. When that was done, he poured a cup and drank it while watching the woman sleeping on his couch. She hadn't moved.

He went over to the diaper bag and rummaged through it more thoroughly, looking for identification. He found a small purse tucked into a pocket and took it out. Inside was her wallet, her car keys, and a tube of lipgloss. There were random business cards, and who knew what else, but he was mostly interested in the wallet. He opened it up and found a Tennessee driver's license. There was forty dollars in cash but no credit cards.

Bailey Jones.

SEX F, HGT 5'-08", EYES HZL.

According to her birth date, she was twenty-five years old. Her address was in Tennessee, so he doubted it was current. A quick check of the town on Google told him it was in the northeast corner of the state, near the borders with Virginia and Kentucky. He put everything back and tucked the purse into the diaper bag.

She jerked in her sleep. A second later, she pushed herself upright, panic written in every line of her body.

"It's okay," he said. "You're fine and the baby is fine. She's sleeping."

Bailey pushed lavender hair from her face and tucked it behind an ear. She had delicate features—a small nose with a slight upturn at the end, a pretty bow mouth that looked kissable and inviting, and smooth cheekbones. Her eyes were big and pretty, with long lashes and amber irises that were striking even while bloodshot.

"I fell asleep. I'm sorry."

"Coffee?" he asked, ignoring her comment.

"Uh, please."

He went and poured another cup. "What do you like in it?"

"Um, black with three sugars would be great. Thanks."

He heaped in the sugar, stirred, and took it back to her. She was smaller on his couch than she'd appeared when he'd opened the door. Probably because she'd been pissed, which had made her seem bigger. Plus he'd been slightly groggy and confused about the situation.

She took the cup in both hands and lifted it to her mouth. When she'd taken a sip, she sighed and fixed him with a wary look. "Thanks."

"You're welcome."

"You got her to sleep." She sounded amazed.

"Five siblings, all younger. Two sets of twins and a brother who's a year younger than me. I had a lot of practice."

She blinked for a second. "Two sets of twins? Oh my God, your poor mother."

He nodded. "Yep. Runs in the family. Both sides, apparently. Mom had her tubes tied after the second set."

Bailey's gaze dropped to his crotch. She jerked it back up again. Her cheeks were pink. "Then I guess I can be thankful my sister didn't have more than one baby."

He snorted, both at what she'd said and at how she was embarrassed to be caught looking. "I guess so. Though I am not this kid's father. That I can promise you."

She tilted her head and frowned. "Can you really? Never forgot the condom? Never ripped one? Never got one with a microscopic hole poked through it?"

Smartass, this girl.

"No, I never forget. Never ripped one either. As for the hole… Well, sure, there are women who might try that. But it wouldn't matter. I pull out."

"Before you pull out then. Pre-come. It happens."

Hearing her say anything to do with come sent a tickle of desire straight into his balls. He wasn't surprised at the reaction. He'd been downrange for weeks, so yeah, sex was on his mind. He'd been intending to head out tonight, call one of his hookups, take care of the itch with a long night of fucking. He didn't do relationships, and there were very few women who could accept that. But he'd found a couple who enjoyed the sex enough to put up with his lack of commitment.

"It happens," he said. "But it would take a super-sperm to get through, don't you think?"

"I don't know. Maybe. Or maybe you're making the whole thing up and you forgot the condom when you were with Kayla."

Kayla? He didn't recall any Kaylas in his life. Not that there couldn't have been any, but this one would have been within the past year and… No. No Kaylas.

"You think with multiple twins running in the family I'd take that kind of risk? Hell no." Because the last damned thing he wanted or needed was to father a bunch of kids right now. His life was *not* conducive to family and relationships. He wasn't sure it ever would be —or that he'd want it to be.

"All I know is what she told me. She said it was you. And that you made it clear beforehand that if there were consequences, you wouldn't do anything to help."

Anger rolled inside him. That was a dick thing to say, and he wouldn't have said it. Not that Bailey would believe him. "She's mistaken."

She lifted her chin. "You're going to have to prove it to me. I can't just take your word for it."

He knew where she was going with this thing. There was only one logical place *to* go. "You mean a paternity test, right?"

She nodded.

He thought about refusing her. But that wouldn't get her off his back. She'd plague him until he got called out on a mission again. And when he returned, she'd still be here.

He liked his peace and quiet too much for that. "Sure thing, sweet cakes. I've got nothing to hide."

Her eyes went flat. Her voice, when she spoke, was soft and hard at the same time. "Don't call me sweet cakes. Don't call me *any*thing but Bailey or Miss Jones."

Alexei studied her. She'd gone stiff and she looked angry. He wondered at her reaction, but then he told himself he didn't care enough to ask why. Probably one of those angry feminist types who hated when guys opened doors and tried to be nice like their mamas taught them. "If that's what you prefer. *Bailey*."

"Yes. Thank you." She took another sip of coffee. Fixed him with those amber eyes, which had softened slightly now that he'd agreed to call her Bailey. "You'll take a paternity test? Really?"

"Yes, really. But you're paying for it. If I'm the father, I'll pay. But not until then." No chance of that though.

The corners of her mouth tightened. "All right. Seems fair enough."

"So where are you planning to get this done?"

She frowned. "I don't know yet. I'll Google it."

Clearly she hadn't expected him to agree so easily. He picked up his phone and tapped on the browser. "I'll save you the time."

A quick check of the results told him there were any number of clinics in the local area as well as several over-the-counter options that you had to mail in. He turned the phone around and held it out. "Which one?"

If he wasn't mistaken, her cheeks started to grow red as she scanned the results. This chick was interesting. The oddest things embarrassed her. "How about a swab that we send in?"

"Fine with me." He wouldn't let her out of his sight until they'd dropped it in the mail. Not that he figured she could tamper with the test, but anything was possible. Besides, it was the nature of his business to be suspicious. "When do you want to get it?"

"Um, today?"

"Today's fine."

She looked confused. "You're being very understanding about this whole thing. Why?"

He decided not to tell her that he wanted to put the question to rest—and get her off his back and out of his hair. Instead, he went with an equally plausible reason.

"Because you seem like you're in a bad situation, Bailey Jones. And helping people is what I do. In a way."

BAILEY CLUTCHED the coffee mug in both hands and blinked at him. He had no idea how true that statement was. She had a roof over her head and money coming in—good money—but her livelihood depended on her job, and that was difficult with a baby. Not to mention she sucked at the whole baby thing. It took her hours to get Ana to sleep, and he'd done it so easily.

She was exhausted, which explained how she'd fallen asleep on a strange man's couch for an hour without waking. Hell, she was still tired, but she couldn't stay here. Didn't want to stay. She just wanted to get that paternity test, find out if Alex Kamarov was the father, and then—

Then what?

Bailey frowned. She didn't know. She'd had some sort of vision of getting help with childcare and support, but the reality was that if he was the father, he had more claim to Ana than she did. The thought sent a chill down her spine that hadn't been there before.

Alex was watching her with those gorgeous green eyes of his. She had the uncomfortable feeling that he could see right into the heart of her, see all her fears and secrets. He was devastatingly handsome. How many women spilled their guts to him—and opened their bodies—before he dropped them like hot potatoes and moved on to the next one in line? Because that's what he'd done to Kayla. Used her and dropped her before the sheets even got cold.

Nervously, Bailey took another drink of coffee. She hadn't been able to make any this morning before setting off for his house. She hadn't eaten either, though she'd made sure Ana had a bottle. Her stomach growled and she cleared her throat to cover it.

He heard it though, because he frowned. "You want some cereal or something?"

"No, I'm fine." She wasn't, but she wasn't going to accept food from him too.

"If you say so."

"I do." She cleared her throat again. "You said you help people. In what way?"

"My job. I get people out of bad situations, though I have to say there are usually criminals involved."

Her heart skipped. "I'm not involved with any criminals." But she probably knew some. The club drew all kinds.

"Never said you were. But you're in a bad situation."

She bristled. He seemed so certain, and even though it was true, she just wanted to deny it. How did he *know?* "What makes you think that? Because I fell asleep on your couch? Babies are hard—and I wasn't prepared to deal with one."

"I think you need to tell me what happened to put you in that position in the first place. Since I'm supposed to be Ana's father."

Bailey swallowed. Did he have that right? Maybe he did. And even if he didn't, she was so close to a breakdown that she wanted to tell *someone.*

"There isn't much to tell. Kayla slept with you, then she took off with a friend and went to California because she knew you wouldn't help her. She didn't tell me she was pregnant. I didn't know anything about it until she came back a week ago with Ana."

"And where's Kayla now?"

Bailey dropped her gaze from the piercing look in his. She didn't like this part. Couldn't make sense of it even now. If Ana was hers, she didn't think she'd be able to abandon her. Then again, she didn't know what Kayla had been through the past few months. "She left. Two days ago."

Alex frowned. "She left her baby with you? Just took off?"

Bailey nodded. The familiar lump was in her throat again. "She's a kid herself. Only twenty-one. She's not prepared for a baby." Anger flooded her belly with acid. "You should have been more careful. You military guys, always fucking with women's heads. She was dazzled by you. Probably thought you would take care of her, but you didn't. You fucked her and sent her on her way."

His face was a thundercloud. "That's a lot of accusation, don't you think?"

"Not if it's true."

His jaw worked. "We're going to find out if it's true. You have a picture of Kayla?"

Bailey reached into the diaper bag and got her phone. Then she scrolled through pictures until she found one. She turned it to him with a surge of triumph.

"Can you deny this is you?"

He glanced at the picture. It was of him and two other men. He had an arm over Kayla's shoulders and they were all grinning. Kayla had sent her the picture when Bailey asked who Ana's father was.

He frowned. "That's me, yeah. She was a waitress at Buddy's. Pretty sure her name wasn't Kayla though."

Bailey felt the acid churning. "Did she go by Harley?"

"Yeah, I think that was it."

"Did you sleep with her?"

His troubled gaze met hers. "I don't know."

Chapter 3

It was surreal to stare at a picture of himself with a woman who claimed she'd had his baby. Cowboy and Money were in the picture too, but he was the one with his arm on her shoulders. Alexei didn't think he'd slept with her, but he couldn't say that with one hundred percent certainty. There'd been a period of time a few months ago when he'd been trying to erase some bad shit that had happened on a mission. Drinking heavily was frowned upon, especially for a sniper, so he'd eased his pain with sex. Lots of sex.

And yeah, he'd made some regrettable choices in partners. He hadn't gotten anyone pregnant though. Not one woman ever came to him with that claim. Not one.

He had an ironclad rule about sex without protection, and he followed it to the letter. So even if he'd slept with Kayla, aka Harley, he wouldn't have gotten her pregnant. But if he *had* slept with her and she thought her baby was his, why hadn't she come to him about it?

"You don't know," Bailey said. "How can you not know?"

"Because I don't. Because it was months ago. Because I don't keep a fucking diary about these things." He leaned forward, pierced her with his gaze. "The baby is not mine. But if she was, I'd do what's right."

"I'm glad to hear it." Her voice was soft, a counterweight to his hard one.

"That picture proves nothing," he pressed on. "It's me and my buddies with your sister. That's not a crime. It's also not evidence of guilt."

She looked down at the picture before clicking the phone's Sleep button. "No, it's not. But it was the only one she had so I could see your face."

"She could have shown you a picture of Justin Bieber and said he was the father. What then?"

Annoyance flashed across her features. "She showed me you. The two of you together. Could she have lied? Sure. But right now all I have to go on is what she told me. And you aren't denying that you *might* have slept with her."

Irritation flared. "So we need to get to the truth."

"The sooner the better." She shook her head. "You know, I have to work tonight and I still need childcare. So if you'd like to head out to the pharmacy, we can do the swabs and I'll be on my way."

"Who's going to take care of her while you work?"

"My neighbor, I hope. If not her, then I have a friend or two I can call."

She didn't look at him when she said it. Alexei felt his gut tighten. Goddamn it, he didn't need to get involved. He would *not* get involved. Especially when there was the weight of this thing sitting between them.

"I can watch her." *Fuck, dude. Where did that come from?*

Her head snapped up. "Why would you want to do that? You don't even know her—and we don't know you."

Alexei rolled his eyes. "You don't know me and yet here you are, accusing me of being her father. Did you think I'd write some checks and leave you to it?"

She had the grace to look embarrassed. "No, of course not. But I figured it would be a process, and I'd get to know you before you spent time alone with her."

"Up to you, Bailey Jones. I'm offering to watch the kid so you can go to work. I don't know why I'm doing it, considering babies are a pain in the ass and I just returned from an overseas mission. I'd like to spend some quality time with my television, a pizza, and a woman, not changing diapers and burping a baby. But if my offer's not good enough for you, I get it. No problem for me if you turn it down."

She was frowning. "If my neighbor can't do it, then I accept."

"Don't sound so excited about it."

"I am excited. It means I can work, which means I get paid." She frowned harder. "But wait—are you planning to use her to pick up women?"

He scoffed. "Lady, I don't need a baby's help. I manage just fine on my own."

"I bet you do," she grumbled, half to herself.

"So where do you work?"

Her gaze skittered away. "At a nightclub."

He'd been expecting her to say she was a hairdresser with hair like that. Apparently not. He got the feeling she didn't want to say anything more about the nightclub. Since it wasn't important to him, he didn't press her. "If your neighbor can't watch her, you can drop her here before you go."

If she took him up on it, he was *so* not getting laid tonight.

She seemed to be thinking about it. "She'd need to stay until about two or so."

"Not a problem. I'll be awake." Awake and asking himself what the hell he'd been thinking to volunteer to watch an infant when he could be getting head instead.

"You won't call someone to come over for a booty call, will you? I don't want you ignoring her to get laid."

He grabbed his keys off the coffee table and pocketed them. "First of all, I wouldn't offer if I was planning to do that. And second—you ready to go get that test?"

She tipped her head back to study his face, and his chest tightened for the briefest of moments. She was pretty. And he was horny. *Down, boy.*

"Fine. And yes, I'm ready."

Her stomach growled again, but he didn't say anything about it. She was reluctant to accept help, so he wasn't going to keep offering. They gathered the baby and went outside. She started for her car, but he stopped her.

"Let's go in mine. There's more room." He didn't point out that her car looked like it could die at any moment. His was a big Dodge truck that he'd bought used two years ago, so he knew it would get them from point A to B and back again. Besides, it would take less time if they traveled together. He could take the test, drop it in the mail, and have her back here in an hour or so.

"Okay. But you have to wrestle the straps on that carrier and get her buckled in."

"No problem." They walked over to his truck and he popped the button to open the doors. It didn't take him long to situate Ana's carrier in the back seat and secure it. Ana goo-gooed at him, her little baby-powder scent reminding him of his childhood. It hadn't been a bad childhood at all, but there were things he'd rather not think about. He folded the body of the stroller and tucked it away.

Bailey stared at him with her jaw hanging open.

"What?" he asked.

"You did that so easily. Like you've been doing it your whole life. It took me *forever* to figure that damned thing out."

"Told you, oldest of six. This one's more modern than what we had, but I'm familiar with the concept."

"Jesus, you're like a wet dream for a woman who wants lots of babies."

He snorted. "Yeah, thanks. Not precisely the reason I was hoping for." And not one that he found any comfort in. Hell to the no when it came to kids of his own. He closed the door gently on Ana before opening the door for Bailey. She was still staring at him.

"And now you're opening doors. Dude, how are you not married?"

That one he could answer truthfully. "I could tell you I haven't found the right person yet, but the truth is I'm not looking. Not interested."

Kids and marriage changed people, and not always for the better.

"I suddenly feel sorry for all those supermaternal women out there looking for a husband."

She climbed into the truck and belted in while he stood there for a second.

"You aren't looking either?" In his experience, most of the women he knew were either looking or planning to look. And a military guy with benefits like his? Total catnip.

"Hell no." She sniffed. "I've got goals—and a husband isn't one of them."

SHE WASN'T LOOKING for a husband, or even a boyfriend, but something about the proximity of this man had her nerve endings jumping like popcorn exploding on a hot griddle. He was big and handsome, and he knew what to do with Ana. Bailey would swear she didn't have a single maternal yearning in her whole body, but there was something very appealing about a hot man taking care of a little baby.

Something that made her stomach twist with longing and desire pool between her thighs. Which was ridiculous, because what did that mean? That she wanted to fuck a man who could take care of babies? Because why? She didn't want any babies. Ana was enough right now, and Ana wasn't even hers.

Her stomach twisted again, but not with longing this time. With fear and doubt and anger. Poor sweet little Anastasia. What was going to happen to her? How was she going to survive being taken care of by an aunt who knew next to nothing about raising a healthy, emotionally well-adjusted kid? And what if Alex Kamarov really was her father? Would he take Ana away?

Probably. And why wouldn't he? It was clear Bailey

didn't know a damned thing. What business did she have with a baby? About as much business as a pyromaniac had with a dynamite factory.

Alex went around and got into the driver's side. He started the truck and backed out of the drive. Bailey considered that she'd just gotten into a vehicle with a man far larger than she was and he was in control of where they went and what they did. Her heart throbbed and her stomach twisted, though her instincts told her she had nothing to worry about.

Still, suspicion was automatic considering she'd grown up with two drug addicts always looking for their next fix. They'd do anything to get it, including sell their own children. Fortunately, it had never come to that, but her trust issues ran deep. Logic told her it didn't apply to this situation though. If Alex was going to hurt her or Ana, he could have done it when they'd been in his house.

They drove the short distance to a pharmacy. He parked the truck and turned to her. "You going in to get it or you want me to?"

"I'll let you pick it out."

He opened the door and went inside. A few minutes later he was back with a package. He handed her the receipt. "You're paying," he reminded her.

"I know." It was money she couldn't really spare, but it was a small price to pay for the truth. Especially if it meant he would help her care for Ana.

She opened the package and read the directions. He read them too. Then he swabbed his cheek, put the swab into the secure pouch designed for it, and sealed it.

"Going to have to get hers," he said, nodding at the back seat.

Bailey's heart skipped. "Okay."

"Do you want me to do it?"

"No, I can get it." She took the swab and got out of the vehicle. Then she opened the back door and looked at the sleeping baby. She absolutely didn't want to wake Ana, but they had to get this done. Carefully, she slipped the swab into the baby's mouth and rolled it against her cheek. Ana protested but didn't start screaming. Bailey removed the swab, dropped it into the secure pouch, and then passed it to Alex.

He put everything in the package, sealed it, and handed it to her. "Post office?"

"Yes."

They drove the short distance to the post office and Bailey went inside this time, dropping off the envelope and getting a receipt. When she came back outside, she stopped and drew in a deep breath. The air was warm and a breeze blew softly. She felt a moment of happiness, like she'd accomplished something big, but then all the usual feelings of worry and fear were back in abundance.

"One day at a time," she muttered to herself as she stepped off the curb and walked over to the white truck where Alex Kamarov waited with a baby that might or might not be his. Because, yes, she had to acknowledge that it was entirely possible her sister was mistaken—or that she hadn't been telling the truth.

Truth was a fluid commodity in Kayla's world. Always had been. It was her way of coping with the terrible situation in which they'd grown up. She'd come up with false identities—Harley being one of them—and she'd told lies. Bailey didn't know why she would lie about something as big as who the father of her baby was, but it was possible. Anything was possible with Kayla.

Bailey worried about her sister, but there was only so much she could do. Kayla was a grown woman, and if she wanted to take off to California for months at a time or disappear after dumping her baby, Bailey couldn't stop her. She'd given up trying. Didn't mean she wasn't worried though. She kept messaging Kayla's phone, but so far she'd gotten no response. Absolutely typical.

She got back into the truck and belted herself in, sudden tears springing out of nowhere. *Dammit.*

"You okay?"

She didn't look at him. "Yeah. Fine."

He reached over and gave her hand a quick squeeze. Her breath stopped. Her nerve endings sizzled to life. A single touch was more electric than anything she'd felt before. But he might be the father of her niece, which made him off-limits. *Off-limits.*

"It'll be okay," he said.

She wasn't sure it would.

Chapter 4

Alexei took her to breakfast. He'd told himself he was going to drive her back to his place and get rid of her now that they'd accomplished what she wanted, but instead he found himself headed for IHOP. Bailey protested when they turned into the parking lot.

He shot her a look. "I'm hungry and I don't feel like going back to my place, dropping you, helping you get that carrier into your car, then coming back. It'll be half an hour or more. So watch me eat or order something. I don't care."

She stopped grumbling, probably because there was nothing she could say. They were here and he wasn't leaving. He helped her get Ana—she still fumbled with the straps—and they went inside. The waitress who usually served him was cute and perky. He hadn't asked her out, but she kept hinting she'd like him to. He'd thought about it a few times, but then he'd thought about what would happen when it didn't work out—and it wouldn't because he really only wanted to fuck her a few times. He'd have to find a new place to eat breakfast,

29

but this one was close to home and he liked their pancakes. A man couldn't fuck up his pancakes for a piece of pussy.

Yet another reason he was pretty certain he hadn't slept with Kayla. She'd worked at Buddy's, and he wouldn't have wanted to fuck up his favorite watering hole for a couple of orgasms.

The waitress gaped as he strolled up with a baby carrier hooked over his arm and a woman trailing behind him with a diaper bag.

"Hi, Marie," he said with a smile. She snapped her jaw shut, but her face grew red.

"Alex. I… Wow, I didn't realize…"

"This is my friend, Bailey," he said, stepping aside to allow Bailey to come up beside him.

Bailey smiled. It was a friendly smile, not the kind of smile that held a territorial claim. He appreciated that since he often got the other kind of smile when he spent time with a woman. "Hi."

Marie didn't smile back. "Hi. Can I get you two some coffee?"

"I'll take one. Bailey?"

"That would be nice, thanks."

Marie spun on her heel and disappeared. Alexei set the carrier on the bench seat and slid in beside the baby. Bailey took the seat opposite.

"I don't think she likes me."

Alexei laughed. "Nope, I don't think so. But you helped me make a decision about her."

She tilted her head. "I did?"

"Yep. I'd been thinking of asking her out. But if she can't be nice to my friends, then I guess not."

"Seriously? I'm not your friend, Alex."

"Alexei," he said automatically and then wondered why. Everyone called him Alex unless they called him Camel, but those were his teammates who did that. Alex was what he went by to everyone else except family. They called him Alexei.

"Alexei," she said. "That's Russian, isn't it?"

"Yeah. My parents immigrated when I was two." And why was he getting chatty about this shit with her?

"So you don't have any memories of Russia."

"Nope."

"Are you bilingual?"

"Trilingual, actually. I have an aptitude for languages, so the military trained me in Arabic as well. I've also been learning Persian."

"Wow. Arabic and Persian." She sounded a little shocked. "That's odd, isn't it?"

"You'd be surprised." Not all the members of his team were linguists, but a couple of them spoke more than one language. It was handy when you were down-range in a foreign country to know the language. And since he deployed to the Middle East quite a bit, Arabic was a good one to know. Persian came in handy in parts of Iraq and Afghanistan. Really handy.

Marie returned with the coffee. She managed to look as if she'd gone in the back and sucked on a lemon, though she pasted on a smile and tried to seem friendly. But he knew now. He had her number. She was one of those women who'd be superpossessive and jealous if he took her out. He didn't do relationships, but he'd date someone for a few weeks if it suited them both. Have a few laughs, fuck a lot.

Marie wouldn't be worth the hassle, that's for sure. Jealousy turned him off. Add in his lifestyle—gone without notice, often for weeks at a time with no way to communicate—and a woman like her would not survive the first deployment.

"Do you know what you want yet?" Marie asked.

"Yeah, I'll take pancakes, a side of bacon, and two scrambled eggs." He'd eaten cereal, but that had been over an hour ago now.

"And you?" Marie said to Bailey, who was still staring at the menu.

"Uh, two scrambled eggs, wheat toast, and hash browns. Crispy."

"Coming right up," Marie said and then flounced away again.

"I think she's mad," Bailey said.

"I don't care if she is. But back to the part where you said you weren't my friend. Why not?"

She blinked. And then she laughed. "Okay, sure. Why not? If you want to be friends, we'll be friends."

"Good thing, because I don't babysit for strangers." Hell, he didn't babysit at all these days. Apparently he was turning over a new leaf. Or an old leaf since he'd spent much of his childhood babysitting his siblings.

Ana was kicking in her carrier, making sounds from time to time but otherwise content. He had to be crazy for not sending Bailey and Ana on their way the instant the cheek swab was done, but something had stopped him. Maybe it was Bailey's stomach growling so insistently, or maybe it was the circles beneath her eyes. Whatever it was, she fascinated him. To a point.

"You're sure the results are going to be negative, aren't you?" she asked, and for the first time he saw her doubts creeping to the fore.

"I am." Because on the slim chance he'd slept with

Kayla Jones—he assumed it was Jones—he wouldn't have gotten her pregnant. He knew that for a fact.

Bailey's gaze went to the baby with the shock of dark hair. "I don't know what to do next if you aren't her father. I'm not equipped to take care of an infant. My job isn't flexible, and I have no other skills to fall back on. Well, none that pay anything."

"What are these other skills?"

"Survival skills."

That wasn't the answer he'd expected.

"Not like Navy SEAL survival skills," she continued. "More like street survival skills. My parents were deadbeat drug addicts. Opioids, not crack. We lived in a lot of sketchy locations. And then my mom OD'd and it was just me and Kayla and our father. A true waste of skin, that man. I walked out at sixteen and took Kayla with me. I kept her in school, but I had to quit so I could work to support us." She twirled the spoon in her coffee and didn't look at him. "We came here a little over a year ago, looking for bigger opportunities. I wasn't ever going to earn the money to attend college while waitressing back in Tennessee."

"But you can here?"

She seemed to hesitate. And then she thrust out her chin and told him, "I'm not waitressing. I'm dancing."

A knot formed in his gut. "Dancing?"

Her eyes were stark and hard. Flinty. Daring him to judge her. "On a pole, Alexei. For money."

Marie returned just then with their plates. She set them on the table and slapped the ticket down. "Anything else?"

"No. Thanks," Alexei said, wanting her gone.

She marched away and he turned his attention to

Bailey again. She shoved a fork in the eggs and didn't look at him. Whoa, that had been some revelation just now.

"So you strip is what you're telling me."

"Yep. You got a problem with that?" There was a challenge in her voice that he wasn't about to rise to.

"Only if you do."

"I don't." She shrugged and reached for her coffee. "It's not what I want to do with my life, but the pay is pretty good and I'm saving as much as I can. I'll walk away eventually, go to college, start a career."

Considering what he did for a living, he couldn't judge somebody else for doing something a little dangerous. Which stripping was, when you factored in the atmosphere and the clientele.

"Which club?"

"The Pink Palace."

He'd been in the Pink Palace, but not lately. A few months ago. He didn't remember seeing her there. But he also had a very clear picture of what it was like inside that club, and he was suddenly feeling very angry and conflicted about the whole thing. Which made no fucking sense. She was nobody to him.

"So tonight, while I'm watching Ana for you, you'll be taking your clothes off for money."

Her head snapped up. "You think you get to judge me? Oh hell no. I do what I have to do to survive. That's what it's all about." She picked up the saltshaker and doused her eggs. "And it's not a guarantee you'll be babysitting. My neighbor will probably do it, and then you don't have to worry about Ana and me anymore."

"Unless that swab says I'm her father." He couldn't help but poke her.

"You're certain you aren't, so I wouldn't worry about it if I were you."

They ate in silence for a few minutes. He chewed his bacon and tried not to be angry. Didn't work, and he wasn't sure why. He didn't know this girl. Didn't care about her. And yet he was getting as pissed as if they were in a relationship and having a disagreement.

"You feel safe there?"

Her gaze sparked. "Safe enough. The guys aren't allowed to touch us, though it happens sometimes. But the bouncers enforce the rules, so it doesn't last long."

He knew what those places were like. The drinking. The hoots and hollers as women bared their bodies on stage. The VIP room and the lap dances. Fucking titty bars were all the same.

"Anybody ever wait for you outside?"

"I'm sure they have, but one of the guys walks us out. Nobody has ever bothered me." She dropped her fork and leaned across the table, eyes flashing now. "What I want to know is this—you can't remember if you slept with my baby sister, but do you remember anything about her? Anything at all?"

He sat back, folded his arms over his chest, and sighed. "She was pretty and she flirted with the guys. Nothing too serious. I remember thinking she had a boyfriend at one point. A guy wearing motorcycle leathers who seemed to hang around a lot when she was there. Didn't say much. Hell, it was months ago, Bailey. I'm not being an asshole, but I didn't spend much time with your sister or I'd remember more."

"She didn't have a boyfriend. She would have told me."

"Okay. Whatever you say."

She brought her thumb up to her mouth and bit it as she stared at him. He thought it was unconscious, but it was still a sexy fucking look. He found himself growing hard as he imagined biting that mouth before thrusting his tongue between her lips and kissing the daylights out of her. She finally dropped her hand and tucked a lock of hair behind her ear.

"I guess we wait for the results and see where we go from there," she said. "I appreciate you cooperating with me about that."

"It's the right thing to do." He picked up the check as she reached for it. "I'll get this. But you still owe me for the paternity test."

She reached inside the diaper bag. A few seconds later, she came out with a wad of bills that she must have had stuffed somewhere besides her purse since that had only held two twenties. She peeled off thirty dollars for the test and another hundred and twenty for the processing fee. He'd used his credit card on the forms because she didn't have one.

He pocketed the money. Ana let out a wail just then and Bailey stiffened, her eyes widening with panic. Alexei reached for the baby and lifted her out of the carrier. The problem was immediately obvious.

"She needs a diaper change."

"Oh. Okay." But Bailey's eyes remained wide and her fingers trembled as she tucked her money away. *Aw, damn.*

"Come on, we'll change her in the truck."

He carried the baby and she took the bag, same as when they'd entered the restaurant. He stopped and paid the bill, then continued to his truck with a crying baby in his arms. A couple of old ladies stood outside the restaurant, chatting. When he walked by, they smiled. He smiled back. Nodded.

"That's a good man you got, honey," one of them said to Bailey. "Congratulations on your beautiful baby."

He didn't hear Bailey's response because he'd reached the vehicle and pressed the button to unlock it. She came up beside him a moment later.

"Here," she said, passing him a portable changing pad.

He unfolded it and laid it on the floor of the truck. Then he shot her a look as he placed the baby on the pad. "You doing this or am I?"

"Honestly, I still gag a bit. But I'll do it if you don't want to."

He couldn't help but roll his eyes at her. "Lightweight."

"Hey, I have all of three days' experience. You've presumably had years."

He stripped the dirty diaper efficiently and held out his hand for the baby wipes, which she handed over. "A few."

He cleaned Ana, applied diaper cream, and put on a fresh diaper. The whole process took less than two minutes. Bailey looked a little stunned when he met her gaze again.

"You know what," she said. "Forget my neighbor. If you're still willing, I'll take you up on the babysitting offer."

Chapter 5

Bailey couldn't stop thinking about Alexei and the way he'd taken care of Ana today. When she'd started pounding on his door, she'd had no idea what to expect. She certainly hadn't expected him to be reasonable. No, she'd been angry and desperate and she'd wanted to take it out on someone. She hadn't truly thought he'd cooperate.

But he had, and then he'd taken it a step further and offered to babysit for her. She hadn't planned to accept, but watching him diaper Ana and soothe her in the restaurant parking lot had changed her mind. He knew what he was doing, and he was good with the baby.

Those old ladies had said as much to her. Yes, she'd blushed and stammered a bit in her reply, but that was because they weren't a couple and Ana wasn't her baby. Not that she could explain all that to two friendly strangers who were impressed with the big man carrying the squalling baby. If they'd watched him change Ana, they would've swooned.

She nearly had. And she'd asked herself, as she stood

there being useless, why she was adding the burden of finding childcare on herself when she already had a willing volunteer. She could go and beg Tiffany, her neighbor, but Tiffany had two kids of her own and looked perpetually tired. Plus she'd want to be paid, and while Bailey agreed that pay was warranted, Alexei hadn't wanted money and he was good with Ana. Better than Tiffany because he wasn't going to be distracted by other children or only doing it for the money.

She'd taken Ana home and settled in for the day. There were chores and the usual unanswered texts to Kayla. Whenever the kid slept, Bailey slept. Ana slept in fits and starts though, so Bailey didn't get a lot of sleep. She even managed a quick shower during one of the naps. She'd applied her stage makeup, which was heavier and darker than she usually wore, then dressed in yoga pants and a tank top for the trip to Alexei's and then the club.

It was around six thirty when she piled Ana and her diaper bag into the car. Alexei had frowned mightily when he'd strapped Ana's carrier into it earlier.

"This car is older than both of us put together," he'd grumbled.

"It's not either."

"Maybe not, but it doesn't look all that reliable."

"It's not, but it's been over a month since the last breakdown. I think it's doing okay."

He'd frowned as she climbed into the car and started it up. Predictably, it sputtered like a drowning cow, but it lumbered into action when she pressed the gas. Her last vision of Alexei Kamarov was him standing with legs spread and arms crossed over his chest, a frown on his face as she pulled away.

Now, as she drove to his house again, her heart kicked up at the thought of seeing him. She didn't like that, but there was nothing to be done about it. He was big and handsome and he pinged all her arousal zones. He was one hundred percent her type even if she'd have said before today that she didn't have a specific type.

Apparently she did. Tall, broad, badass Navy SEALs did it for her, it seemed. She drove the five miles to Alexei's house, feeling better the closer she got to it. He lived in an older neighborhood with houses, not a low-rent apartment like she did. She'd wanted to save money, and she hadn't had the cash for a huge security deposit. Then there was the fact she didn't have a credit card, which meant she was limited in the kinds of places that would accept her.

Still, she hadn't looked too hard because it had been her and Kayla at the time and their needs weren't great. But now that she had Ana to care for, the apartment seemed shabbier than she liked.

Bailey parked in the driveway, behind Alexei's Dodge, and got out of the vehicle. She started around the car to get Ana, but Alexei came outside and strode off the porch toward her.

"I wasn't sure you'd go through with it," he said as she opened the passenger door and pushed the seat forward so she could get to Ana.

"Free babysitting? Of course I was going through with it. Unless you've changed your mind?"

"Nope."

She freed the carrier and lifted it out, handing it to Alexei. His fingers brushed hers, and electricity shot down into her toes and up through the follicles on her head.

Wowza!

She grabbed the diaper bag, but he took it from her and shouldered it. Then they stood there staring at each other for a long minute.

"You want to come in for a second?"

"I shouldn't. I need to get to the club."

His gaze searched her face. She knew he was taking in the makeup—the heavy eyeliner, the fake lashes, the crystal jewels beneath her eyebrows. She applied it at home because it was often difficult to get a mirror at the club. She'd do her lipstick later, right before she went on. That at least didn't take too long.

"If you need anything, call me," he said.

They'd exchanged numbers earlier, before she'd left the first time. In case she changed her mind about the babysitting, he'd said. She'd looked at his number in her phone a few times. Not to cancel. Hell, she didn't know why she did it. She'd thought about texting him, to see if he'd answer, but she couldn't think of any reason to do so.

"What I need is childcare. You're already doing that."

His brow furrowed. "I mean if anyone harasses you or you feel unsafe. I'm the kind of guy who can fix that."

He stood there with a baby carrier and a diaper bag, all muscled and hot and somehow menacing as well, and she knew he wasn't lying. He could totally fix anything he set his mind to. Including the longing swirling inside her belly at the sight of him.

Nope, not happening.

He'd plowed Kayla and planted a seed. Or had he?

"I'll keep it in mind. But Deke doesn't allow any

harassment in the club. Men who get rowdy get thrown out. It's safe."

Not always, but she wasn't telling him that. Shit happened sometimes, but not often.

He frowned as if he didn't believe her. "I've been there, Bailey. I know what goes on in that place."

"Same as any nightclub," she replied. "But I'll call you if anything changes. Though what's your plan? Put Ana in your truck and come kick some ass? Should I get you one of those pouch thingies people wear their kids in?"

"Very funny. I've already got backup if I need it, so no, I won't be bringing the munchkin."

She was relieved to hear it. "I gotta get going. I'll text you when I'm on my way to pick her up. It won't be before two."

He was looking angry again. "Okay. Let me know. I'll be awake."

Bailey got into the car and started it up. It rumbled in its usual sickly fashion as she put it into reverse and backed out of the driveway. With a last look at Alexei and Ana, she pressed the gas and left them behind. She ought to feel relief that she was free for a few hours to work and not think about a baby's needs.

But she was strangely sad instead.

"YOU HAVE GOT to be kidding me," Cash "Money" McQuaid said as he walked inside, pizzas in one hand and a six-pack in the other, and stopped dead in his tracks. "Where the hell did you get a baby?"

Cody "Cowboy" McCormick was shaking his head

and laughing. Remy "Cage" Marchand came over with paper plates while Adam "Blade" Garrison hovered nearby, ready to leap on the pizzas as soon as the boxes hit the table.

"I answered an ad for a part-time nanny job," Alexei said. "Where do you think?"

"Dude, seriously." Money was the last one to arrive at Cage's house because he'd stopped to pick up the pizzas, and he wasn't up to speed yet.

Though they'd just gotten back from deployment yesterday, when Cage called to ask if they wanted to get together at his place for pizza and beer, most of the guys had jumped on it. Dane "Viking" Erikson couldn't make it, but Ryan "Dirty Harry" Callahan and Zach "Neo" Anderson were on the way.

Alexei had almost said no, but he'd decided that taking Ana would be acceptable so long as Cage said yes and he informed Bailey. Both of which had happened. Cage had seemed amused and Bailey sent back a terse reply that basically said *whatever, dude*.

Damn, that girl fascinated him. When she'd rolled up to his place tonight with all that damned makeup enhancing her facial features, he'd gotten harder than stone. Not that she needed the makeup, but the way she applied it made her eyes bigger and more golden. In other words, striking as fuck. Add in the clingy yoga clothing, which he knew she'd trade for a G-string later, and his mind was working overtime. He seriously needed to get laid. Which wasn't happening tonight with the pip-squeak for company.

"Girl accused Camel of being the kid's father," Cowboy said, always one to jump right to the point. "So he swabbed his cheek and offered to babysit."

"No fucking way," Money said, jaw dropping. "Really?"

Laughter drifted from another room. The women were upstairs in the living room, chatting and drinking cocktails while the guys did their thing in the basement, aka man cave. Their thing including poker, of course.

"Yeah," Alexei said, hardly believing it himself. Was he going fucking soft? "Really. Pounded on my fucking door this morning loud enough to wake the dead and accused me of knocking up her sister."

"Whoa. So where's the sister?"

"Good question. Bailey doesn't know either. Skipped town. She was a waitress at Buddy's for a while last year. Harley was her name, though it's really Kayla."

"I vaguely remember her," Money said. "Might have picked her up."

"So maybe you're the kid's father," Alexei said dryly.

Money had given up the pizzas and beer, so both hands went in the air. "No fucking way. I don't play that game."

"None of us do—or did," Cowboy said.

And they didn't, because their careers as SEALs were too important to them. They didn't need to knock up a random woman and possibly get busted off the team because of accusations and paternity battles. Now that they were HOT, the best of the fucking best, it was even more critical to keep their lives as simple as possible. Not that they all adhered to that plan anymore—some of them had gotten married or engaged lately. No doubt there'd be babies one day soon for this crowd. But who was taking that plunge first?

Certainly not Alexei. Because this baby wasn't his, and no matter how cute she was, he wasn't going to be in her life for very long. She kicked in her carrier and made goo-goo noises just then, as if to remind him how adorable she was.

"So you took a paternity test, huh?" Money said. "How long will that take?"

"A few days according to the package."

"You trust it?"

"Why not? It's a pretty straightforward process. Determine if our DNA matches. If it comes back positive, I'll go for a more formal test to prove it. But it won't."

"Man, you don't even date the same girl for more than a couple of weeks. No way is that your kid," Cowboy agreed.

"Pretty much what I said to the pip-squeak's aunt. She declined to accept that explanation."

Money walked over and peered at Ana. "Sure is a cute baby. Definitely not yours then."

Alexei snorted. He knew how to get Money back for that remark. "Want to hold her?"

His teammate backed away, shaking his head as if the hounds of hell were about to be released. "No way, man. I don't do babies."

"Yet. What if Ella wants a few?"

Money let out a breath. "She will, and that means I will—but not yet."

"No time like the present to figure out how to hold one without panicking," Alexei teased.

"Nope, not happening."

Cowboy came over and peered at Ana. "I'll try."

Money snorted, relieved to be off the hook. "Miranda getting the urge?"

"Not yet. But you never know."

Alexei picked Ana up and snuggled her for a second. She really was a cute little bundle. Then he handed her over, telling Cowboy how to hold her and where to place his hands. His big teammate took her like she was made of glass, then tucked her into his beefy arm and supported her head and neck the way he'd been told.

"She's so little."

"Bailey says she's a month old."

"And her mother left her?"

"Yeah."

"Wow. Poor kid."

The other guys came over and looked at her then. When she started to fuss a little, Cowboy thrust her at him. Alexei took her, rocking and soothing her until she quieted again.

"Man, that is weird," Blade said, munching his pizza.

"What?" Alexei asked.

"Watching you with a baby. You're a stone-cold sniper, capable of blowing a hole in a man from over a mile away, and yet you're holding that baby like you were born to do it."

"Oldest of six, dude. You get used to babies."

"All right, we eating or what?" Cage asked, grabbing a plate and piling on the pizza.

"Give me a sec," Alexei said. He spread out the blanket he'd brought and placed Ana on her tummy in the center of it. After he grabbed a slice, he went back and sat on the floor, taking out one of Ana's toys and letting her grasp it.

His man card was about to get pulled for this shit, but hell, the kid needed attention. It wasn't her fault she'd been abandoned—or that her aunt meant well but knew dick about taking care of her.

"What the hell are you doing?" Cowboy asked.

"Tummy time," he replied with a straight face.

"What the fuck?" Money looked puzzled. "What's tummy time?"

Alexei rolled his eyes as if it was obvious. It wasn't, but he wasn't going to pass up the opportunity to rib these guys. "Man, you two are married and you don't have a clue. Better read up on this shit before those wives of yours start wanting kids. Tummy time is important because it helps strengthen their necks. She can't do a lot of it yet, but you do it every day and gradually she'll get stronger and do more time on her tummy. Helps her learn to roll over and then eventually crawl and shit."

"I can't believe you know this stuff," Money said. "I gotta agree with Blade—it's kinda weird."

All right, so it was weird. He wouldn't deny it. They knew him as their team sniper, the guy who picked off the difficult targets so they could go in and get the job done. They'd fought a lot of battles together, but this was a side of him they'd never seen before.

But they were his teammates, and despite a bit of ribbing, they accepted it. They gathered around, sitting on couches and chairs, and ate pizza, talking and watching Ana. Alexei rolled her onto her back after a few minutes. She was still too young to spend much time on her belly. He'd have to ask Bailey if she'd been doing this with Ana. He somehow doubted it. Bailey was as clueless as these guys when it came to the kid.

After a while, the women came downstairs. They'd already seen Ana once, when he'd walked in earlier, though Ella hadn't because she and Money arrived after he did.

"We wanted to see Ana again," Christina Marchand said.

They gathered around, exclaiming over the baby's cuteness. Christina and Ella were brave enough to hold her, though Miranda was the natural. Cowboy looked a little stunned at that revelation. Miranda gave him a wry look.

"Oldest of six, babe," she said when he commented on it.

Alexei held up his hand. Miranda gave him a high five.

"Don't worry," she continued. "I don't want one. Yet."

"Thank God for that," Cowboy muttered. "Not that she isn't cute, but she seems like a lot of work."

"What will you do if she's yours?" Christina asked.

"She's not. But if she is by some chance, I'll make sure I'm on her birth certificate. Claim her as a dependent. Beyond that, I'd have to think about it."

Because how could he take care of a baby when he wasn't home for weeks at a time? Tonight was a one-off. It wouldn't happen again. That test would come back and he'd be off the hook. Ana and her prickly aunt would move along—and he'd get back to his life.

Except now that he'd spent time with Ana and knew that her mother was gone and Bailey was overwhelmed —not to mention in a job that wasn't all that stable—he couldn't help but wonder what was going to happen to her. He thought of Bailey in the Pink Palace, that dive of a strip club, and his doubts multiplied. The munchkin needed structure, and it didn't look like she was getting much of it right now.

Because how the hell was Bailey Jones supposed to take care of a baby when taking care of herself was probably a full-time job?

Chapter 6

Bailey tried to push Ana and Alexei from her mind as she prepared for the show. But the memory of that handsome man holding her tiny niece wasn't going to leave her anytime soon. He was just so assured with Ana, and he made her so very aware of how badly she sucked at dealing with the baby. Not that he did it on purpose. No, it was just his competence and confidence that did it. She had no maternal instincts at all. He did though. Or paternal ones. Whatever.

Bailey applied red lipstick, then stripped out of her clothing and put on one of the bejeweled G-strings she danced in. Then she donned the jeweled bra and covered everything with her costume, which was a leather jacket and a skintight faux-leather miniskirt with Velcro at the seams. Thigh-high boots, a cap with sequins on the brim, and a jeweled whip rounded out the look.

Bailey thwacked the whip against her leg and told herself to concentrate. Money was the goal tonight. Not handsome Navy SEALs. Not babies. Not anything but the next dance and what paid the bills.

The dressing room was a madhouse, as usual, with girls coming and going, touching up their makeup, donning costumes, cursing and smoking and laughing about something that had happened onstage.

Deke stopped by on occasion, moving the dancers along when necessary. Bailey strode toward the stage, taking one last drink of water from the bottle that one of the attendants handed her. The music cued up, and Bailey strode onto the stage to a raucous welcome from the patrons.

The entire routine was under ten minutes, but it brought the house down. She'd never been able to afford gymnastics or dance as a kid, but she'd watched and she'd learned. She'd practiced all by herself in the front yard of their trailer, learning how to do backbends and splits and all the moves it took to be a cheerleader. Because she'd desperately wanted to be one, though her family would have never been able to afford the uniforms or the camp even if she had made the team.

She'd never made the team though. Too poor, too untrained probably. Too many things she hadn't even known about when she was a kid longing for a dream. The cards had been stacked against her, and she hadn't realized it.

She realized it now, so she danced her ass off and she got those dollar bills tucked into her G-string so she could succeed where her parents had failed. She was determined to make a better life for herself—and for Ana, apparently.

When she finished her routine, she left the stage, donning a robe and guzzling water from the attendant, then continued toward the dressing room. A shape loomed out of the darkness, barring her way. She crashed to a halt.

"Nice tits," a man said.

Bailey's blood went cold. "How did you get back here? Nobody is allowed backstage."

He chuckled as he moved into the meager light. He wasn't very tall, an inch or two taller than her, but he was broad and he looked about as mean as a cornered bear. There was a scar that went from his upper lip to his cheek, and his eyes gleamed as he raked them over her. He wore biker leathers, and there was a chain hanging from his belt that went to his pocket.

"Where's Kayla?"

Bailey froze. "Who are you?"

"Doesn't matter. What does matter is where Kayla is. She's got something that belongs to me. And you're going to tell me where she is or I'm going to hurt you, Bailey. *After* I fuck you hard and long."

Shock flooded her system. Fury and fear followed. "I don't know where Kayla is, but even if I did, I wouldn't tell you, asshole. Who the fuck do you think you are?"

He took a menacing step toward her.

"You need any help?" one of the bouncers called to her.

Bailey's heart was racing, but she swallowed as she made eye contact with Brian. "Yes, please. This asshole is bothering me."

Brian lumbered forward, his hand going beneath the jacket he wore to touch the butt of his weapon. "You need to clear out, man," he said. "We don't want any trouble, but we won't shrink from it."

The man smirked. "I was just going." He started

toward the exit, then turned around and shot her another look. "I'll be in touch for that information. You can count on it. If you'd like to save yourself some trouble, you tell that sister of yours she knows where to find me. It'll be a lot better for her if she comes willingly."

He left without another word.

Brian came over, frowning. "You okay? He touch you?"

Bailey's heart was pounding. Willingly? What the fuck had Kayla gotten herself into? "No, he didn't touch me. I'm fine. He was just a creep."

"I'll let the guys know. We'll keep an eye out for him. He won't get back in the club."

"I know. Thank you."

Brian tipped his chin at her. "You were looking fly tonight, girl. Awesome routine."

"Thanks. I appreciate it."

"You're better than this, Honey," he said, using her stage name. "Some of these girls… Well, you can tell it's all they got. Not you. You can do better."

She was oddly touched. "Thanks, Brian. It means a lot to hear you say that."

"Think about leaving this life before it touches you too hard, you know?"

"Yeah, I know." She knew because of the girls she worked with. Some were stuck. Some were just like her, trying to find a better way and working hard to get there.

He nodded. "I know you gotta get back to work. I'll make sure you're safe, don't worry."

Bailey headed for the dressing room to prepare for the next show. But she couldn't shake the memory of that man or the meanness in his voice. He'd known her.

He'd known Kayla. And he wasn't going to give up his search for her sister easily. He'd said Kayla had something that belonged to him. But what?

ALEXEI TOOK Ana back to his place around eleven. She was sleeping soundly, so he wasn't worried about the time. When they got there, she woke and wanted a bottle. He fed her, burped her, and changed her before putting her down again. Then he settled in to watch some television until he heard from Bailey. Pretty pitiful night for his first full day back from deployment. He should be at a club, hooking up with a chick or two.

But he was here, babysitting an adorable infant and waiting for a text from her aunt. The text came at precisely two a.m. *Heading your way. Be about twenty minutes or so.*

I'm awake.

About twenty minutes later, he heard her car pull up. She shut off the engine and he went to open the door and let her in. She was dressed in the yoga pants and top, but her makeup wasn't perfect anymore. She also smelled like smoke. She looked spent.

"Hey," she said with a small smile.

"Hey." He stood back and opened the door wide so she could walk beneath his arm and enter.

She did so and he let his gaze slide over the street, looking for anything that might be out of place. It was sheer habit, but it was a good one, so he didn't make himself stop.

He shut the door and turned. She stood there with defeat written in every line of her body. Or maybe that was exhaustion. When she looked up, there were tears glistening on her cheeks. She dashed them away, but it was too late. He'd seen.

His senses went on high alert. "What's wrong, Bailey? Did something happen?"

"No, of course not. Everything is fine."

He stalked toward her. She didn't lift her head to look at him. "You're lying."

She blew out a breath, but she still didn't meet his gaze. "It's not your responsibility to take care of me, or even of Ana. If the test comes back positive, well, that will be different where she's concerned. But me? I'm nobody."

Shit. He put a finger under her chin and tipped it up, ignoring the electricity zipping through his nerve endings at that light touch. "You aren't nobody. Tell me what's wrong."

She sniffed. And then she smiled sadly. "Has it ever occurred to you that I might be playing you? That this whole thing is an elaborate hoax to get your sympathy and support?"

"Well, yeah," he told her honestly. "But I don't think it is." If she'd been planning a hoax, she'd have been more prepared. Of that he was certain. Anyone with a half a brain would, and she definitely had a brain in her pretty head.

"Why not?" she whispered.

He thought about kissing her, then discarded the idea. Not the right maneuver at this very moment. She was too raw, too emotional. Something was bothering her.

"You might lie about a lot of things, I don't really know, but you aren't lying right now. I've got an instinct for these things." He had to or he'd have been dead by now.

"You're a good guy, Alexei Kamarov. I kinda hope you fucked up your condom and you *are* Ana's dad. She'll be safe with you."

Aw fuck. "She's not safe with you?" He'd wondered precisely that earlier, but he wouldn't dare say it. She cared about her niece. She was trying.

Her eyes filled with fresh tears. "I don't think so, no." She spun away from him and dashed her fingers against her cheeks. "Sorry. I'm tired. I don't usually fall apart about stuff."

"Tell me what happened tonight."

She sucked in a breath. He could see her warring with herself. And then he saw the moment she made up her mind. Her chin went up and her eyes sparked. "A man came to see me. He thinks I know where Kayla is —he said she had something of his and he demanded I tell him where he could find her. He threatened me."

"A man threatened you." His voice came out hard, cold—but she didn't seem to notice.

"Yes. He came backstage. When I said I didn't know where she was, he said he was going to hurt me if I didn't tell him." She sniffed and waved a hand as if it was nothing. Her next words filled him with hot anger. "Oh, but he plans to rape me first."

Alexei tried to process what she said with a cool head. He really did. It did *not* work. His protective instincts took over. His training kicked in. "You can't go back there," he growled.

She gaped at him. "I have to. It's work. It's what pays the bills. I'm not quitting, Alexei. I need that job."

He made a decision. "You aren't taking Ana

anywhere tonight. You'll stay here. I'll protect you both."

Her eyelids fluttered. And then she shook her head. "No. No way. If I give in to fear, he wins. I won't do it. I won't help him, and I won't run from him either."

Alexei closed the distance between them, took her firmly by the shoulders. She was slender and light, but she was also strong. He could feel the strength in her arms as she tensed beneath his touch. He eased his grip to reassure her, but he didn't let go.

"I have three bedrooms in this place. If you go home, I'll be forced to follow you and set up operations outside your door. You don't want that, Bailey. Trust me when I tell you that you want to stay here tonight."

She frowned. Bit her lip. Need flooded him as the desire to suck that lip pounded through him. *What the hell?* She was cute, but she was off-limits. She had a *baby* to take care of—and he wasn't getting involved in that beyond what it took to keep the two of them safe for the time being.

"I don't have any of my stuff here."

"I'll have your things delivered. Tell me what you need and it'll be here."

She gazed at him in wonder. "You're serious."

"Of course I'm fucking serious."

"But I don't like giving up. Giving in to fear. If that asshole knew where I lived, he'd have gone there first."

He liked the way her mind worked. But she was also wrong. "Possibly. But even if he doesn't know yet, he'll find out. Are the bills in your name?"

"Yes."

"The rental contract?"

"Yes."

"Trust me, he'll show up. Maybe not tonight, but soon."

"So what are you suggesting? That Ana and I stay here for a few days?"

Alexei frowned. Was that what he was saying? Bailey Jones and an infant in his house? Cramping his lifestyle? Preventing him from getting laid and walking around naked whenever he felt like it?

Yeah, it was. *Jesus, he was losing it.* "That's exactly what I'm suggesting."

She shook her head vigorously, her lavender hair flying. "I can't do that."

"Why not?"

"I…" She looked perplexed.

"Exactly. You can't come up with a reason other than we're strangers and you aren't sure about me. But I haven't threatened you, and I'm good with Ana. That's enough of a reason, don't you think?"

She looked militant. "I'm not a coward. I don't quit."

He squeezed her shoulders. "I know that. But there is such a thing as retreating to fight another day. It's what we do when the conditions aren't right, when waiting another day or two will swing everything to our advantage. Patience is the long game, Bailey. And it's fucking rewarding as hell. Trust me."

What the hell was he saying? Yeah, he was patient on a mission. He had to be. He could spend days getting into position and setting up for the shot. But now that he was home? No, his patience was at an end. He wanted to be selfish, take care of himself… Didn't he?

She frowned hard, and he knew she was about to

capitulate. "I won't stop going to work. I won't let one misogynist jerk keep me from making a living."

"Fine. We'll figure something out. I'll make sure you aren't alone there."

He didn't like it, but he was smart enough to fight his battles one at a time.

"I'm never alone. The bouncers are there. Deke— the manager—is there. Tonight, Brian scared the guy off. They look out for us."

"I'm glad for that, but unless Brian is a former SEAL, he's got nothing on me and my brothers. We'll take care of you, Bailey. We'll take that motherfucker apart if he comes back."

She sighed, defeat settling over her features. He could see it happening, and he relaxed a little. Which was crazy because he shouldn't want her to stay here at all.

"Okay, fine… But Alexei?"

"Yeah, baby?" He forgot for a second that she hated endearments, but she didn't react and he didn't apologize.

She looked worried. "Do you think you can find my sister and stop this guy before he gets to her?"

He almost lied to her. But he couldn't do it. "Honestly, I have no idea. But I'll try."

Chapter 7

Bailey couldn't believe she'd agreed to stay, but it was a done deal now and there was no backing out. She scrubbed her hands up and down her forearms, chasing away the chill. He noticed. Of course he did.

"You cold?"

"A little."

After he'd said he would try to find Kayla, he'd let her go and retrieved his phone. He'd called someone, outlined what had happened and what he wanted, and then ended the call. That's when he'd turned and witnessed her rubbing her arms.

He picked up a blanket off the back of the couch and brought it to her. She shrank away for a second and he frowned.

"I smell like smoke and sweat," she protested.

He wrapped the blanket around her shoulders anyway. She didn't try to stop him this time. "It washes."

"So do I," she said jokingly.

His hot gaze swept her face. Her nerve endings

tingled to life beneath her skin. What was it about him that did that to her? *He's a player, girl. Don't forget it.*

"You can shower if you like."

"I don't have anything to change into. All I have in my gym bag are my work clothes. Or lack of clothes," she added, trying to make him laugh.

He didn't. "Someone will bring clothes for you. Anything else you need from your place?"

Bailey started to shake her head, then blinked. "Wait a minute—I never told you where I lived."

"You didn't have to."

"You know? Just like that?"

He nodded. "It's my job. I know shit."

She hugged herself, oddly comforted and also a bit intimidated. "So you're a professional stalker?"

That earned her a grin. "Not a stalker. But Bailey, your information isn't a secret, okay? I didn't go searching for you— but the second you told me someone threatened you, I needed to know how easy you were to find. My guys found you with a simple Google search while I was on the phone just now."

She was boggled by the whole thing. "But how will they get in? Don't you need a key?"

He looked amused. "No, we don't need a key."

It occurred to her that if he'd found her that quickly and didn't need a key, then perhaps the man who'd threatened her earlier could do the same. And that was a scary thought, especially if she'd been home alone with Ana.

She shivered again. "I think I'll have that shower after all. I want to wash off the stink of the club."

"Sure. Down the hall, first door on the left. There are towels. There's a robe too. On the back of the door.

It's clean. My sister gave it to me for a gift. I don't use it."

The thought of wearing his robe was oddly arousing. She wouldn't have thought she was in the mood to be aroused, but apparently she was wrong. Except it wasn't a jump-his-bones aroused. More of a *I could fall into him and not come up for air for hours* aroused.

Which was totally wrong because he wasn't the kind of man you counted on to be there for you after the novelty of sex wore off.

"Do you have anything to eat?" She was usually pretty hungry after a shift. She typically stopped at McDonald's and grabbed something quick, but she'd been unnerved by that man earlier, and she'd wanted to come straight here. Brian had walked her to her car and waited for it to start. Once it had, she'd freaked a little. She'd been certain someone was following her, so she'd driven around a couple of blocks, doubled back on herself, and then headed straight here.

"I have a few things. What do you want?"

"Carbs and fat," she said. "Though I really should say I want something healthy."

He laughed. "Carbs and fat. How about a frozen pizza?"

Bailey's mouth watered. "Sounds delightful."

"I'll stick it in the oven while you shower."

She wanted to melt into a pile of relief and gratitude, but she told herself she had to stay cool. "I should have asked this originally, but how's my niece?"

"You've been dealing with some shit. It's understandable. Not only that, but not asking right away says that you trust me with her. Which I appreciate."

"I do trust you with her." Probably more than she

trusted herself since she didn't know babies as well as he did.

"I know." He smiled. It was a beautiful smile. And a cocky one. Dude was seriously confident about himself. "She's fine. She was fussed over at my buddy's place, and now she's asleep in her carrier."

"Thank you."

"You're welcome." He frowned, and she bit her lip in anticipation. She knew he was about to say something else. "She's going to need a crib. Something she can be a little freer in."

Bailey gulped. She'd been thinking about that. "I know. But I don't know where to start."

"You can start with a pop-up crib. It's actually a playpen and a bassinet too—I'll show you," he said when she started to get confused.

Bailey gulped in a breath. Did he have any idea how sexy that was? That he knew such things? Probably. There probably wasn't much he didn't realize about how women perceived him. Strong, beautiful, sexy man. He was big and lean and so pretty it almost hurt to look at him. No wonder that waitress had gotten so upset at IHOP. She'd thought he was going to be hers.

Truth was, he probably wasn't going to be anybody's. He didn't have to be.

"Kayla didn't bring much with her," she told him, forcing her mind back to the topic at hand. "The stroller. A diaper bag. Bottles and diapers and some clothes. I've done what I can, but I'm not really knowledgeable. Though I've spent a lot of time on YouTube lately."

That was an understatement. She'd watched videos on so many things to do with babies—feeding, burping, diapering—and she still hadn't scratched the surface of all that needed doing. When she thought of it like that, the weight of responsibly threatened to squash her. No wonder she'd pounded on his door this morning. She'd been terrified of all she needed to learn. Terrified she'd fuck it up.

Wow, was that only this morning? It seemed a lifetime ago at this point.

"Shower," he said. "We've got time to talk. I'll put the pizza in the oven."

Warmth filled her at his tone. She was determined to make the best of this thing. Let him help her. Let him do what seemed to come naturally to him. Pray he found Kayla before the asshole from tonight did. "You really are a good guy, Alexei."

He hesitated a moment. "No, I'm really not." A chill slid down her spine at the coolness in his voice. "But I am right now."

THE PIZZA WAS hot and cheesy. Bailey ate more than she should, but she was hungry after a night at the club. Dancing took it out of her. But it had been a good night. Between the stage and a few lap dances, she'd gotten nearly eight hundred dollars, though she'd had to give some of it to the club and some to the bouncers and waitstaff for their services. Not a bad gig if you could get it.

But not enough to save for college, pay living expenses, and care for a baby. Bailey took another bite of pizza and sighed. She was warm and safe for the moment, but she wasn't worry free. She'd taken a hot shower, scrubbed off the makeup and sweat, and wrapped Alexei's robe around her body. He'd said he didn't use it, and that was true. She could tell because it smelled like laundry detergent, not him.

He sat across from her and ate a slice of pizza, though he didn't eat as much as she did. She told herself she didn't really care, but then she wondered if he was judging her for eating so much fattening food.

That's your mother talking.

Yes, it was. Her mother had been obsessed with her weight. She'd gotten addicted to drugs in the first place because she'd wanted to maintain her figure. When she'd injured her back pushing herself too hard during a workout, she'd started taking painkillers. That was the beginning. By the end, she'd been skinny, but she'd also been dead. One overdose too many and she'd departed this world.

Bailey wasn't going anywhere. She had a baby to care for and a sister to find. And if she had to do it with a little extra fat on her thighs, so fucking what.

A high-pitched wail came from one of the bedrooms. Bailey froze. Alexei dropped his pizza, wiped his fingers on a napkin, and stood. She tilted her head back to look up at him, thinking he resembled nothing less than a warrior headed into battle.

It took a second for her brain to kick in, but she stood as well.

He frowned at her. "I've got it."

"I want to see her." And she did, because even though the tiny baby scared her, she was also the sweetest thing in Bailey's life right now, as well as a physical connection to her sister.

He didn't argue. Instead, he led the way into a darkened bedroom where he'd placed the carrier. She thought it must be his room because the bed was large and the covers were thrown back. She tried not to think about the fact he slept here. She focused on Ana and then felt guilty about the baby lying in her little carrier for hours on end when she needed a crib.

Ana kicked and screamed, and Alexei picked her up. He determined she needed changing and immediately set about the task with an efficiency that stunned Bailey. He whipped off the dirty diaper, cleansed, powdered, and diapered her again in a matter of minutes. Ana stopped fussing and started kicking and cooing when Alexei put her back in her carrier.

"You amaze me," Bailey said.

He glanced at her, his green eyes soft and sensual as he gazed at her. "It's nothing," he said. "You'll get there."

"I hope so. Otherwise I'll have to figure out how to hire you to be her nanny."

He arched an eyebrow. "You'll figure it out. How to take care of her, I mean."

An intense relief washed through her at the sight of him rocking Ana in the carrier. Without this man, she would be totally lost right now. "Maybe so. But I'm grateful for your knowledge at the moment. I don't think I could deal with any of this otherwise."

He rocked Ana, his eyes boring into hers. "Tell me what that guy looked like tonight."

She hesitated, but then she asked herself why. Alexei was cool and competent—and he was a SEAL. That meant something. "Not all that tall. Maybe five-ten. A little on the heavy side, but beefy instead of fat." She closed her eyes for a second. "Dark hair, a wide face with a flat nose, and a scar from his upper lip to his cheek. Looked like someone's idea of a former football player, you know? No neck, bulky, but not exactly fit. He wore a biker jacket with chains. I didn't see the patch."

"Name?"

"He didn't give one." She chewed her lip. "He said Kayla had something of his. What do you think that could be?"

"Maybe she owes him money. Maybe she stole something from him. Or maybe he's just a possessive asshole who can't fathom that she left him." He looked down at the baby, whose eyes were drifting closed. "Maybe he's Ana's father."

Bailey didn't like the cold finger of dread that slid inside her chest and touched her heart. She didn't like to think that evil man could be sweet Ana's biological father. "Can you find out who he is?"

He straightened and she realized that Ana was asleep again. Magic man. Sexy man. "I intend to, sweetheart."

Bailey heard the endearment. It was the second time tonight. But it didn't make her cringe the way it did when one of the men in the club said it. The way Alexei said it, the word was like a caress. Not that she planned to tell him that, of course. He was already too smooth for his own good.

"Thank you."

"You comfortable in that robe?"

She hugged it tighter. It was a thick robe, falling to her ankles. But she was very aware she had no clothes on under the fabric. "It's great. Very comfy."

"If you're tired, you can go to sleep. I'll put your

stuff by the bedroom door so you can grab it when you wake."

Bailey swallowed. She *was* tired, but she was keyed up too. The club, the man, the fear. Alexei Kamarov. It was a lot of shit to process. "I can't sleep. Not yet."

"Need a drink? I've got wine and beer."

She shook her head. "No, I don't drink."

He looked perplexed. "You don't?"

"My parents were addicts, Alexei. Opioids. I don't touch addictive substances."

"That's admirable."

"Thank you... but I think of it more like it's a matter of survival. If I drink or take pills, then what will I be?"

He was looking at her with an intense expression. She couldn't tell what he was thinking at all. But then he spoke, and it wasn't what she expected.

"You're pretty special, Bailey Jones. I hope you know that."

SHE AMAZED HIM. Alexei stared at the girl with the purple hair, her body engulfed in his robe, and he wanted to drag her into his arms and hold her tight. She was so lonely. So alone. Not unlike him.

Not that he usually minded. He liked being alone. Until he didn't. Right now he didn't. He wanted to tangle with someone in a bed, bury his cock in her body, caress and kiss and come hard and deep before falling blissfully asleep. Tomorrow he might want to do it all again. Or he might want to be alone for a while. Never could tell until morning came.

None of that was about to happen with this girl.

Baby. Complications. Here there be dragons...

"Let's get out of here," he whispered. "Let her sleep."

They tiptoed into the living room. He tried not to watch Bailey's ass as she walked in front of him, but he couldn't quite stop himself from doing so. Girl had a fine ass. She also had a narrow waist and big tits, which occasionally gapped the robe open as she moved. He tried to keep his eyes on hers when that happened, but those tits drew him. Especially when he thought they might pop out at any moment.

Just what he fucking needed. A gorgeous girl with a hot body who was off-limits.

She smelled fresh from the shower, not like smoke and liquor and sweat anymore. He tried to picture her on that stage, her smudgy, smoky makeup alluring as fuck, her long limbs supple and graceful, her hips undulating in rhythm to some music, and he couldn't quite reconcile it with the sweet-smelling girl wearing his robe.

Bailey Jones was an exotic dancer, but she wasn't like other dancers he'd known. They were always a little hardened by life, but Bailey didn't seem to be yet. If anything, she seemed determined and overwhelmed at the same time. Innocent and sexy, contrasts that he found far more tempting than he should have, given the circumstances.

There was a hard knock on the exterior door, and Bailey started. Alexei pulled his Glock as he went into protector mode. Bailey squeaked at the sight of the weapon, her hand covering her heart, her eyes widening.

"Is he here? Is he coming for me?

"I doubt it. It's probably my guys with your stuff. But just in case."

She licked her lips. His groin tightened. *Bad timing, dude.*

"Why don't you go into the guest room and wait. Third door on the right."

She spun and went back down the hallway. Alexei glided over to the door, put his eye to the peephole. Blade and Neo lurked on the porch, two badasses scanning the surrounding area suspiciously. Across the street, Mrs. Tucker's curtain whipped back. Nosy old biddy. But sweet. She often baked him cookies. She was under the impression he was a traveling salesman, which was why he was often gone. She watered the plants in the flowerbeds—nothing he cared about, but the landlord did—and kept an eye on things.

Alexei holstered the gun and yanked open the door. "Why didn't you text?"

"I did," Blade said. "You didn't answer."

Alexei reached for his phone. It wasn't there. "Shit, it's on the table. I had to change the baby and forgot to take it with me."

Blade grinned. "Slipping, old man?"

Too much thinking about Bailey and her tits probably. Alexei stood back so they could come inside. "Maybe so."

Neo carried a duffel bag. He dropped it on the couch. "Got a bunch of clothes and the diapers she had lying around. There's also a laptop computer. Not much else to take, really."

"Thanks. I appreciate it. See anybody while you were raiding the place?"

"There was a car out front with a man inside."

"He drove away when I approached," Blade added. "But dude, the place where she lives… It's pretty sketchy. Could have been anything. Drug dealer, pimp, john. Who knows?"

"So he could have been there for anybody in that building," Alexei said.

"Yep."

"It's not the best place, but it's affordable. And easy to rent when you don't have credit."

They all whirled. Bailey appeared in the opening to the hallway, her lithe body engulfed in his robe, her eyes flashing with heat. She looked like a warrior princess the way she glared.

He didn't know if she was mad or embarrassed or something in between. But he moved to defuse the situation. It was late and she had to be tired. Not to mention the stress of the threat tonight. "Bailey, these are my teammates. Blade and Neo."

"Ma'am," Blade said.

"Ma'am," Neo said a split second later.

She frowned. Then the frown melted away as she made up her mind about something. "Hi."

His teammates stared at her. Alexei tried not to feel annoyed, but it didn't work. Dammit, he wasn't going to bang her for very good reason—but neither were these two assholes. "You two got stuff to do?"

Neo snapped out of it first. "Yeah. Guess so."

"Yep," Blade added, shooting a grin at Bailey. "There's a pillow with my name on it waiting for me at home. Nice meeting you, Bailey."

"You too," she said, her voice smoky.

"You get tired of hanging out with this grumpy asshole, call me. I promise not to be a jerk."

"Thanks. I'll keep that in mind."

Alexei growled. "Blade, mind your own fucking business."

His teammate grinned and gave him a mock salute. "Just saying, man. If you get tired and want to split a shift. You know."

"Out," Alexei said. "Now."

Blade grinned, and Alexei knew his teammate was ribbing the hell out of him. And enjoying it too. He walked them both to the door while Bailey went over and started rummaging through the duffel.

"Got a plate number on the car," Blade said quietly, all business now. "We'll run it."

"Thanks," Alexei replied, his annoyance fading. Hell, Bailey was beautiful. Of course they were going to stare. And flirt. He'd have stared too if he were them. He'd already stared, though he'd tried to keep it on the down low. And he damn sure wasn't flirting. No sense going there when it couldn't lead to anything. If there were no sister, no baby, and they'd met at a club, things would be totally different. He'd have been all up in that by now.

But he couldn't, which meant they couldn't either. No fucking way.

Neo lifted an eyebrow. "Don't do anything I wouldn't do, Camel."

"What wouldn't you do?"

Neo grinned. "Exactly."

Alexei closed the door behind them and locked it. When he turned, Bailey was gone. He went over to the table. The pizza was cold, so he took it and put it in the oven again for a quick reheat. In case she wanted more, though she'd eaten half of it already.

She came back a few minutes later, dressed in a formfitting tracksuit that left no doubt about her curves. Her hair was mostly dry now, and it fell to her shoulders in soft purple waves. He wondered what color it really was. It'd been pink in her driver's license photo. Girl clearly liked color.

"You still hungry? I put the pizza back in the oven."

She shook her head. "No, I'm good. Thank you for fixing it."

"It's not a problem. In fact, it wasn't even difficult. Read the package, follow directions." He shrugged. "Not rocket science."

"Well, I still appreciate it. Can I put the leftovers away for you? Or do you plan to eat it?"

"Nah, I got it." He turned off the oven, then took out the pizza and wrapped it in foil.

"You don't let anybody do anything for you, do you?"

She was standing behind him and he turned, met her soft gaze.

"Sometimes," he said, his voice a bit lower and sexier than he'd intended. Suggestive. *Shit.* Not what he'd meant to do.

She cocked her head to the side. Then she smiled. "Are you flirting with me, Alexei Kamarov?"

He could lie. Or he could tell the truth. Then he could play it off. "Yeah. A bit. You mind?"

She hugged herself. It was a defensive gesture, and that bugged him. He didn't think she was aware of it though. "I should. But no, I don't mind."

"Look, you don't need to worry about anything while you're here. I don't expect payback and I'm not hinting you owe me, okay? It's just that you're kinda sexy and I'm a man who hasn't had sex in a couple of months because I've been working."

She frowned and laughed at the same time. "Well, thanks. I think. And I didn't think you were suggesting payment in sexual favors. Honest. But working where I do—well, I don't get the normal kind of flirting, you know? It's kinda nice."

He hated to think about what happened to her at the Pink Palace. He knew the bouncers took care of it, but that didn't mean guys didn't grab her anyway. Or hang out waiting for her because she'd smiled at them or given them a lap dance they couldn't forget. Men should know better, and yet they didn't. He'd dragged plenty of sailors out of bars around the world for precisely that reason.

But he did know better. He put the pizza in the fridge. "You don't have to be uncomfortable with me, Bailey. I've got your back."

He'd like her front too, but he wasn't going to say it.

"And what about when the test comes back? If the results are what you think they'll be?"

She expected him to bail. He could hear it in her voice. He should bail. Why wouldn't he? Most guys would, given the circumstances. He'd already gone above and beyond. He could walk away free and clear. Not his problem. Not his kid. Et cetera.

But she looked so certain he was going to toss her out. Her and the pip-squeak. His gut twisted at the idea. He couldn't do it. He just wasn't wired that way. If he had been, he wouldn't be HOT.

"We'll figure it out," he told her. "Don't worry."

Chapter 8

Bailey didn't want to rely on anyone, and yet the conviction in his voice soothed her. Because she *was* alone, dammit, and she didn't always know how to look after Ana and take care of herself too. It was nice to know someone had her back, even if his answer changed in the next few days. For now, it was enough.

For tonight, it was enough. She'd go to sleep feeling secure even if she woke up feeling totally different.

"I want you to be Ana's father. But I don't as well."

He tilted his head like a puppy that'd heard an odd noise. "Really? Why not?"

"Because you seem like an honest, stand-up kind of guy. If you're her father, does that cease to be true?"

And then there was the part where if he really was Ana's father, she felt like he belonged to Kayla and Ana. Which made her inconvenient attraction to him very inappropriate. Hell, it was already inappropriate. She'd known him less than twenty-four hours and she was already fantasizing about what it'd be like to have him in her life, standing between her and the world.

He did things to her insides just by existing that she hadn't experienced in a very long time. Or had she ever? She wasn't sure. Whatever, she'd like to experience them guilt free, thank you very much.

"If I'm her father, then no, it doesn't cease to be true. It just means that all my precautions failed."

"It also means you fucked my sister and forgot about it."

"Yeah, it would mean that."

"I'm not sure how I'll feel about you then."

"First of all, I'm not convinced it happened. But I'm a man, Bailey. I sleep with women I forget. I'm pretty sure it happens in reverse as well. Men don't have a corner on one-night stands or fucking because it feels good."

Her heart thumped. Just hearing the word *fuck* on his lips made her insides squeeze tight. Other parts of her responded as well. Parts she'd rather did not.

"Well, if you slept with Kayla, she didn't forget you. She knew your name and she had a picture of you and your friends. I'd say she remembered you pretty well." Bailey grabbed her bottle of water from the table and went to sit on the couch. She was tired and she couldn't do this standing up. "Why did you take that picture with her, Alexei? Do you even know?"

He came and sat across from her, a beer bottle in his hand. He twisted it back and forth, eyes and mouth broody. His answer wasn't what she expected. "It's a bar. People take pictures. I know that's not what you want to hear. I remember she was a waitress named Harley. I remember that she was young and sweet and she served us quite a bit. She might have asked for the picture. It happens. Chicks ask for pictures with us sometimes."

She could believe that. All three of the guys in that picture were freaking fine. Tall, muscled badasses who inspired confidence—and maybe a bit of envy out of a girl's friends if she had a picture with them.

Alexei sat back and gazed at the ceiling, tapping his fingers on the arm of the chair. The tapping stopped and he sat up again.

"Wait a minute. That guy tonight. Stocky, dark hair. Neck like a football player. Biker jacket. Fucking hell, I wonder if it's the same guy who used to hang around when your sister worked? Not sure he had a scar though. Could the scar have been reasonably new?"

Bailey's heart tripped a little faster. Was it that easy? Was the guy tonight the same one who'd waited for Kayla almost a year ago at Buddy's Bar & Grill? And if so, what did that mean for Kayla? For Ana?

"I-I don't know. It was dark, but maybe it was kind of reddish. Like new scar tissue." She frowned hard, trying to recall the scar in detail. "Maybe I should tell Brian and Deke to let him back into the club. That way you could see if he's the same guy."

He nodded after a long moment. "Yeah, that could work."

"I don't perform again for another two nights, but if we can find someone to watch Ana, you can go with me. Maybe he'll come back, and then you'll know."

He nodded. "We'll try it. But it's more than ID'ing him, Bailey. If this guy comes back, regardless of whether he's the same one from a few months ago, I'm going to make him regret he threatened you."

A shiver rippled down her spine. His words were filled with dark conviction. She liked it more than she should. Brian was threatening enough in his own way, but he wasn't a Navy SEAL badass like Alexei.

"Don't do anything that'll get you in trouble."

"Don't worry. I have a lot of practice at not getting caught."

"Thanks. I think." What did one say to that anyway?

He glanced at his watch. "One of us needs to get to sleep because the pip-squeak will wake up wanting a bottle in a couple of hours."

She still couldn't reconcile that a guy as big and badass as he was could be so in tune with Ana's needs. It was seriously sexy in ways she didn't want it to be.

"The pip-squeak?" She smiled. Then she waved her hand. "You go. It'll take me a while to come down from the night." It wasn't quite true because she felt a yawn welling up inside. She held it back, but only barely.

He peered at her. "I didn't mean one of us has to stay awake until then. We can both sleep—but one of us is waking in two hours or so."

She sighed. "It should be me. You had her all night."

He shook his head. "You need the sleep. You haven't been sleeping since Kayla left."

"No, I haven't." She hated that he knew, and yet she liked that he was sensitive enough to figure it out. "But I won't always have you to help, so I need to get used to it."

He stood and held out a hand to her. She took it and he lifted her effortlessly to her feet. "Not tonight, Bailey. Go and catch up on your sleep. We'll make plans tomorrow. *After* you've had at least eight hours."

As if in response to his order, she let out a jaw-cracking yawn. She hated that she couldn't hold it back.

He grinned. "Go to bed, Bailey."

"Thanks, Alexei."

"No problem, babe."

She gave him an answering grin before turning on her heel and heading for the guest room. Five minutes later, she was sound asleep.

———

BAILEY SLEPT UNTIL ALMOST NOON. Alexei prowled around the house, feeling restless as hell. He was trapped—and he'd done it to himself.

He flopped onto the couch at one point, opened his laptop, and did some online shopping. He ordered stuff for the pip-squeak. Nothing big, but stuff she'd need, like extra onesies, booties, caps, and a Boppy pillow. He rolled his eyes that he even fucking knew what that was. But his sisters used them, so he knew.

A little while later, he fed and changed Ana, played with her, and gave her some tummy time. When he put her down for a nap, he called Blade to see if there was any news.

"You find anything on Kayla Jones?" he asked.

"Nope," Blade said. "Can't find a trace of her since she left here six months ago. It's like she didn't do anything that required her to use ID. She has no credit cards, so there are no purchases and nothing to track down. She didn't rent a place, didn't change her driver's license to another state, nothing."

"And the baby?"

"If she had the baby in a hospital, she used a different name."

"Birth certificate?"

"None that I can find. Yet. If she had the baby

somewhere other than a hospital, it's possible it hasn't been filed yet. Ana's only a month old, right?"

"Yeah."

"I'll keep digging. I popped over to see Hacker. Got him looking too."

Hacker was Sky "Hacker" Kelley, Echo Squad's IT guy. He'd been damned useful when the team had gone to help Viper, aka Mendez, in Russia a few months ago. If there was anything to find, Hacker and Blade would find it.

"Thanks, man. Appreciate it."

"You got it."

They hung up and Alexei checked on Ana, who was sound asleep. He pulled the door to, not closing it, and went back to the living room to clean his weapons. He unfolded the pad on the coffee table, got out the supplies, then reached into his range bag and pulled out a Glock. He'd just taken apart the slide, barrel, and spring, and placed them on the pad with the grip when he saw movement in the hallway.

Bailey emerged, lavender hair mussed, eyes sleepy. She moved with a sexy grace that drew the eye. He had a quick vision of her lying in his bed, naked, with those same sleepy eyes and tousled hair. His dick started to throb.

Down, boy.

"Hey, sleepyhead," he said. "You get enough rest?"

She shuffled over to him and flopped down in one of the chairs nearby. "I feel like I slept a week. Why didn't you wake me?"

"Why should I? You don't have anywhere to be. I don't have anywhere to be. May as well rest while you've got a babysitter."

She frowned slightly. "Don't make me feel any guiltier. Did you get any sleep at all?"

"Yeah. A couple of hours at a time. She's sleeping pretty well for an infant, actually."

"I don't think she stayed down for more than half an hour the past few nights when I've had her."

"Well, you might not have figured out what she needed."

"You might be right. So she slept, huh?"

"Yep."

"But you still had to get up every couple of hours."

He could tell she felt guilty about that. He thought about teasing her but decided not to. She'd take it seriously anyway. "It's how I sleep on missions. I'm used to it."

She laid her head back against the cushion. "So you're a Navy SEAL. Do you really do the kind of stuff they show on television?"

"You mean those prime-time dramas about Navy SEALs that have popped up lately?"

"Yes."

He oiled the gun, then picked up the slide and ran a nylon brush over it, cleaning away all the gunpowder and grit. "I wouldn't say they're one hundred percent accurate, but they certainly give the general idea of what we do."

"It's dangerous."

"It can be." He brushed the outside of the barrel and spring as well as the grip before wiping off all the residue. "But we're well trained."

She watched him start on the inside of the barrel with a wire brush and more oil. "So you could be killed."

He met her gaze. "Could be. But that could happen whenever you get behind the wheel of a car."

Her lips twisted. "Well sure, but you don't typically drive a car at a hundred miles an hour on an icy road with no seat belt, right?"

"The job isn't *that* dangerous, Bailey. It's more dangerous than driving a car, but it's not like playing volleyball on a minefield or anything. We're not only trained, we're also outfitted with the best equipment and technology that money can buy. Besides, what we do is important."

"And what is that? Chase terrorists and drug dealers?"

"Partly. It's important to eliminate those people and the threats they present. It's also important to rescue civilians caught in the cross fire."

She pushed a hand through her hair. It fell in an artfully tousled wave across her cheek. She curled it behind her ear. "If Ana is yours, how will you care for her with that kind of job?"

Instead of denying the kid was his, he answered the question. "You'll help me."

She blinked. "What makes you so sure about that?"

"Because you will, Bailey. If you didn't care about her, you'd have dumped her off somewhere the minute your sister left her. But that's not who you are."

She dipped her chin, hiding her gaze from him. Now why was he going and being all sensitive and shit? He didn't need to encourage soul-baring. That kind of thing gave women ideas.

"No, it's not. I know what it's like to be left alone and uncared for, so no, I wouldn't do that to Ana." She ran her fingers along the arm of the chair. "Our parents would leave us, sometimes for days at a time. I think I was about eight the first time it happened, which made Kayla four. I didn't know how to cook, but I could use the microwave. I microwaved bacon, bags of popcorn, cans of soup. Whatever I could find to feed us. There wasn't much there, quite honestly. But I used what we had and I got us to school every day."

There was a sudden ache in his chest. "I'm sorry. No kid should have to go through that."

He didn't know what that was like because his mom had always been there. She'd been frazzled and torn in too many directions quite often, but she'd taken good care of them all.

Bailey shrugged. "I did what I had to do. I got really good at taking care of us—hiding food, hoarding supplies, making contacts I could trust when my parents disappeared on one of their drug-fueled weekends. I was scared most of the time, and then I was numb. At a certain point, you just don't give a fuck anymore."

She'd stunned him into silence. He'd seen the dregs of humanity in his job and he knew how low a person could sink. To think Bailey had suffered at the hands of her dysfunctional parents filled him with a kind of rage that surprised him.

She didn't seem to notice. She dashed a finger beneath her eyes, and he wondered if she was crying. But then she looked up, her jaw hard and her gaze clear. He recognized determination when he saw it. "I won't let that happen to Ana. I can't. And if it means I have to give her up to foster care, then I'll do that too—only it'll be the absolute last fucking resort, believe me."

Chapter 9

Alexei looked angry. Maybe she shouldn't have said any of those things, but then again, what the hell. It was true and she wasn't going to hide it. There was too much at stake.

"I'm sorry, Bailey. Your sister left you in a pretty shitty position, didn't she?"

"She did." Bailey had tried not to be angry with her little sister, but she couldn't quite help it. She *was* angry. Their childhood had been harder on Kayla, mostly because she'd been so young when the bad stuff started, but Bailey was having a hard time giving her sister a pass for abandoning her baby.

And now she was worried about what kind of trouble Kayla might be in. What if Kayla hadn't left Ana because she'd wanted to? What if she was trying to protect her baby?

Because Bailey thought that if Kayla had learned anything from their childhood, it would have been that family had to stick together. Maybe their parents hadn't been so great at it, but Bailey sure had. She'd kept Kayla with her no matter what, and she'd taken care of them both. There were times when it would have been easier to leave her behind, but Bailey had never done that. She'd worked and scraped and fought for two people, not just one.

So if Kayla was giving up now, was there more of a reason behind it?

"Do you have any idea where she might go?" Alexei asked.

Bailey shook her head. She'd been racking her brain, but she couldn't think of any particular place to look for Kayla. Kayla went where she wanted to go, where she felt called to go, which was part of what made this so difficult now. Was she being flighty or was she in trouble?

"She's always taken off for a while—weeks sometimes—but she comes back. Except when she went to California and had Ana. That was the longest absence."

"So what about it—do you think she could have had a boyfriend?"

Bailey chewed her lip. If the man who'd threatened her last night had been Kayla's boyfriend, she'd certainly never told Bailey about him. "I don't know. I mean, why wouldn't she have mentioned him if she did?"

"Maybe she thought you wouldn't approve of him."

"If it's the same guy, I probably wouldn't have."

"Did she ever talk about any guys?"

"Sometimes. She was impressed with the military guys coming through Buddy's. But I don't recall hearing your name until I pushed her to tell me who Ana's father was. And then she blurted it out, like maybe she said the first thing that came to mind." She shook her head sadly. "There, I've admitted it—you've got me thinking you might not be Ana's father after all. And I think that scares me more than if you are."

Because he was a decent guy and he knew how to take care of Ana. He'd be a good dad for her. But if he wasn't really her father, then what? Bailey's stomach twisted as she considered all she would have to do to make permanent room for a baby in her life. All the things she didn't know, all the things she'd need to provide. She'd have to find a more stable profession, something with insurance. She'd wanted to go to nursing school, but how would she afford that with a kid? She'd need to work out childcare and think about good schools and paying for college someday—

Panic squeezed her throat, but she closed her eyes and forced herself to concentrate on her breathing. Within moments, her heart rate slowed again and the panic receded to the edges of her brain. When she opened her eyes, Alexei was still there. He was calmly sliding the parts of the gun back together, his gaze on her the entire time. He didn't even need to look at what he was doing. That level of competence was terrifying in a way.

"You done freaking out now?"

She nodded, her heart in her throat. "Yeah," she finally managed to croak. "How did you know?"

"Could be the pasty-white skin that gave it away. Or the throbbing pulse in your throat. Or maybe it's the way your nostrils flared while you closed your eyes and counted methodically."

Bailey gaped at him. "How in the hell did you know I was counting?" She knew she hadn't done it out loud. Hadn't moved her lips either.

He wiped down the gun and laid it on the pad before meeting her gaze again. "Because it's my business to pay attention to signals. I'm good at it. Get dressed and I'll take you to lunch. I fucking starved to death waiting for you to wake up."

She couldn't get over how he just knew what was going on in her head. It was kinda freaky. She shook herself mentally. "You could have woken me up earlier."

"Nope, couldn't. You needed the sleep." He stood. "Now come on and get ready. We can head over to Walmart or Target after lunch and get that portable crib I was telling you about."

All she could do was stare up at him. He was so freaking handsome, so rugged—and he made her insides melt just with the tone of his voice. She didn't need that in her life right now, but she'd be damned if she wanted to let it go.

"Why are you so nice about this? About me being here and upsetting your routine? I showed up on your doorstep with a baby, screeching like a cat, and you're just so fucking nice to me."

He slid a loaded magazine into the weapon, racked the slide, and then calmly tucked the gun into his pants. Once it was there, she couldn't even tell he had it. How did he do that? And how did he look bigger and more intense between one breath and the next?

"I've told you before, Bailey. I'm not nice. I'm not cuddly or soft or biddable. I'm not looking for love, and I don't particularly want children. But I don't turn people away when they need help. Goes against everything I stand for. You need help. Ana needs protecting."

Her gaze slid over hard muscles and thick limbs. It occurred to her that overpowering her would be nothing for him. And yet he didn't. He stood there waiting for her, and her heart melted more than she wanted it to. *Don't make this into something it's not, Bailey. Men leave. Men fail. Men can't be trusted.*

"You're helping us because we need it, not because I can pay you or anything, right?" She didn't wait for his acknowledgment. "Yeah, Alexei, I call that nice. You call it what you want, but you're just about the nicest person I've met lately."

He shook his head like she was a few bricks short of a load. "Then wait until the asshole who threatened you turns up again. You won't think I'm very nice after that."

She couldn't help but smile at him. "Pretty sure I still will."

THEY WENT to lunch at a small diner where the waitresses fussed over Ana and the hamburgers were amazingly good. After lunch, they went to Target and picked up a thing called a Pack 'n Play. It was a playpen, a crib, and a bassinet in one. It also folded so it was portable. There were so many things Ana needed. Naturally, Alexei navigated it all with the cool confidence that Bailey had come to expect.

She was a couple of hundred dollars lighter when they left, but at least she had the right stuff now. When they got back to his place, he showed her how to set up the portable crib, and they put Ana in it so she could kick and play with her feet. Alexei explained tummy time to her, and they put Ana on her tummy for a few minutes before turning her again.

Bailey gazed into the crib at the tiny baby and felt overwhelmed by responsibility but also by tenderness. She reached out to touch a tiny hand. It immediately closed on her finger, and Ana squeezed with a surprisingly strong grip.

"Why don't you want children?" she asked Alexei. She hadn't forgotten what he'd said earlier—that he wasn't looking for love and didn't want children. The first part made perfect sense. The second, considering how much of a natural he was, didn't.

He shoved his hands into his jeans pockets. He looked broody and intense. She thought he wasn't going to answer.

"My parents had six kids, and they were constantly overwhelmed. Add in being immigrants and trying to learn a new language and new customs, and I don't think I ever saw them happy together. They were always fighting, always in over their heads. They tried to hide the fighting, but I knew. They divorced two years ago, as soon as the youngest twins hit high school. They were good parents, but I think having so many children broke them as a couple."

Ana let go of her finger, and Bailey straightened. "But that's six children, not one or two."

He snorted. "Magic sperm, Bailey. I could father six kids before I knew what happened to me. Hell, my luck, it'd happen all at once."

Bailey winced. "Ouch."

"Yeah, ouch is right."

She grinned at him. "Well, sure, ouch for you too— but I was thinking more about the poor woman who would have to carry six babies in her belly before popping them all out. What a nightmare."

"And now you know why I wrap it tight."

Unexpected heat flared beneath her skin. Holy shit, was that a blush? Really? But the thought of this man standing in front of her with a hard-on, his hand wrapped around it as he slid on a condom, was almost unbearably sexy.

He cocked his head. "Are you blushing?"

Hell. So much for being cool. "A little. Maybe." Why deny what he could clearly see happening?

"Over birth control?"

Bailey rolled her eyes. "Not over birth control, you idiot. More or less the thought of you putting the condom *on.*"

His gaze went smoky—and then it dropped over her body, slowly, before rising again. Their eyes met. Held. Her heart pounded. *No, no, no. Bad idea. So bad.*

"I'd be happy to give you a personal demonstration."

As if on cue, her nipples tightened. Her pussy grew wet.

She wanted to groan. She *so* did not have time for this. She had goals, plans. And a huge responsibility with baby Ana. There was no time to get involved with anyone. Especially not with a hunky Navy SEAL who did dangerous things for a living—and who might still be Ana's father even though she didn't really think so anymore.

"I don't think that's a good idea." Her voice was hoarse. Strained. "I can't afford distractions right now."

The fire in his gaze flickered but didn't cool. "I don't think either of us can. But it's been a long time for me, and I'm about to lose my mind. Stripping you naked and tasting you doesn't seem like such a bad idea to me at this moment."

Her belly flipped. Butterflies swirled. She wanted to lean into him. Kiss him. See if it was as exciting as she imagined it would be. Stroking herself into orgasm was getting old, but maybe just one kiss would reignite the thrill of getting off by herself.

No.

"I can't," she whispered.

He pulled in a breath. Took a step back, the heat in his gaze banking. "Then don't look at me like you can, Bailey. Because no matter what you think, I'm *not* nice. I'll make you feel good, but I *will* walk away when it's over. Remember that."

Chapter 10

Living with Bailey for the two days before she went back to work was more torture than he liked. She was sexy as fuck with her lavender hair and lithe body, and Alexei kept catching himself watching her, thinking of the way she'd looked at him when she'd confessed she'd been imagining him rolling on a condom.

He'd grown harder than fucking stone when she'd said that. If she'd dropped her pants then and there, he'd have lost his mind and fucked her before he remembered that he wasn't supposed to do that.

At night when he lay in bed, it was worse. He pictured her in the makeup she'd worn when she'd dropped off Ana—and then he thought of her gyrating on a stage in a tiny G-string. He'd had some massive hard-ons at those thoughts—and he'd been massively pissed off too.

He understood the hard-ons. He didn't know why he was pissed. She wasn't his, he didn't want her to be his, didn't care that other men were ogling her—

Okay, that was a lie. He did care. What he didn't

know was why. She didn't mean anything to him. Their only connection was the pip-squeak, and that wasn't going to last much longer. Once the test came back and proved he wasn't Ana's dad, he was off the hook.

Not that he would kick them out or anything. Alexei wouldn't leave Bailey on her own to deal with a man who'd threatened her and her sister. He'd take care of that motherfucker if—when—he reared his head again.

Still, even when Alexei tried not to—even when he opened his laptop and surfed over to some porn—he found himself thinking about Bailey and what she looked like in a G-string. Wanting to see her in it. Wanting to run his palms down her body and over her curves and mounds. He wanted to explore her. Wanted to hear her moan and call his name. Wanted to see her bite her lip when he made her come.

Jesus. These urges for one woman were nuts. As soon as he got Bailey settled at home again, he'd arrange a hookup with one of the women whose numbers he kept for just such a reason. Women who didn't expect a relationship but enjoyed a good fuck.

He was on edge after two days alone with Bailey, looking at her but not touching her. They ate meals together, talked companionably, and took care of Ana. He taught her several things. Some of it he had to look up on YouTube because it had been a while. But most of it he remembered from his childhood and from visiting his very fertile sisters.

The Boppy pillow came, along with the rest of the crap he'd bought. Bailey's eyes grew shiny as she insisted she couldn't accept. But he'd told her she had to or he was dumping it all at the local thrift shop. So she'd relented, but she kept shooting him thoughtful glances when she figured he wasn't looking.

Drove him fucking nuts.

Bailey grew more confident under his tutelage, changing diapers, feeding, and rocking Ana to sleep. She took the crib to her room the second night, and he never heard a peep all night long. She emerged from the bedroom the next morning with a triumphant smile. He gave her a high five.

The night she was supposed to return to work, he arranged for Miranda to watch Ana. Cowboy was horrified, but Miranda merely laughed and said she'd be delighted. She was between cases right now anyway.

"It'll probably be overnight, unless you want us to pick her up at two a.m."

Miranda waved a hand. "Honey, I got it. Don't you worry. Pick your jaw up off the floor, Cody," she said to her husband. "You might as well learn sometime."

Apparently Miranda hadn't warned Cowboy when they were headed over to Alexei's place what they were doing. Alexei watched them go, silently laughing at his teammate. Dude was about to get a crash course in Baby 101. Alexei would pay to see that if he didn't have other things to do.

Bailey was still getting ready. She'd said goodbye to Ana earlier. When she emerged from the bedroom, she was wearing her tracksuit and the heavy makeup she'd had on two nights ago. His groin started to ache.

She carried a gym bag, and she smiled tentatively at him. "You ready for this?"

"Baby, it's beer and boobs. How can I not be ready?"

She frowned, but she didn't say anything about him

calling her baby. "Pretty sure you can't be drinking beer if you're supposed to be watching for that asshole tonight."

"You're right. Just testing you." He grinned.

She was still frowning. "What are you going to do if he comes back?"

He didn't tell her what he wanted to do, which was put a bullet between the guy's eyes. Instead, he told her what he thought might be believable—and palatable. "I'm gonna have a little chat with him. Find out why he wants your sister—and what he knows."

"Why do I get the impression none of this is going to happen without threats and coercion?"

"Because you've been here for two days. You know enough by now to realize I'm not planning to ask nicely. Wouldn't work anyway."

"Just don't get arrested, okay? I don't have a key to your house or your car or anything. I'll have to go back to my place, and most of my clothes are here now."

He went over to the kitchen and opened a drawer. Then he pulled out one of the spare keys he kept there. He liked to have them on hand, though Money had a key for emergencies. He handed it to Bailey.

"Just in case."

She folded it in her palm and looked up at him with eyes rimmed in smoky charcoal. "This doesn't inspire confidence, Alexei."

"It'll be fine, babe. Come on, you ready?"

"Yes."

They went out and got into his truck. It was about a twenty-minute ride to the Pink Palace. Alexei parked near the building, his truck facing out, and turned to look at Bailey.

She seemed thoughtful. "Deke isn't going to let you in the back. You'll have to go through the front like the other customers."

"Wanna bet?" This Deke was no match for him. He opened the door and put a booted foot on the ground. Then he went around and opened Bailey's door. He shouldered her bag. She huffed a breath like she was going to say something, but then she shrugged and headed for the entrance.

The club was dark, even at the rear entrance. There was a man standing just inside. He was a big man, stocky, and shorter than Alexei. His gaze narrowed when it reached Alexei.

"No boyfriends, Honey. You know that."

Honey?

"Not my boyfriend, Brian. This is Alexei. He's my bodyguard."

Brian looked up, meeting Alexei's gaze. "What, you hired a Russian guy to protect you? Where'd you find him, the mafia?"

Alexei smiled his stone-cold-killer smile. "Brian, is it? Not mafia, man. Navy SEAL, and I'm coming in with the lady tonight. Anybody touches her, they gotta go through me."

Brian puffed up like a rooster. He started to reach around to his back, but Alexei pulled his Glock before the man could even get his fingers on the grip of his own gun. He held it at his side. Casual. Cool. Nonthreatening.

Well, not really. Definitely threatening.

"Wouldn't do that if I were you," he said.

Brian's face reddened but his hand dropped to his

side. "You know this isn't the kind of shit we allow in here, Honey," he ground out.

"I know. But he's here to protect me. And he wouldn't go in the front entrance when I told him to. So what am I supposed to do?"

"What the fuck is going on here?" a voice said. Another man came out from the hallway. He was tall, thin, and he wore gold chains around his neck and one wrist. His gray hair was spectacular because it was clearly a comb-over, but a puffy comb-over that was impressive in its height.

"Honey brought a bodyguard," Brian said. "A Navy SEAL."

The man came into the light. He looked curious rather than pissed. "Oh yeah? Prove it, fancy-pants."

"I can't prove it," Alexei replied, sizing the man up as he holstered the Glock. The man had a shrewd gaze and he was clearly waiting. "But I'll tell you my name and the class I graduated in. If you have access, you can verify it. Or maybe you can tell me your class."

"Yeah, I could. But let's hear yours first."

Alexei didn't mind saying it. BUD/S classes weren't secret. It was the work you did afterward that was. Your assignments, your missions. But every man who'd ever graduated from BUD/S was listed, just like in a high school yearbook. Though only those in the know could access the lists. It'd be interesting if this guy was a brother-in-arms. You never could tell where a former SEAL might end up. A strip club was a little odd maybe, but then again maybe not.

Alexei rattled off the class, year, and date. "Alexei Kamarov. I'll wait," he finished.

"I'll be back in a few minutes. You can wait for

Honey outside the dressing room—but if you're lying, I want you the fuck out of here."

"Fair enough." Alexei followed Bailey to the dressing rooms. There were chairs outside and he took a seat. What he really wanted to do was go in and clear the dressing room, but he could hear feminine voices, so he was pretty sure there was no man waiting inside for Bailey to walk in.

"I told you it was better to go in the front," Bailey said with a sigh as she stood outside the door. "Sorry about that, but Brian and Deke are protective."

"I'm glad they're careful. But leaving your side is not what bodyguards do, Bailey. I can't protect you if I'm not nearby."

She made a face. "I thought you were coming with me to watch for the man who threatened me, not shadow me everywhere I go."

"If I'm shadowing you, then I'll see him if he shows up. You're the one he's after."

She was still standing there when Deke—he assumed it was Deke since she'd called the other guy Brian—came strolling down the hallway. He held out his hand. Alexei took it.

"Deke Mitchell. Graduated BUD/S in 1975. Served twenty-two years."

"Thanks for your service."

"Thanks for yours, Alexei."

"Call me Alex."

Deke nodded. "You taking care of this girl?"

"Yes."

"She hire you?"

"It's complicated. But I'm not going to let anyone hurt her."

Deke nodded. He was a SEAL. He got it. "That's my goal too. I watch out for these girls, and I don't let anyone abuse them. I can still kick ass pretty good for an old guy."

Alexei didn't doubt that was true. Being a SEAL meant something no matter when you graduated BUD/S. "I'm looking for the guy who harassed her the other night. He might have something to do with the disappearance of her sister."

Deke's gaze swung to Bailey. "Your sister go missing? You didn't mention that."

"I didn't think you'd be interested."

"Of course I'm interested. You said she left the baby with you for a few days—that's not true?"

"No. She left the baby. Period."

"Holy shit."

"Yeah, that's pretty much what I thought." Bailey held out her hand and Alexei handed her the gym bag. "I have to get ready, if you two don't mind. You can continue the reunion without me."

She disappeared inside the dressing room, shutting the door behind her. Deke lifted an eyebrow. "You tapping that?"

Alexei liked the old guy, but the question irritated him. Probably because he wasn't but he wanted to. "Not sure that's any of your business, Deke."

Deke snorted. "Nope, sure isn't. But I'm old. I can dream."

"Well, dream about somebody else. She's got enough on her plate."

"All right, sailor. I got a club to run. Make sure you don't shoot anybody on my premises, got it?"

"Aye, aye, sir."

"Atta boy."

A blinking light on the ceiling caught Alexei's eye as Deke turned away. "You got cameras in this joint?"

Deke turned back, nodding. "Of course."

"Think I could get a look at that guy from the other night?"

Deke studied him for a second. "I'll get my guy to review the footage. See what we can find. If we got a good shot, I'll let you know."

"Thanks."

Deke nodded. "See you around, kid."

Alexei took out his phone and called Blade. He trusted that Deke would tell him if he had anything, but there was no sense waiting for the old man if Alexei's team could hack the system and get the information sooner.

If they were lucky, they'd have an ID on the guy before the night was over. Assuming he didn't show up first...

Chapter 11

"Holy mother of God, Honey—where did you find that guy?"

Bailey turned from the mirror to look at Cherry, who'd just walked into the dressing room. She had her red hair piled on her head and she wore a maxi dress and sandals. She was pretty, petite, and Bailey felt an uncharacteristic twinge of jealousy at the thought she'd been outside this room talking to Alexei. Because how else would Cherry know that Alexei was here with her?

"Giant. They stock them on aisle six," she dead-panned, naming the popular grocery chain in the area.

"Har-dee-har." Cherry slung her bag onto the bench and reached up to untwist her hair. "I could use one of those. Maybe even that one when you get tired of him. There's just something… delicious about him."

Delicious? Yeah, that was the word. Definitely the word. Tall, dark, handsome—and Cherry had no idea the man was tender with babies. Holy ovary explosion, that would be nirvana to the girl. She already had three kids with three different guys. What was another one— or maybe two, considering Alexei's magic sperm?

"He's a friend. And he's helping me out."

"I hope he's helping you find your G-spot. Because whoa, he looks like he'd be fun to take for a spin."

The other girls worked on makeup and hair, not paying much attention to the two of them. Though they'd definitely notice Alexei when they left the room.

And he'd notice them. That fact wasn't lost on Bailey. Especially when she considered that he had to go into the club and watch for the man who'd threatened her. He'd be out there for all the shows. Maybe he'd see something he liked. Something he wanted to take home.

Bailey frowned. She couldn't think like that. It wasn't her business and it didn't matter. Besides, even if he did see someone he wanted to take home, he wouldn't right now. She and Ana were there. But what if he did?

No. He wouldn't.

"I'm not taking him for a spin, Cherry. He might be the father of my sister's kid, so no, not going there."

"Wow, really? Lucky sister."

Bailey started to tell her no, not so lucky since Kayla was missing and Alex hadn't even known Ana existed until a few days ago. But that wasn't Cherry's business, and Bailey didn't owe anyone an explanation.

"I said might. Might not too."

"Well if he's not, you need to get him naked and ride that cock until you can't walk. That's what I'd do."

"You'd ride any stiff cock pointed in your general direction," one of the other girls said as she painted on her lipstick.

Cherry laughed. "When it's attached to something fine to look at, you bet I would. I like cock—but not so much I'll fuck any guy with a stiff one. I got standards, girlfriend."

"Yeah," another girl muttered behind Bailey's back. "If he's breathing, that's good enough for Cherry."

Bailey stifled a laugh. Cherry glared, though she hadn't heard what was said. "Mind your own business, Delilah," she told the other woman.

"I am minding it," Delilah said as she sat down and started to brush glitter powder over her shoulders and face.

Bailey adjusted her leather miniskirt and tapped the whip against her thigh. Her heart thumped just a little bit harder tonight, and she didn't know if it was because of the guy or because of Alexei. Probably both. If the guy was here, he didn't scare her because she had Alexei. But what Alexei might possibly do worried her more than a little bit.

She took her phone out of her bag and checked for messages. There was nothing from Kayla. She sent another text anyway, because she was worried, and then scrolled through email. Nothing there either.

On a whim, she sent a text to Alexei. *Behaving yourself out there?*

His reply was swift. *Always.*

Any sign of the creep?

Lots of creeps out here. But none that fit the description you gave.

Bailey snorted. Alexei was funny even when he wasn't trying to be. *You in the audience or waiting outside the dressing room?*

Outside the dressing room. Not letting you head for the stage without me.

All righty. Be out soon.

In fact, there was no reason to wait. She could go and stand offstage and watch Tracey bump and grind through her routine. Bailey often watched the other girls, looking for techniques.

"Break a leg, Honey," Cherry said as she headed for the door. "And then jump that man's bones."

Bailey laughed. "Thanks. And we'll see."

Not that she had any plans to jump Alexei, but a girl could certainly dream about it.

She opened the door and stepped into the hall. Alexei leaned against the wall, one foot propped on the bench, scrolling through his phone. He looked up when she appeared—and if she hadn't been watching him, she'd have never believed the way his green eyes darkened or the way his entire body seemed to go utterly still.

She grinned at him, more than a little self-conscious about the skintight leather and the very little she wore beneath it.

"Jesus H. Christ," he said. "That ought to be illegal."

"What?" She tapped the whip against her thigh-high boot. "Tight clothing and whips? Tsk-tsk, Alexei. I had no idea you were a prude."

"Prude? Hardly. But that outfit— Christ, it's giving me ideas I'd rather not have right now."

"Never been to a strip club, big boy?"

He smirked. "Of course I have. I've just never seen you in a strip club before."

Oh yeah, her heart was thumping now. Almost in time to the music coming from the club. "Then prepare for a great show, Kamarov. I'm gonna knock your socks off."

His gaze skimmed down her body. Up again. His eyes, when they met hers, were smoking hot. "You already do, baby doll."

"Flirting, Alexei?"

"Flirting? This is a full-court press come-on, Bailey."

She told herself not to do it, but she closed the distance between them anyway. Pressed her leather-clad body against his torso. Practically moaned at the heat and hardness of him.

What are you doing, Bailey? Red alert!

She put her hands on his chest, slid them up to his shoulders, the whip still in one palm. She put the whip behind his neck, grasped both ends, and dragged his head down to hers. His mouth was a whisper away when she stopped. They stared at each other for a long moment. She closed her eyes, tilted her head, felt him relax the tiniest bit as he anticipated the kiss. She waited another second until she thought he would have closed his eyes.

That was the moment she let go of the whip with one hand and pushed him away as she ducked aside. His eyes popped open as he stepped back.

He looked shocked for a second. And then he laughed. "Glad you aren't a Special Operator."

"A what?"

"Another name for SEALs and other military Special Forces. Means that I'm glad this isn't combat and you aren't the enemy. I think I'd be dead right now if you were." His voice dropped to a low growl. "Though what a way to go."

A thrill shot through her.

"Hey, you ready to go, Honey?" It was Jenny, the

stage manager, peering down the hall at the two of them.

"I'm ready." She glanced at Alexei. "Any instructions?"

He shook his head slowly, his gaze burning into hers. "None that I'm willing to share right now. Just go out there and do your thing. I'll take care of the rest."

Chapter 12

The girl was smoking. Not that Alexei didn't already find her attractive, but when she'd walked out of that dressing room in head-to-toe leather, her cleavage on magnificent display, thigh-high boots taking his eye up to the barely there miniskirt, he'd wanted to toss her over his shoulder and abduct her before anyone else got a good look at her.

When she'd pressed her body to his, his breath had stopped for the space of a heartbeat. And yeah, he'd expected the kiss. She'd prepped him for it, focused his attention on nothing but her, her mouth moving closer, her cherry-red lips a whisper away. And then she'd punked him. Moved out of his grasp before the kiss ever came.

She'd left him standing there with a throbbing cock and a powerful urge to snatch her back and complete what she'd started. Not that he would have done it, but he'd wanted to.

Alexei watched her ass sway as she strode away from him. It took him a solid minute to collect himself and head for the door that would take him into the club. He found a good spot near the front, at the edge of the stage, and settled in to wait. He didn't sit. Instead, he stood and let his gaze rove over the crowd. It wasn't a huge crowd, but it also wasn't a weekend. Still, there were a good number of men sitting at tables and drinking beer, or harder stuff, hooting and hollering at the woman on stage as she pranced up and down and then stooped to let them put dollar bills in her G-string.

One of the guys tried to cop a feel, and the woman playfully smacked him. A bouncer came forward and pushed the guy back as the woman rose and continued her strut as she collected all the money waiting for her. The bouncer bent close to the guy who'd tried to feel her up. Alexei could tell by the body language what was going on—and it seemed to be working because the customer looked more than a little intimidated.

Alexei forced himself to study the other men in the club. None fit the description of the guy Bailey had told him about, and none looked like the guy he remembered seeing at Buddy's a few months ago.

"Gentlemen, another round of applause for the lovely Tracey Del Mar!" The emcee leaned forward into the mic as Tracey departed the stage. "Are you ready for Honey Payne, our beautiful dominatrix?"

Honey Payne?

The cheering intensified. The lights went down. The heavy pumping beat of a song Alexei didn't recognize boomed into the darkness. And then a spotlight shone down on the figure that appeared on the stage.

Her head was turned to the side, her lavender locks curtaining her face, her bejeweled hat sparkling. She had a fist up to her chin. Her other hand held the whip that hung at her side. The music reached a crescendo—and Bailey sprang into action.

She strode down the center stage like a model on a catwalk, all graceful limbs and exaggerated movements. And then she stopped and began to gyrate her hips, grabbing the pole and twisting around it, her hair flying, the whip's jeweled handle blazing like it had been set on fire.

Holy fuck. Alexei was mesmerized. He had to force himself to look at the crowd, to see if anyone was paying more attention to Bailey than they should or if the man he was watching for had arrived. But Bailey was his focus whenever he turned to the stage again. She was beautiful, her dance seductive and hotter than fuck. She used the whip as a prop, sliding it between her breasts, between her legs. Humping the damned thing. Making his balls ache harder than they'd ever ached before.

When she began to peel off her jacket, his breath stopped. She worked the damn thing, slowly revealing gleaming skin until she finally let the garment fall completely away before tossing it behind her. He swallowed hard, thanking God for the sparkly bra she wore beneath it. If she'd bared her tits, he didn't know how he'd have tolerated these hooting assholes ogling her.

And they did hoot. They whistled and catcalled and said suggestive things, though not enough to get them kicked off the premises.

"Come down here and suck it, baby!" a man yelled.

"Sit on my face!" another screamed.

Alexei dragged in measured breaths. He knew how to be calm, how to slow his heart rate. He did it as a sniper all the time. He was as cool as motherfucking ice out there in the field.

He was cool now. Or he was trying to be. Because inside? Holy hell, right now, he was boiling like a fucking volcano. His dick was hot and hard and his anger was high. But he'd get through it, because that's what he did.

The dance went on for much longer than he wanted. Torturing him. Teasing him far more than his imagination had done the past couple of nights.

Bailey strutted and gyrated. The miniskirt went flying with one tug of the Velcro, revealing a glittering G-string that left nothing to the imagination when she turned and shook her ass. She had a tattoo on one cheek, but he couldn't tell what it was because she whirled again.

By the time she unhooked her bra and teased the audience with glimpses of flesh, Alexei was so fucking pissed he didn't know how he was going to contain it much longer. What he didn't quite get was *why.* Bailey wasn't his girlfriend, or even someone he'd known for years. He had no claim on her.

But watching her graceful body gyrate, knowing how hard she worked and why she did it, spending time with her over the past two days—well, he wanted her. Badly. Even though he knew he shouldn't. Even though it would be a disaster because Bailey had commitment written all over her face and Alexei didn't do commitment. Didn't want it.

The bra went sailing behind her, landing on the stage, and Alexei had to physically restrain himself from going up there and covering her body as the screaming in the audience reached a fever pitch.

And why wouldn't it? Her tits were gorgeous. Full, firm, with pink nipples that stood up straight and proud. They tilted up slightly. He wanted to fill his hands with them, and then he wanted to suck and nibble those tight peaks until she couldn't take anymore before finally slipping his cock inside her and taking them both to nirvana.

Hell, every man in this room wanted the same thing. He could see it in their faces. Hear it in their whistles.

Bailey strutted up and down the stage, the same as the girl before her had done. She stooped to let men put money in her G-string while Alexei gritted his teeth. She cupped a few cheeks, smacked a few arms and asses with her crop, reached into a few belts when directed. Alexei growled. What the fuck was Deke Mitchell thinking to allow that?

The grabby guy from earlier put money in her G-string, but his hands stayed to himself. It probably helped that Bailey had the whip, which she used to great effect whenever one of the guys seemed a little too pushy. Still, Alexei watched them all like a hawk, ready to pounce if one of them so much as put a frown on her face. He skimmed his gaze over the room again, noted nothing new before going back to Bailey.

But then it happened. Bailey had stood and turned toward another group when one of the guys—not the grabby one from earlier, but one of his friends—wrapped a hand around her ankle, sliding his other hand up her calf and heading for her inner thigh. Bailey swatted at him, but he ducked away from the blow. She said something to him, her expression angry.

Alexei didn't remember crossing the room. But he was suddenly there, grabbing the guy's arm, wrenching him backward and twisting until something popped. The dude dropped, screeching. One of his buddies aimed a punch at Alexei's head.

It didn't go well. Alexei caught the fist and redirected it, then took down the next two men who threw themselves at him. Another man launched himself, and Alexei felled him with a blow to the head. He heard shouting, but he didn't heed it. Two other men swarmed in, but before he put them on the ground he realized they were the club bouncers and he stepped back, letting them take over. They mopped up what he'd started, grabbing the men by their shirts or arms and shoving them toward the door.

Deke was there too, looking pissed as hell at the disruption to the evening's entertainment. "Get in the back with your girl, sailor," he growled as he went by.

Alexei stood there for a moment breathing hard, fists clenching at his sides. Music throbbed. Wide eyes watched him from every direction. Not that he fucking cared, especially if they got it into their heads that it was a bad idea to touch Bailey. He sprang onto the stage and stalked toward the back where Bailey had retreated moments before. When he went through the curtains, it was quieter. The stage manager didn't say a word as he stalked by, though her eyes were wide as she followed his progress.

Alexei ignored everyone, heading for the dressing room where he paused outside the door for several moments while he worked to calm down. Then he knocked on the door. It jerked open in his face. A black woman he hadn't seen before stood there, looking pissed. She was gorgeous, with silky dark skin, tawny eyes, and a sneer that said she could eat him for breakfast if she so desired. Any other time and he'd let her just to see how it felt.

"What do you want, pretty boy?"

"Bailey."

"Ain't no Bailey in here. Go away."

"Honey then."

The woman looked over her shoulder. "You want to see anyone, Honey?"

"Let him in, Shasta," Bailey said, and the woman swung the door wide.

Bailey was sitting on a chair, a robe wrapped around her body, her fingernails tapping on the arm of the chair. A couple of other women were there too, but they glanced at each other and at Shasta. The three of them gathered up their things and then strolled past him and into the hall. Shasta was the last one and she stopped, her tawny gaze eating into his as she walked a pointed nail up his chest and tapped it beneath his chin.

"Don't you go punching anything else, lover boy. Especially not Honey."

Alexei blinked. *What the fuck?* "I'm not going to hit her."

"Good." Shasta looked over her shoulder at Bailey, who still hadn't moved. "You okay being alone with this guy?"

"Yes. Thanks, Shasta."

"You got it, girl."

The women left and Alexei stood in the door for a moment before closing it behind him and walking over to her. Her makeup was still perfect, though beads of sweat stood out on her brow and her cheeks. "You okay, Bailey?"

"Yes. I'm fine." She blew out a breath. "You shouldn't have done that, Alexei. Brian and Chris would have handled it."

"That guy was about to grab you."

"I know. And he wouldn't have gotten there. The guys really do handle it. They throw those douches out too." She closed her eyes and laid her head back on the chair. "God, I wish I was a drinker. I could use a shot right about now."

Alexei sank onto a knee so he could meet her gaze better when she opened her eyes again. "Look, I'm sorry. But I wasn't going to let him touch you, Bailey. Nobody has the right to do that without your permission."

Her eyes opened. She gave him a soft smile. "Deke is probably angry—but truthfully? I'm not. It's about time someone beat the hell out of one of these assholes."

Alexei blinked. Not what he'd expected. "Wait a second—you don't mind that I dislocated that guy's shoulder and punched his friends out?"

"Nope. The girls don't either, by the way. They're just being protective of me. But it can't happen like that again. Guys getting beat up on a regular basis could affect revenue. We can't have that. But tonight? Oh yeah, those fuckers deserved it. They've been harassing the girls, especially in the VIP room, but not quite enough to get kicked out. Just enough to get by with a warning here and there."

"I thought you said the bouncers were pretty good about protecting you."

"They are—but what a woman considers harassment and what a guy considers harassment are two different things. Especially in a place like this. Innuendo is harmless, according to them. Besides, shouldn't we expect that kind of talk considering we take our clothes off for money?"

He was about to be so pissed off he couldn't see

straight. Which was going some because he'd already been so pissed tonight he couldn't think straight. Hell, what was happening to him? He was usually way cooler than this.

He stood. Folded his arms over his chest. His knuckles ached, but he didn't mind. Bailey's gaze went to the skinned spots where he'd landed a blow against some guy's teeth.

"I doubt those douchebags will be harassing anyone else anytime soon," he told her.

"Certainly not at the Pink Palace." She sighed and ran her fingers through her hair. He focused on her mouth, on the pretty red bow in her top lip. He hadn't tasted her yet. He wanted to. "I have two more sets tonight. Do you think you can refrain from beating up the customers?"

Alexei started. "Two more sets? You're going back out there after that?"

She frowned at him. "Of course I'm going back out there. The rent doesn't pay itself. Neither does college tuition. And neither will Ana's pediatrician visits if you aren't her father."

"No," he said, his voice hard. He didn't want this for her. He didn't want her going back out there. Taking off her clothes and baring her breasts again. He couldn't deal with it. With men ogling her and lusting over her, jerking off later to fantasies of her and that jeweled whip.

Like you will?

Shut up.

Her eyebrows lowered over her amber gaze. "Wait a minute—are you *telling* me I can't do my job?"

Okay, so he'd stepped in it now. But the thought of

her out there again. *Fuck no.* "Yeah, that's what I'm telling you. Get your shit together, Bailey. We're going home."

"Home? Whose home? I don't have a home right now, thanks to some asshole threatening me." She rose from the chair, her slender body vibrating with anger. Her face was splotchy red, and the color dipped down into her cleavage, which he could see in the gap of her robe. "You aren't telling me what to do, jackass. I need to work, and you're only here to find out who that guy was and what he knows about Kayla. If we leave, how the hell are you going to find him? He's coming *here*. Not to your place. Not prancing down Main Street with a sign proclaiming him The Dude You're Looking For. We have to be here to find him, and I need to work to afford to live!"

His teeth were going to crack if he ground them any harder. "I'll float you a loan. You can stay with me. I'll find him another way. Trust me."

She folded her arms over her chest. Her eyes blazed. "Trust you? Trust you with everything I have when I barely know you?" She shook her head, hair flying. "No. No, I can't do that. I can't take that chance."

Frustration hammered through him. There was something else too. Something that was a lot like, well, possessiveness. He didn't want anyone looking at her in that getup. Didn't want those dudes jacking off to fantasies about her. He wanted to do that— Wait, no, he didn't want to jack off to fantasies. He wanted to fuck her good and long and make her feel pleasure like she'd never had before. He wanted to make her scream.

"We can find another way, Bailey. You don't have to go out there again."

116

She reared back. Blinked. "Why does it matter to you? I've been doing this damned job for a year now. I could do it in my sleep—hell, I think I sometimes do. It's not real, Alexei. I strip for money, but it's not me. It's Honey Payne. She's not me."

He took a step closer to her, anger boiling in his veins. Her scent wrapped around him. There was sweat and powder and whatever body wash she'd used in his shower. She smelled good. Intoxicating. He reached for her. Dragged her into him, his hands wrapped around her upper arms.

She felt good pressed against him, her body soft and warm, her curves apparent beneath the robe. Her palms flattened against his chest, her head tilting up, her smoky eyes searching his with confusion and maybe even wonder. If she'd acted scared or affronted in any way, he'd have let her go.

But she didn't. She stayed.

"It's you I'm worried about," he growled. "Bailey Jones. I don't want you going back out there. I don't want those guys looking at you. Jerking off thinking about you."

She smiled softly. Smoothed her palms over his chest and up his shoulders. Then she cupped his cheeks, her hands soft. He wanted to turn his face into one, press a kiss to a palm. It wasn't like him, and he didn't.

"That's sweet, Alexei. I appreciate it more than you know. But I have to go out there or I lose my job. Strippers are contractors. We don't get benefits like paid time off or sick leave. If we don't work, we don't get paid. I can't afford that right now. Not unless you can find me a new job that pays $70K a year right away. Or maybe you can marry me instead and make me your dependent. Then Ana and I won't have to worry about a thing."

She chuckled at what must have been horror on his face. The *m*-word did that to him. Hell, any word to do with commitment and relationships did that to him. Which meant she knew where the line in the sand was, and she'd just pushed him past it. To prove a point.

"Yes, I know how it works when you marry a military guy. And no, I wasn't serious." She patted his cheek, stood on tiptoe, and placed a very chaste kiss on his mouth. He barely had time to react or he would have gone in with tongue and kissed the hell out of her.

In spite of the *m*-word.

She was too quick, however. She took a step back and yanked the ties of her robe. "I need to dress for the next show. If you could close the door behind you, please."

Chapter 13

Bailey made it through two more sets in spite of being distracted by Alexei's brooding gaze. She could feel him watching, could feel his gaze boring into her. Tracing the lines of her body. She could feel it like a touch.

He'd dragged her against him and she'd melted like wax. She shouldn't have let it happen, but she had. Because she knew if she'd protested, he'd have let her go. But of course she hadn't. She'd stood in his arms like she belonged there.

Except that she didn't and she never would. Alexei had made it clear that he wasn't into relationships, and if she let him into her bed, that's exactly what she'd want. Because, damn him, no matter how he protested and growled, he *was* a decent guy. He'd bought baby things for Ana. He called her pip-squeak and sang songs to her in Russian when he was rocking her to sleep. He was gentle with the baby, honorable, and she knew now that he could sweep through a room and take down six guys with his bare hands without breaking a sweat.

She thanked her lucky stars there were no more

gropes that night. She didn't need Alexei doing the commando routine again. None of them did, because the customers would flee, and that wasn't good for business.

She didn't know what had passed between him and Deke, but it must have been something because he didn't even react to the catcalls and whistles. Or the guy who yelled for her to come down there and suck his dick while she spanked him with her crop.

She almost snorted, pondering how she was supposed to do both those activities at once, but mostly she ignored it and moved on. By the end of the evening, she'd made about five hundred dollars. Not bad for a Wednesday. And not bad considering she hadn't performed any lap dances tonight. She'd figured Alexei didn't need to witness any of those after the incident earlier. She also wasn't in the right head space to disconnect herself enough to do any this evening. They weren't the most fun part of the job, but they were often the most profitable, which was why all the girls did them.

Alexei held the door for her while she climbed into his truck. He went around to the other side and started it up. They sat there in silence for a long minute. She didn't know what to say, so she said nothing.

"You want to stop and get something to eat?" he finally asked.

"Something from the drive-through is good. I don't want to go inside."

"Anywhere in particular?"

She appreciated that he didn't ask her why she didn't want to go inside a restaurant. He understood. Or maybe he didn't, but he wasn't going to grill her about it. "Chicken sandwich and fries. Doesn't matter where."

"Copy."

"What?"

He glanced at her, looking dark and serious, and yeah, delicious. "Military speak. Means I heard and understood."

He didn't say anything else and she didn't either. He took them through a McDonald's drive-through, ordered, and when she handed him a twenty, he looked at it for far too long before he spoke. "I got it."

Her emotions were too near the surface tonight. "Afraid you'll get dirty?"

"Not sure where those things have been," he said as he pulled up to the window and took cash from his pocket.

Oh, that was rich. *Asshole.* Just when she'd been killing herself thinking about what a good guy he was and how much she wanted him but couldn't have him. "I'll have you know that one came from my purse, not from tonight."

He shrugged in a way that said he wasn't in the least bit sorry. "My bad."

"Yeah, your bad." Okay, so it had been a long night and tensions were high. She could ignore him or she could be pissed. She chose to ignore him.

He got the food from the next window, handed her the bag and their drinks, and drove back to his house. Bailey munched fries as they glided through the streets.

"You said you've been doing that job for a year?" he asked moodily.

"Yeah, just about."

"How much longer, Bailey?"

"Being judgy, Alexei?"

"No. I seriously want to know. Because if you have

to take care of Ana, how can you maintain the schedule?"

She'd been wondering that herself. "I don't know," she answered truthfully. "It was always supposed to be temporary. But what is temporary? I thought a couple of years maybe. Get enough money to go to college, transition into being a waitress or a receptionist or something. But it's easy money in a way. Easier than waitressing. You get abuse in a waitress job too—and the tips aren't nearly as good."

"You like showing your tits like that?"

She stiffened. And then she shook her head. "Wow. Really? Fucking wow. You pretend to be so enlightened and nice—*nobody can touch you without your permission,*" she mimicked. Fresh fury swirled hard in her belly, churning up the fries she'd just eaten. So much for ignoring him. "You beat a man up for presuming I'm a cheap whore, but then you treat me like one with a comment like that. What the fuck, Alexei?"

His knuckles whitened on the wheel. His nostrils flared. Handsome asshole. Jerk with an awesome body who made her feel safe. Dickhead she wanted to slap.

"You're right," he finally said. "I'm sorry."

He was giving her whiplash with that reply. She hadn't expected an apology. She'd expected a typically caveman answer of some sort.

"Damn right I'm right."

He shoved a hand through his hair. Squeezed the wheel again. "I didn't like seeing you up there like that. Seeing those men leer at you like you were a piece of meat. And I couldn't help but think that if you weren't standing there with that gorgeous body on display, none of it would be happening."

She didn't know what to say. And then she did. Because he didn't understand. She reached over and put her hand on his arm. The zip of electricity in her fingertips wasn't a surprise anymore. But it was still thrilling.

"It would still happen, Alexei. That's what men do. Doesn't matter if you're covered from neck to toes, they'll still find a way to leer and marginalize you with a comment."

He glanced at her, anger sparking in his gaze. "Not all men."

She leaned back on her seat again. Ate a fry. "I know. But enough of them that I've come to expect it. It's what being a woman is all about. Watching out for yourself, always wondering if some guy means you harm. Thinking about where you're safe and when you're safe. Clothes, or lack of, don't make you safe. A man who'd abuse you because you're scantily clad would do it even if you were fully clothed if he was given the chance."

"You're pissing me off at my gender right now."

"Am I? Sorry. Just telling the truth. But if you don't take anything else away from this conversation, take the fact that my current profession has nothing to do with the assholish behavior of those men tonight. That's who they are. The men who come in and have a good time, enjoy the show, and tip well even though they might leer and whistle? They're just being men. I can appreciate the difference."

"I hear you, babe—but you aren't going to make me feel any better about the fact you're standing there with that magnificent rack on display."

He thought she had a magnificent rack? Now why did that make her blush like a virgin all of a sudden?

She knew she had nice boobs, firm and perky, but no one had ever called them magnificent.

"It's the job, sailor man." She'd heard Deke call him a sailor, so she figured it was the correct term. "And no job is perfect."

"No, definitely not."

They pulled into his driveway and he shut off the truck. She didn't wait for him to come around and open her door, but he made it in time to take her gym bag. She followed him to the front door. He inserted the key and opened it, but he didn't let her go in first. He always went first, blocking her body with his until he deemed it was safe. She didn't understand it, but she didn't complain.

Bailey went over and dropped the food on the coffee table. "Do you mind if we eat here, or do you prefer the dining table?"

They'd sat in front of the TV with food a few times the past couple of days, but she still asked.

"It's fine."

She flopped onto the sofa and rummaged through the bag, finding her sandwich and the rest of her fries. Alexei put her drink down and she took a sip.

"I'm so tired I could crash right here," she said as she unwrapped the sandwich. "But I'm keyed up too."

He sat beside her and grabbed his food. "I get that. Happens to me too."

She peered at him thoughtfully. Was this an awkward truce, or was he going to mention the club again? Before he got the chance, maybe it was time she took charge of the conversation for a while.

"What precisely do you do in the Navy SEALs?" She had a good idea what some of it was after tonight. It involved lightning-fast maneuvers and people who screamed bloody murder.

"Stuff."

She laughed. "That's what they show on those nighttime SEAL dramas—*stuff.*"

"You don't really want to know what my job is."

"Why not? You know mine."

He studied her, his gaze boring hotly into hers. "All right, but don't say I didn't warn you… I'm a sniper. I shoot people, Bailey. From the kind of distance where they don't know it's coming. Among other things."

Her heart throbbed. "I… Wow."

"Upset?"

Was she? "No. I'm assuming they're bad people."

"The worst. Terrorists. Drug dealers. Human traffickers."

"There was a movie about a sniper," she said.

He nodded. "Chris Kyle. *American Sniper.*"

She remembered that movie. It had Bradley Cooper in it. "Didn't turn out so well for him, did it?"

"No, but that wasn't combat. It was a crazy asshole with a weapon."

Bailey swallowed. "But life in general… It seems like he had a hard time adjusting to life outside a battlefield."

Alexei shrugged. "It happens. Every time we come back… There's an adjustment period."

"When was the last time you were there? On a mission, I mean."

"I got back the night before you woke me up banging on my door."

Bailey set the sandwich down. She couldn't eat it now. She couldn't eat anything while thinking about

Alexei dressed in camouflage, weapons strapped across his chest. About the mental load he carried. "Oh."

He frowned. "Is this conversation bothering you?"

She started to lie. But then she didn't. "A little bit, I guess. Maybe because I'm already keyed up. Maybe because, even though I'm pissed at you for trying to tell me what to do, I like you. And the thought of you in pain…"

His gaze hardened. "Stop. Just stop. That's not what this is, Bailey. We aren't a thing. There's no relationship here. You aren't supposed to get twisted around the axle about my work or my state of mind."

Bailey blinked at him. So many things in that statement to piss her off. She snorted a laugh because he didn't even see the irony in what he'd just said.

"Oh really, Captain America? The same as you didn't get twisted around the axle about my work or the fact there might be men jerking off to thoughts of me right now? Because we aren't a thing and this isn't a relationship, right?"

He had the grace to look sheepish. But then he opened his mouth and ruined it. "Right. But it's not the same thing."

Now he was making her mad. "Oh yeah? Is that because I'm stripping while you're out there protecting the world? Is that the difference? Or is it because I'm just a woman and you're a big strong man who knows what's right for me?"

"Fucking hell, you make me insane," he growled, pushing both hands over his face and glaring at her.

"Pot. Kettle. Black, Alexei." She crossed her arms over her chest and leaned back on the couch, propping a foot against the coffee table and glaring back at him. "Explain to me how it isn't the same thing."

"My life is fine. I'm not doing something to get by or make enough money so I can do something else. I'm doing something that makes a difference. What I do helps my country."

"Oh, I get it. Geez, why didn't you say so?" Lava boiled in her veins. "You do something noble while I'm just a dirty stripper, right?"

"Not what I said," he growled.

"You implied it." Bailey got to her feet. "I'm showering and going to bed."

He frowned. "You didn't finish your food."

She stuck her nose in the air and glared down at him. "I'm not hungry anymore. Your hypocrisy has killed my appetite."

JESUS, he was an asshole. There was no other word for it. The bedroom door slammed. A moment later it opened again, and then the bathroom door slammed. The water turned on and Alexei tried not to imagine Bailey stripping down and stepping beneath the spray.

Yeah, he failed.

Alexei didn't blame her for being pissed. He'd been a dick. But when she'd gotten that moist-eyed look, her breath hitching when he'd told her he'd just returned from a deployment, he couldn't stand her sympathy. He didn't need it and he didn't want it. He was fine.

Naturally, it all fell apart after that and he'd made a mess of it. He didn't think she was a dirty stripper at all. He understood doing what you had to do to survive. But her job wasn't important to *her*. It was a means to an end until she could find something better. His job *was* important to him, and being HOT was everything. That's what he'd been trying to say, but she'd gotten pissed and stormed off.

He finished his food, crumpled the wrapper, and threw everything away, then headed for his room. When he heard Bailey leave the bathroom, he went in and took a piss and brushed his teeth. The air was still steamy and smelled like her. Flowery and fresh. If he closed his eyes, he could almost picture her in the shower.

He glared at himself in the mirror, then flipped off the light and went to bed. Naturally, sleep didn't come as quickly as he'd like. He replayed Bailey's striptease even though he tried not to. His cock turned to stone. His balls ached for release.

He smoothed his palm down his abdomen, beneath the waistband of the boxers he'd worn to bed. He took his stiff dick in his hand, nearly groaning at how sensitive it was. How ready.

He hadn't intended to do it, but maybe if he cleared his head, he could think logically about all this shit again. He pushed the boxers down and stroked himself from root to tip. His body responded, the pleasure singing through his veins, his balls tightening in anticipation. He stroked faster, the image of Bailey with her gorgeous tits strutting on that stage foremost in his mind.

It didn't take long before his balls squeezed tight and semen surged up his shaft and shot onto his belly. Alexei groaned as he jerked every last bit of pleasure from his body. Then he collapsed on his pillow, breathing hard.

He stripped off his boxers and used them to clean

up. Then he threw them on the floor and turned over, punching the pillow and settling in for sleep.

But sleep eluded him for a long time. Instead, he lay there and thought about Bailey. Not her tits this time. Her eyes. Her soft, soulful eyes and the way they'd filled with emotion when she'd said she was bothered by the idea of him in pain. It was more than he could take. More than he probably deserved. But what he didn't understand was why he cared what she thought. Why it bothered him.

Why he couldn't get her out of his head no matter how he tried.

Chapter 14

Bailey had to pee. She woke up when she couldn't push off the inevitable any longer. It was still dark out, which meant she hadn't been sleeping for very long. Shouldn't have drank that soda before going to bed.

She threw the covers back and got up. She didn't need a light to see her way to the bathroom. The hall was dark, but the light of a streetlamp filtered inside, lighting the way. She shuffled to the bathroom, leaving the light off as she shut the door and took care of business.

When she finished, she opened the door—and froze as she came face-to-face with Alexei. He was tall and broad, and her gaze skimmed over his bare chest, down his abdomen—and then stuttered to a halt when she encountered no clothing to halt her progression. The happy trail trailed… and ended in a dark mass of hair from which a long, thick cock protruded.

Her heart stopped. Her mouth watered. And she jerked her gaze to his, determined not to look. Not to *want*.

"What the hell, Alexei?"

"Sorry," he said, though he made no move to cover himself. "I didn't know you were up."

"I flushed the toilet! Washed my hands! How could you not know?" she hissed.

He snorted. "Because I was asleep. I woke up when I had to fucking pee. Drank too much before bed."

She let her gaze drop again. His cock was semihard. Magnificent. She wanted to drop to her knees and take it in her mouth. And that was a feeling she hadn't had in a very long time. Too many guys at the club telling her to suck it had kind of ruined the idea.

But now? Oh, now she would suck that thing until he exploded on her tongue. Bailey shook herself. What the hell was she thinking? She was pissed at him, not wanting to suck his dick. She snapped her eyes back to his. Was he smirking at her?

"Like what you see?"

"Seen one, seen them all," she retorted.

"Sure, I'll grant you that dicks aren't all that different—but what I can do with it… now that's something you might want to know."

Bailey was so glad it was dark. Heat flared beneath her skin. Bloomed in hot waves across her body. She was also wet. Her panties were going to be soaked if this continued. But then she thought of his smug superiority earlier. The way he'd shut her out of his life while simultaneously trying to control hers.

She dragged her gaze back to his. "Not particularly," she told him. "If I want to fuck a guy who refuses to respect me, I can just pick one up at the club. Dime a dozen there."

The heat in his gaze banked. "I'm not those guys, Bailey."

"No, maybe not, but you aren't much better. Oh sure, you're helping me. But you don't respect me enough to keep from insulting me when you feel threatened."

He made a sound that might have been a growl. "I don't feel threatened by you. I just… fucking hell, are we really talking about this while I'm naked and have to piss?"

She stepped aside from the door. "By all means, don't let me stop you."

He hesitated as if he might say something, but then he breezed past her and went inside, closing the door. She waited for a few moments, her heart hammering, and then she went back to her room and shut the door. She was just climbing into bed when the door opened.

Bailey squeaked. "What now?"

He stood in the entry, imposing as a Greek god— and every bit as naked. "I'm not threatened by you. I like you. I'm attracted to you. I want to fuck you blind, Bailey. I shouldn't, but I do. So yeah, I get pissed when I have to stand there and watch you baring your body on a stage—and it's not for me."

Oh my…

Hello, melty panties. Hello, hammering heart. Hello, throbbing pussy. She swallowed and forced herself to think.

"That's… Wow. I like you too. I think. But not when you're being judgy and bossy. I've been on my own for far too long to let anyone tell me what to do. And we barely know each other, as you've pointed out many times. It's been three days—even assuming you didn't knock Kayla up, that's not enough time for me to decide to jump into bed with you. No matter how gorgeous you and that cock of yours might be."

He dragged in a breath. "Fair enough," he finally said. "But Bailey—I'm sorry for being an asshole earlier. I don't want you to feel disrespected. It's not who I am or what I do."

He turned and walked out, shutting the door behind him. Bailey sat up in bed for a long while, staring at the door, her body jumping with nerves and thwarted arousal. Now why did he have to go and be decent when she'd been pissed at him for being a jerk? It was easier to turn him down when he was a jerk.

She fell onto her pillow face-first, her screams of frustration disappearing into the cushion.

"YOU AWAKE?" Blade asked.

Alexei pushed a hand through his hair and yawned. "Yeah, man. I'm awake," he said into the phone. It wasn't quite true, but it would be. It didn't take him long to get functional. It couldn't in his job.

"We got the footage," Blade said. "The club uses a local alarm company and they record twenty-four seven. It's real motion footage too. Good stuff. Anyway, found the guy and managed to get a still. His name is James Dunn. He's part of the Kings of Doom motorcycle club —and he's a suspected sex trafficker. He was stopped in West Virginia last year with a nineteen-year-old girl, some marijuana, and a suitcase of condoms. The girl refused to give evidence and there were no charges on the trafficking. The marijuana charge remains, but he left before it went to trial. There are charges against him in several states, including this one. He's wanted for possession of stolen goods, forging checks, and assault and battery."

"Shit."

"Yeah, shit is right. Money thinks he's seen him before. Maybe he's the guy who was dating Kayla Jones at Buddy's."

"Can you send me a pic?"

"Yep. On the way."

Alexei's phone dinged and he pulled it away from his head to open the picture. The meaty face was a little grainy, but Alexei was pretty sure he was looking at Kayla's boyfriend. And the dude was a trafficker in addition to being a fucking douchebag criminal? Man, the feeling in Alexei's gut was not a good one right now.

"That's the guy," he told Blade. "We need to find him."

Alexei didn't like the dread forming inside. Sex traffickers like Dunn were insidious. They recruited girls with promises of love or a better life, then kept them high and traveled around pimping them out, hence all the condoms. The girls were usually complacent because of the drugs. When they were caught, they didn't rat out the trafficker because they were too scared. It was a petty operation, but no less sickening or criminal than the bigger operations that sold girls into slavery in other countries.

"So far we've got nothing, though we're checking hotel registrations and local businesses for any trace of him. I can't say for sure, but he might have been the guy in the car outside Bailey's building the other night."

"He thinks she knows where Kayla is. But what does

he want with Kayla?" It wasn't a question he expected an answer to.

Blade didn't attempt to provide one. "I can't find a trace of her, Camel. Not in California and not here. It's like she doesn't exist."

"She had a baby. She has to exist."

"I know, dude. But she's hiding. She's scared of something."

"Jesus," Alexei said. "If she was really with Dunn, and he was pimping her out—Ana could belong to anyone. Or she could be Dunn's if Kayla was really his girlfriend."

"Holy hell," Blade said. "It makes sense now."

Alexei's senses prickled. "What does?"

"There's something about an adoption agency here. James Dunn visited an adoption agency in Baltimore— the Stork's Nest. They specialize in high-end adoptions. People with a lot of money who are willing to pay exorbitant sums for a baby of their own."

Anger was a drumbeat in his brain. "Any records on the visit?"

"No, just the single entry that he went there. The police were keeping tabs on him, but that didn't extend to the purpose of his visit."

Alexei thought of baby Ana. If Ana was Kayla's and James Dunn's, would he have offered her to the adoption agency for a price? *Of course he would have.*

"Fucking asshole," Alexei said. "Thanks, Blade. I appreciate the information."

"Hey, man. We're like the musketeers and shit. One for all and all for one." He paused. "No problem."

They hung up and Alexei got out of bed. He was still naked, so he found a pair of sweats and dragged them on. They hung low on his hips, but they weren't in danger of falling off. He headed for the kitchen, intending to fix coffee before hitting the shower.

Bailey looked up as he strolled in. He crashed to a halt. She was sitting at the kitchen table, scrolling through her phone. She was completely dressed in skinny jeans, sandals, and a fitted tee that emphasized how luscious her breasts were. Alarm bells began to ring deep within him.

"Going somewhere?" he asked as he went over to the coffee maker and pressed the Start button.

Her expression was cool. "I think maybe I should go home. Get out of your hair."

He gaped at her. "Is this about last night?"

She dropped her gaze for a second. "No."

He didn't believe her. "What the hell are you thinking, Bailey? That asshole is still out there, still looking for you." He shook his head. "I can't let you go."

"I'll buy a gun. He won't get very far if he tries to break in."

"First of all, there's a waiting period. Second—ever shoot a gun before?"

She hesitated too long. "Once. It's not that hard."

"Sure, it's easy to pull a trigger… It's not so easy to hit what you're aiming at."

She threw up her hands. "I have a life, Alexei. I can't put it on hold forever. I need to go home and do my own thing. Without *you*, because you won't always be there to bail me out."

He couldn't even process what she was saying. "A man threatened you with physical violence—or have you forgotten?"

"I didn't forget. But guys say shit all the time at the

club—doesn't mean they mean it." She snorted. "Hell, *you* say shit and you don't mean it."

He was too pissed to ask her what she meant by that last sentence. "Bailey. Jesus." He paused, gathered his thoughts. "All right, how about this? His name is James Dunn. He's definitely the guy I saw last year at Buddy's waiting for your sister. Multiple times, I might add."

She looked only mildly shocked. "Okay."

He stalked over to where she sat, glared at her. "No, not okay. He's a sex trafficker, Bailey. He sells women into sexual servitude. He keeps them high and pimps them out."

Her eyes widened. Her jaw dropped. Her eyes were clear one minute and then glistening with tears the next. He felt like an ass for putting that look on her face, but she had to know. And she had to believe she was in danger.

"Oh my God. I… Are you sure?"

"Yeah, I'm sure." He couldn't tell her about the existence of HOT, much less that it was state of the art and had access to more secret shit than she could imagine. And even if they didn't have access, their IT guys were good enough to break in. Not that it was always kosher to do so—or that Mendez would approve in all instances. In fact, he might knock some heads together and bust some ranks before it was all through.

"And you say he was Kayla's boyfriend?"

"She said he was, yeah. They were dating when she was working at Buddy's."

She tilted her head. "How do I know you're telling me the truth?"

What the actual fuck? "Seriously?" He spread his arms out, anger coursing through him. "Why would I lie? I swabbed my fucking cheek for you, Bailey. I'm not trying to direct you down another path when the test is already done. If I'm Ana's father, which I am *not*, I'll do the right thing."

"But if you aren't?" she shot back. "What then?"

He knew what she was waiting for. She was waiting for him to say he was gonna cut her loose. And he should. God knew he should. She was a pain in the ass. The pip-squeak was adorable as hell, but not a good fit for his lifestyle. He needed them gone. Sooner the better.

But first he had to make sure they were safe. He couldn't live with himself if he didn't. "I'm not quitting, Bailey. We're going to find Kayla, I swear it. We'll get Dunn and make sure he can't hurt you or Ana or Kayla. I'll fix this."

Bailey's eyes glistened. He thought she might cry, but she put her head in her hands and breathed in and out. "My God, it's all so complicated. Just a little over a week ago I was planning my schedule and going about my business. Now I have a baby, a missing sister, a sex trafficker—and a Navy SEAL who wants to be the boss of me."

Yeah, he wanted to be the boss of her all right. In bed.

"I'm not trying to tell you what to do." He paused as her head snapped up so she could glare at him. "All right, fine, I am trying to tell you what to do. But it's my job, okay? I have experience with this shit. I keep you safe, get the bad guy, and then you're free to do whatever the fuck you want to do."

One eyebrow went up. "Really? Whatever I want to do, huh?"

His dick started to tingle. *Down, boy.* She was too pissed to flirt with him right now. She was being a smartass. "Yeah. Just stick with me for a while, okay? Let me help you."

She blew out a breath. Shook her head. "Fine," she finally breathed. "I don't suppose I have a choice anyway."

Chapter 15

Bailey yawned as she applied her makeup that night. She hadn't gotten much sleep the evening before. After her encounter with Alexei, she couldn't stop thinking about the full package. The *full* package, because she'd seen everything. It had been dark, sure, and she hadn't gotten as good a look as she wanted, but she'd seen enough to realize the dude was hung. She'd already known he was hot. She hadn't known he had the equipment to go with the rest of the package until that moment.

But, wow, he did. So she'd tossed and turned and, yes, finally caved and sank her fingers into her wet heat so she could get some relief. She'd been so certain when she woke this morning that she had to put some space between them. Before this craving got worse. Before she gave in and slept with him—and then got her heart broken because he wasn't a guy who did relationships, as he'd stressed more than once.

Not that she wanted a relationship. She didn't have time for one, not really. But she also knew herself. She'd been lonely for a long time. If she started down the path of a physical relationship with Alexei, she could fall for him all too easily. Not because he was hot and sexy, but because he had a tender, honorable side that drew her to him with every second they spent together. He was nothing like the men she'd known growing up, or the ones who came to the club and only saw her as a body.

If only he was bad with babies, or he'd slammed the door in her face when she'd first showed up on his doorstep. Then again, she'd probably be in bigger trouble right now if he had, considering what he'd told her about James Dunn.

Bailey shuddered. What the hell had Kayla gotten herself into? Why was her little sister so bad at making decent choices? And why had she hidden James Dunn's existence last year? Because Kayla had never mentioned a boyfriend. She'd talked about the military guys at Buddy's, but never one in particular. Not even Alexei.

And all the while, she'd been hanging out with Dunn. Had she gone away with him too? Had she and Melanie really gone to California, or was that all a lie? And what about now? Was Kayla hiding, or had Dunn found her after all? Was that why he hadn't been back yet?

Bailey picked her phone off the counter and opened her text messages. There was an endless string of texts from her to Kayla, but nothing in return. She sighed, then brought up the keypad and began to type.

Why didn't you tell me about James Dunn?

She stared at the screen for a long while, then finally hit Send and set the phone down again. She finished her makeup, fluffed her lavender hair—maybe it was time to go back to being blond—and grabbed her gym bag with all the stuff she needed for tonight.

When she emerged from the bedroom, Alexei was watching television, his feet propped on the couch. He shot her a look over his shoulder, his gaze darkening as it slid over her body. Then he turned away again, and she felt the loss of his heated gaze.

He turned off the TV and stood. "You ready to go?"

"Yes."

They walked out to his truck, and he held the door for her, like always. She watched him walk around the front and then stared straight ahead while he climbed inside. He was wearing dark jeans and a black polo shirt tonight. He looked good enough to eat with a spoon, damn him.

"It's so quiet without Ana," she finally said as he backed out of the drive and headed down the street. She hadn't thought she'd miss her niece, but she did. Not everything about her, that's for sure. But some things. Her little face—when she wasn't crying. Her snuggles. Her sweet baby smell.

"I'm sure she's being spoiled rotten right now. Miranda's having fun. Cowboy, probably not so much."

He snorted a laugh and Bailey couldn't help but grin. "You're seriously having fun thinking about your poor friend dealing with a baby, aren't you?"

"Oh yeah. Cowboy needs someone with his maturity level to play with."

"Cute."

"Okay, so Ana is more mature. My mistake."

Bailey laughed. "Your friends are great. You sure they don't mind keeping her?"

"I'm not sure of anything—but I know that Miranda and Cowboy will take care of her and keep her safe."

Bailey sighed. It must be great to have friends like that. People you could count on to watch your back whenever you needed it. To be there for you. She'd been taking care of herself—and Kayla—for so long that she didn't know what it was like to have a tribe. Oh, she had the girls at the club and some of them were awesome. But they all had their own lives and their own problems to deal with.

"Are you friends with the rest of your teammates?" She knew that SEALs had teams or units or squads or something. But were they close or did they just work together?

"We're brothers. We'd do anything for each other."

She thought of his conversation with Deke last night. "Was Deke a SEAL too?"

He glanced at her. "Yeah, he was. Decorated too."

"Decorated?"

"Medals. He saved people. Did important shit. He's a good guy."

He was, though he was also a hard-ass sometimes. "You're not going to piss him off tonight, are you?"

Alexei laughed. "Can't guarantee that, but it's not my goal."

They were nearly to the club when her phone chimed with a text. She fished it from her bag, thinking it might be one of the girls giving her a heads-up about something. They often did that for each other. Schedule change, someone couldn't make it, et cetera.

But it wasn't any of the girls. It was Kayla. Bailey started to shake as she hit the Call button. If Kayla had just texted her, surely she could talk.

"My sister," she said to Alexei as he pulled into the club parking lot and swung into a spot. He didn't turn off the truck. Bailey let the phone ring and ring, but Kayla didn't pick it up. "Dammit!" she yelled, stabbing the button to end the call. Because Kayla wasn't going to answer no matter how many times Bailey kept trying.

"Let me see the text," Alexei ordered.

She swiped back to the message box. Swallowed as she read it again. Then she turned it to Alexei. A muscle in his jaw flexed as he read it too.

Stay away from James. He's dangerous. He'll kill you. Does he know you have Anastasia? Don't TELL him, Bale! Please don't tell him!

———

DUNN HADN'T SHOWN. Alexei waited for Bailey outside the dressing room door, anger humming in his veins. He hadn't wanted her to do this tonight. In fact, he'd tried to stop her, tried to convince her that it would be better if she went back to his place and chilled the fuck out for a while.

Predictably, she didn't like that idea. She'd argued. He'd argued. They'd yelled. He'd asked himself, at one point, what the fuck he was doing because it sounded like two people in a relationship having a fight. And he was intimately familiar with those because he'd had to listen to his parents' fights when he lay in bed late at night and they'd thought no one could hear.

To be fair, he hadn't heard the words, but he'd heard the voices. Angry voices. Pleading voices. Crying—his mother. More yelling—his father. And then silence. Sometimes he heard other noises. Noises he couldn't quite identify. He knew now what he didn't know then—they were the sounds of make-up sex.

So he'd argued with Bailey while a disconnected part of him watched the whole thing and shook its head in disbelief. *What are you doing, dude? Why are you fighting over this? Let her fucking dance. Watch the show. Watch for Dunn.*

In the end, that's what he'd done. But he'd hated it. Hated every damned second of Bailey's routine. Her sexy little gyrations, her spins on the pole. The mother-fucking lap dance she'd performed for some kid cele-brating his twenty-first birthday. Alexei had watched the whole thing in stunned, angry silence.

It also made him hard, which pissed him right the fuck off. He wasn't a deprived kid getting hard at the slightest hint of sex. And certainly not while watching a woman grind on another dude.

A woman he wanted pretty badly if he were being honest with himself. He wanted her to grind on him like that. Naked.

He was still pissed off when the door opened and she came out. She'd changed into her usual tracksuit. Her makeup was still in place, though it was smokier and more smudged than when she'd started.

She didn't smile. He didn't either.

"You ready?"

"Yes."

They walked out to his truck in silence. He held the door for her. Got in and started it. "McDonald's?"

"That would be great."

They rode in silence. "Same as last night?" he asked when they turned into the parking lot.

"Yes, please." She held out a twenty. This time he took it. Not because he wanted her to pay for the food but because she'd gotten so mad at him last night for refusing. For making her feel dirty and cheap, she'd said.

He didn't want to do that. He hadn't intended to do that. He'd been a broody bastard though. Tonight he wouldn't be. Even though anger and frustration hummed through his veins like an alcohol buzz.

After he handed her the food, she started eating fries. But she still didn't speak. He sighed.

"You still mad?"

"No. I'm hungry." *Chomp, chomp, chomp.*

"You sound mad."

She closed the bag. Blew out a breath. "Okay, fine. I'm irritated. I'm also worried about my sister. Worried about Ana. What the hell did Dunn say or do to scare Kayla so badly? Why won't she answer my calls and tell me what the fuck is going on?"

Alexei white-knuckled the wheel. He was used to fixing things for people, but so far he hadn't fixed anything. "I don't know. I intend to find out. If I could fix everything for you right now, I would. But I can't."

She sniffed. "You can fix one thing."

"What's that?"

"You can apologize for being bossy. There was no reason for me to skip tonight and every reason to be there."

Shit. "He didn't show up."

"He *could* have. And you'd have been there to get him if he had."

"I wasn't going to abandon the plan, Bailey. Deke could have looked out for him. A couple of my guys could have gone and watched for him too. If Dunn showed up, one of them would have bagged him."

Her head dropped. "Maybe I just needed something

to do. Did you think about that?"

He wanted to give her something to do. "Like a lap dance?" he ground out, unable to stop the words from escaping.

She snorted suddenly. "Oh geez, that poor kid. I didn't even touch him—but he was so aroused."

Alexei growled. *Not* what he wanted to know. "Of course he was. You were grinding on his lap like—"

She arched an eyebrow. "Like?" Before he could think up a suitable answer that wouldn't piss her off more, she shook her head. "I wasn't touching him, Alexei. It only looked like I was. If I'd ground on his lap for real, he'd have embarrassed himself in front of all his friends. Which I think they wanted or they'd have gotten him a private dance."

Private dance. He didn't even like to think about it. He turned into the driveway and shut off the truck. But he didn't move. Neither did she. Because she clearly hadn't forgotten what she'd told him she wanted when she'd finally started speaking to him. Alexei blew out a breath.

"I still think you could have skipped tonight, but I'm sorry for being an ass about it. Happy now?"

She laughed. It wasn't at all the sound he'd expected. "Wow, I didn't think you were actually going to do it. Just for the record, Alexei, you're lousy at apologies. You did it, but you sound pissed off about it. Not to mention you still don't think you're wrong."

He flexed his hands on the wheel. Let go and scrubbed a hand through his hair. "I wasn't wrong that you didn't need to be there. It was handled."

"I couldn't let the girls down though. And I still need the money, let's not forget. Unless you turn out to be Ana's father, and then you can marry me and support us both— Oh my God, your face!" she howled. "So funny. You really do get totally horrified at the idea of marriage, don't you?"

She was teasing him? Of course she was. Alexei opened his door, put a boot on the ground. "Ha ha," he said. "You're a real comedian, Bailey Jones."

———

OKAY, so maybe she shouldn't tease him, but she'd had a hell of a night, and she could use a good laugh. So fine, she'd pressed his hot button. Lain on it, in fact. He'd been a bossy ass earlier, so he deserved it.

She got that he was trying to protect her, but the only thing that had changed before she walked into work was that text from Kayla. It upset her, sure. But, if anything, it made her more determined to go in there and perform. Because Kayla was safe for the moment, and maybe Dunn would show up again. And then Alexei could do his thing and stop Dunn from threatening her and Kayla and Ana.

More than ever, she believed that Alexei wasn't Ana's father. Kayla had pulled his name out of her ass when confronted, but Bailey suspected that Dunn was really Ana's father. And Kayla hadn't wanted her to know it. But why? And why run off like that? Why not answer any fucking phone calls? Was Ana the thing of Dunn's she'd taken?

Bailey waited behind Alexei while he unlocked the house and went in first. She palmed her phone while setting the food on the coffee table, checking again for any messages. Of course there was nothing. She tapped out a text while eating fries.

Why won't you answer me? Are you safe? We're fine here. I'm with AK. Did you lie about him being the father?

She sent it before she could change her mind. Kayla probably wouldn't answer anyway. Alexei dropped onto the couch beside her and dragged his food from the sack. He flipped on the television and went to cable news. She'd noticed that he watched a lot of cable news, much of it international.

She checked her email, placing the phone on the table so she could eat and read at the same time. There was the usual shopping stuff, a Groupon offer—and an email from a genetics lab.

Her heart thumped. It had to be the test results. The kit's information sheet had said they'd send an email notifying her once the results were in. Her sandwich was suddenly dry in her mouth, and she picked up her soda to take a deep drink.

She glanced at Alexei. And then she opened the email and read the contents. It directed her to a site where she could log in with the PIN they'd given her. She followed the directions and then she was in. There were disclaimers. Jargon. And then a page to tap for the result.

"Alexei?"

He turned his head. "Yeah?"

"I got the email from the DNA test company. I've logged on to see the results."

His brow furrowed. He pressed the Mute button. Was that concern in his eyes? Oh hell, she did not need to see that. She melted when he was nice. When he was an ass, it was much easier to maintain her distance. He needed to be an ass right now.

But of course he wouldn't be. He'd be sensitive and amazing.

"You okay?"

She swallowed. "I haven't looked yet. I thought we should look together."

His expression softened. "If that's what you want."

Her finger hovered over the link. She almost wished she could make time stand still for a little while. Let Ana at least have the possibility that a man like this one was her birth father.

"Whatever the result," he said softly, his deep voice stroking her nerve endings, both soothing and arousing at once, "I've grown kinda fond of that pip-squeak."

She smiled in spite of the hammering of her heart. "She does that to a person." She pulled in a breath. "You ready?"

"Yeah."

He leaned in to look at her phone, and Bailey tapped the link. She had to scroll past a data table with percentages, but then the result appeared in black and white.

JOHN DOE IS EXCLUDED as the biological father of Jane Doe.

"WOW," she said, sudden tears pricking the backs of her eyes. "I guess you were right."

"Guess so."

"I'm sorry for everything," she began, but his gaze snapped to hers and his fingers pressed against her lips. Softly, but firm enough to make her hesitate.

"No. You did what you had to do. You're a fierce aunt, Bailey. Kayla told you I was Ana's father. That's not your fault."

"I don't know why she lied to me." She bit the inside of her lip. "She lied about so much, you know? I ask myself who this girl is, who she's turned into. We were close growing up because we had to be. I took care of her, looked out for her, tried to make things right for her."

"You did your best. But we all make our own choices, right? Your sister made hers for reasons you may never understand. Doesn't mean you didn't do a good job raising her."

"Maybe that's it," she said as his words sank in. "Maybe I was more parent than sister to her the past few years. She certainly hid stuff from me like she thought I wouldn't approve. And I probably wouldn't have."

She pressed her hands to the sides of her head as the import of the test sank in. Really sank in. She wanted to hyperventilate. Wanted to have a good freak-out for once in her life. But she never got the luxury of having those. It was her job to be strong. To do whatever it took to survive and not let life beat her down.

"What the hell am I going to do now?"

Alexei's strong fingers wrapped around her wrists, pulled her hands away from her head. He entwined his fingers with hers. Her body sizzled to life with sparks of excitement that she did not need to feel.

"You'll do what you always do, Bailey. You'll take care of the people you love." He squeezed her hands. "I'll help you figure it out."

Chapter 16

Alexei couldn't sleep. He was restless as fuck. How the hell was he restless when he'd gotten the news tonight that he hadn't accidentally fathered a child after all?

He'd known he wasn't Ana's father, but there'd been that small sliver of doubt that sometimes crept in when he was alone. Had he fucked up somehow? Gotten drunk and forgotten the condom? Forgotten to pull out?

But he hadn't done any of that. Ana wasn't his.

He was relieved. And yet he felt a little melancholy about it too. Which was odd because he didn't want kids. He didn't want the responsibility of caring for another human being and making sure they had everything they needed. Then there was the problem of possibly fucking up their life by being gone on missions all the time or, worse, getting killed out there and never seeing them grow up.

Fuck.

He threw back the covers and stalked to the kitchen for a beer. Maybe that would help. He snagged one from the fridge, popped the top, and took a healthy swig. The sound of a door opening in the hallway made him freeze. He heard her footsteps, and then she appeared in the light coming in the window.

"Can't sleep?" he asked.

"No."

"Want a beer?" He remembered that she didn't drink. "Strike that. I forgot."

She shrugged as she walked into the kitchen. She was wearing a long T-shirt that hung halfway down her thighs. It wasn't meant to be sexy, not like the clothing she wore at the club, but it was. Or maybe it was sexy because he knew what was under it. He'd seen everything but her pussy at the club. Hell, everyone at the club had seen everything but her pussy.

Alexei gritted his teeth and tried not to think about that. It pissed him off, and he wasn't quite sure why. "Anything else then?" he asked as she climbed up on a barstool next to the kitchen counter. "Soda? Juice? Water?"

"No, I'm fine. I just… I heard you get up, and I didn't want to be alone. I think too much when I'm alone."

God, he knew what that was like lately. "What were you thinking about?" As if he didn't know. Ana. Kayla. How she was going to get by with an infant to take care of all on her own.

She shrugged. "A lot of things. And you…"

"Me?" He hadn't expected that. "Why me?" His blood started to hum.

"Because you're interesting. You speak Russian. You come from a big family and you know your way around a diaper. You stepped up and you stuck by my side even when you didn't have to. You could have brushed me off until the test results came back, but you didn't. You started acting like Ana could be yours even while you insisted she wasn't. And you bought her things I didn't know she needed."

Why was his face growing warm at that recitation of facts? "I didn't spend a fortune, Bailey. It's just some stuff."

She ran a fingernail back and forth along a crack in the laminate counter. "Maybe so, but you still didn't have to do it. It was sweet of you."

Sweet? He was not sweet. Not usually anyway. He was just… raised right. "Okay, so it was sweet of me. Now what?"

"Nothing, I guess. I just wanted you to know that I appreciate everything you've done. I know we haven't always seen things eye to eye."

He took another slug of beer. His cock was still tingling. Still interested. He really wished it wasn't, but it most certainly was. Bailey Jones had *trouble* written all over her. And not in the usual sense of the word, because that kind of trouble he could deal with.

No, she had *commitment* written all over her, no matter that she'd said otherwise the first day he'd met her, and that was the kind of trouble he definitely wasn't looking for. Still, his cock tingled and his balls ached and he wanted to tug her off that stool and into his arms. He hadn't even kissed her yet. Hadn't tasted her lips at all. She'd pressed her mouth to his once, so quickly he hadn't gotten a taste, but now all he could think about was what he'd missed.

"If you really want to thank me," his mouth began while his brain pounded out a warning, "you can start with a kiss."

Her eyebrows went up. He thought there was a good chance she might get angry and stomp out of the room. After all, he'd told her that she didn't owe him a thing—and certainly not sex—in exchange for his help.

But fuck it, he wanted to kiss her. And since he wasn't going to make a move without permission, there was only one way to get it. Tell her what he wanted.

She blinked. Licked her lips. He suppressed a groan. His dick was growing stiffer. If she let him kiss her, he'd probably have to go back to his room and whack off before he could get to sleep again.

Her gaze dropped over his body, and he knew there'd be no hiding his erection for much longer. She trailed her eyes back up again, her long lashes lifting slowly until her amber gaze met his. Was that interest he saw there? Or maybe it was disgust that he'd stooped to such a low. She was used to propositions, most of them not as nice as what he'd just said. But still a proposition.

"Okay," she said. "I think I can do that."

SO MAYBE IT was a bad idea to agree to a kiss, but the truth was she wanted it. She'd lain in bed thinking about Alexei's body, his naked body that was utter perfection, and she'd once more found her fingers drifting beneath the covers and down toward her wet center. But then she'd heard his door shut and his footsteps head for the kitchen. She'd lain there for five minutes, debating with herself about whether or not to get up and go talk to him.

Not because she'd expected him to ask for a kiss, or even expected anything to happen between them. Just because she'd wanted to see him and talk to him. Because this was almost over, whatever this was. He wasn't Ana's dad and he wasn't going to want her and Ana around for much longer.

Oh, she believed him when he said he was going to protect her from James Dunn. But how long would he keep looking for the man? He had a job, and one day soon he was going to have to go back to work. Even if he wanted to, he wouldn't have time for her and Ana and their drama. It was a lot of drama.

She slipped off the stool and went over to his side. He set his beer on the counter and turned to face her. She hesitated for a second and then pressed forward, into him, her palms sliding up his bare chest. Her heart skipped a beat. He was warm and hard, his skin silky smooth to the touch.

He put his arms around her, held her loosely. She tipped her face up to his. He was taller than she was, her forehead coming up to his chin.

"So how do you want it?" she asked, her voice on the verge of cracking. Heat flowed through her, pooled between her legs. Her sex ached with a need she found surprising. She hadn't had sex in over a year, but she also hadn't wanted it. Working at the Pink Palace had kind of burned the desire for a man right out of her. Not in the generic sense, but in the specific sense. She found every man who propositioned her lacking—and that's what they did. Proposition. There was an expectation that, because she stripped, they didn't need to ask her on a date or court her in any way.

Which was sad, because inside she was still the small-town girl who wanted a guy to take her out, talk to her, get to know her a little bit before trying to ram a hand down her pants.

And then there was Alexei. He was different. He'd pissed her off in more ways than one, but he still managed to be a good guy in spite of it all. They'd talked a lot over the past few days. He'd asked about her life. She'd asked about his. They'd talked about Ana and babies in general. He might not be the kind of guy who wanted a long-term commitment, but she wasn't convinced she wanted it either.

Right now she'd just like to be with a guy who knew her as more than a chick he'd watched strip in a bar. Sure, Alexei had seen that too—but he'd never actually treated her differently because of it. He'd growled and grumbled and been a little judgy, but he'd never treated her like she was easy simply because she danced. So many guys did.

"Maybe don't ask me that," he said very seriously. "Because my mind goes places that are way beyond a kiss."

She skimmed a hand down his arm, over his hard biceps, back up again. "What kind of places?"

"Bailey." His voice sounded strained. "Seriously, I haven't had sex in a couple of months now. I'm ready for it. More than ready. But I'm not sure you're the right person to do this with. It's too complicated between us."

Okay, that hurt. She stopped moving her hands on his body and took a step back. Maybe she was the only one affected here. Last night he'd said he wanted her, but maybe he'd changed his mind. Or maybe he'd decided she wasn't worth the hassle.

"You asked *me* for a kiss. What did you want? A peck

on the cheek and a pat on the head? Because that's not what you led me to believe when you said it."

He blew out a breath. "I shouldn't have done that. Asking you for a kiss was wrong. You don't owe me anything for my help. Besides, I know I'm not in the right frame of mind for a kiss from you. I'll want more, because I've been staring at your body on that stage for two nights in a row. You're sexy as hell, Bailey—and I want to do things to you that are going to make us both hot and sweaty. Last night you said you weren't ready for that. I'd rather not find out you only want to go so far when I'm aching from how much I need to be inside you. Like I said, complicated."

Oh my.

Bailey drew in a deep breath. Her nipples tingled. Her sex ached. She wanted to break this tension. She wanted to get naked with Alexei Kamarov. Would it burn her in the end? Maybe. But what a way to burn.

"I wasn't ready last night. I am now."

He stared at her for a long moment. "It's the test, isn't it? I'm not Ana's father, so now I'm okay?"

She frowned. Twisted her fingers in the hem of her tee. "Partly, yes. If you'd been her dad—if you'd slept with Kayla—it wouldn't be right of me to sleep with you too. She's my sister. For all I knew, she was madly in love with you."

"You still don't know if I slept with her," he said. "Hell, I don't even know—I'm pretty sure I didn't, but there were nights back then…" He shook his head. "Things were rough for a while. Substance abuse is more than a little bit frowned on in the military. I might have self-medicated with sex instead."

Her heart throbbed. She had an urge to wrap her

arms around him, but she didn't do it. What if he pushed her away?

"I'm sorry it was rough for you."

"It happens. Just like in the movie, Bailey. Sometimes it's hard to leave what you do out there behind."

He was referring to *American Sniper*. She shivered a little as she imagined him hurting over things that had happened in a battle zone.

"I'm not worried about whether or not you were with my sister. Kayla lied to me about a lot of things. I think she pulled you out of her head because I demanded a name and yours was the one that occurred to her. It's a little more memorable than Joe Smith."

He frowned. "I guess it's also possible mine was one of the only last names she knew. The guys tease me about it sometimes. I also end up explaining why they call me Camel."

"Camel?" She thought of the desert beasts—ugly and sorta elegant at the same time—and didn't know how anyone could compare Alexei to a camel. Unless it had to do with his ability to keep going…

Oh…

"Kamarov. Camel. The first sound is the same when you come at it like an American with no knowledge of Russian."

She blushed a little. "Guilty, huh?"

He smiled. "Yeah, guilty. But how would you know the correct way without being told?"

"So it's KAH-ma-roff, right?" she asked, mimicking what he'd said.

"Yeah, that's it."

She waited. Sighed. He didn't move. Didn't say

anything to indicate he'd heard her say she was ready. "All right then. Guess I'll go back to bed."

She turned on her heel, confusion and disappointment swirling together, and started for the bedroom. She could lie in bed and toss for a while, or maybe she'd take care of business herself. And maybe that was better. Less complicated, as Alexei would say.

He caught her arm and she stopped, though she didn't turn around again. He moved closer, behind her, until she could feel the press of him against her backside. His hard body, his harder cock behind his athletic shorts. He didn't hold her tightly. He put both hands on her upper arms. She could escape if she wanted.

She didn't want to. She pressed herself backward, a little harder, rubbing against his cock. His breath hitched in.

"I want you, Bailey. That's not an issue. I just can't promise you anything in the morning. I don't want to hurt you."

"I didn't ask for anything," she whispered. "I haven't had sex in a long time either, Alexei. Over a year. You seem safe. And nice, though I know you hate that word. Maybe I want what you want out of this—to feel good and walk away when it's done. I'm a big girl. I know what I'm getting."

His grip tightened for a second. He reached up to push her hair off her neck. Softly, gently. Goose bumps rippled down her spine at the brush of those fingers on her skin.

"One night. We feel good together. No promises in the morning. Is that what you're saying?"

Bailey bit her lip. Could she do that? Of course she could. She was a grown ass woman. She could handle it.

"That's what I'm saying."

"We shouldn't do this," he said. "But we're going to, aren't we?"

She nodded, her breath catching in anticipation.

A moment later, his mouth skimmed over her throat. A big, solid arm went around her and pulled her even tighter to his body.

She tipped her head to the side, seeking his lips. He let her go and turned her, tugging her against him again. Their mouths met in a clash of tongues that was anything but tame—there was no turning back now.

Chapter 17

Holy hell, kissing Bailey was like walking into an inferno. The fire was out of control and raging, and all he could do was take more of it. So much more, until he thought he would combust. His cock didn't waste any time before turning to stone. His hands slid down her body, grabbed two handfuls of delicious ass through her T-shirt, and lifted her until she put those legs around him.

That's when he realized she wasn't wearing any underwear. Alexei groaned as her slick heat met his bare abdomen. That sweet pussy he'd wanted to see was right there, naked and hot and wet, and he couldn't wait to slide his tongue into it and taste her.

But first he couldn't seem to stop kissing her. Her arms were around his neck, her mouth on his. Her tongue stroked his, tangling and dueling. Their kisses were deep, sucking kisses that only heightened his excitement. He didn't want to stop, and yet he had to stop if he wanted more of her.

A vague part of him seemed to stay apart,

wondering how the hell this was happening. He hadn't made a conscious decision to stop her from leaving the room. One second she was walking away and the next he was launching into action, grabbing her arm, stopping her.

He'd told himself it was a mistake as soon as he did it, but it didn't feel like much of a mistake at the moment. She hadn't had sex in over a year.

Jesus.

He needed to change that—he was going to change it. There was no turning back now, no way in hell he was letting her go, no matter the small voice at the back of his brain that told him this thing with her wasn't going to be as cut-and-dried as he thought.

A one-night stand, walk away in the morning. No promises. She knew the score. They both did. This wasn't going anywhere, no matter how hot it might be at this moment. How necessary it suddenly seemed to living.

He carried her into his bedroom, still kissing her, put a knee on the bed and laid her back on it, coming down on top of her. Then he glided his hands down her sides, hooked his fingers into her hem, and dragged her shirt up and off.

She was utterly naked beneath it. Not that he could see because their mouths fused together again and he hadn't gotten the chance to look. But he could feel. His fingers moved over her tits, tweaking her hard nipples, shaped her waist, her flat abdomen, and then continued downward, seeking her wet heat.

She was smooth, soft, silky. He realized with a shot of pure lust to the brain that her pussy was bare as he skimmed his fingers over her sex. She arched up toward him, seeking his touch between her legs.

He wanted to give it to her—but he wanted to give her his tongue even more. Somehow, with what seemed like a superhuman effort, he dragged his mouth from hers, dragged it down her chest and over to one of those sweet nipples. Her fingers dug into his hair as he sucked the tight bud into his mouth, flicking it with his tongue as he watched the play of desire on her features.

She caught her lower lip between her teeth, her eyes heavy with need as she watched him. He abandoned the effort and continued down her abdomen, licking her skin as he went. When he shouldered her legs apart, she opened them without hesitation and he finally got a good look at her body in the predawn light coming between the blinds.

"Fuck me, Bailey," he said as he met her eyes across the beautiful delta of her belly, the mounds of her fabulous tits, the silky column of her neck. "You're gorgeous."

She smiled. It was a shy smile, which he found kind of amazing. Surely she knew how hot she was? How could she not?

"Thank you."

He slipped his fingers into the wet oasis before him, inhaled her scent, tried not to come in his shorts. "I've been dying to taste this," he said, spreading her open. "Dying to lick all the pretty folds of your pussy before you explode on my tongue."

Her breath caught. "I don't think you're going to get much chance of that. I'm planning to explode pretty much instantly."

He grinned at her. "Then we'll just have to do it again, won't we?"

SHE COULDN'T BELIEVE this was happening. From the first moment their lips had touched until now, fire had consumed her. She wanted nothing more than this —him, her, naked skin and cool sheets and hours of potential pleasure ahead of them.

Bailey's back bowed off the bed with the first touch of his tongue. Her fingers slid into his hair again, clasping him to her as he licked the length of her seam. He pressed the flat of his tongue against her clit before concentrating on that single spot, licking and sucking and flicking until he drove her mad with it. He knew just when to stop, when to back away and let her come down just a little bit before attacking again.

It was absolute torture—but of the *best* kind.

Still, she needed to come. *Needed it badly.*

She'd thought it would happen immediately, but she hadn't reckoned on his skill in building her higher and higher without letting her fall.

"Alexei," she gasped as stars began to pop behind her eyes. "Please don't stop—like that—oh my God…"

He didn't stop this time, didn't leave her hanging while he built her up again. He licked hard against her most sensitive spot, over and over—and then he inserted a finger inside her passage, fucking her while he took her over the cliff's edge.

The stars became a whiteout. Color faded. Her voice didn't work as she gasped for air. Her orgasm slammed her body into the mattress, bowing her back as she lifted her hips and rode his face, trying to make the pleasure last.

When it was too much, when she was too sensitive for another moment of his tongue on her body, she pushed him away and collapsed on the bed, her heart racing as she dragged in breaths and tried to regulate her pulse.

He kissed the inside of her thighs and then crawled his way back up her body, licking her flesh, kissing her, until he reached her nipples and sucked them both lazily while she twirled a finger in his hair and closed her eyes.

"I'm guessing that worked for you," he said with a laugh.

She opened her eyes and met his gorgeous green ones. Oh, a woman could drown in those eyes. *Don't go there, Bale. Commitmentphobe, remember?*

"It wasn't bad," she said coolly, teasing him.

He arched an eyebrow, but the grin didn't go away and she knew he wasn't taking the bait. Her heart did a hitch thing that it hadn't before. She pushed it out of her mind and concentrated on him. On that handsome face, his mouth slick with her juices, his eyes sparkling and filled with desire. For *her*.

"Wasn't bad, huh? Need another round?"

"Not yet," she squeaked when he slid back down her body. She was too sensitive, her soul too raw—

But when his tongue slid into her body again, she groaned with the utter perfection of it. Within seconds, he was lapping at her clit, driving her insane with the feelings crashing into her. Bailey bit her lip, moaning and thrashing on the bed as he held her hips and brought her to another shattering climax before he let her go.

"You taste so good, Bailey," he said, his big form rolling up her body again. "I could eat you all night."

She glanced down his torso, past those lean hips. He was still wearing his shorts, but there was a giant tent in the front. As good as he'd made her feel so far, she knew there was even more waiting for her.

"Out of those," she said, pushing him over onto his back. He went willingly because she wouldn't have been able to shift him otherwise. She grasped the waistband and dragged the shorts down his hips.

And oh my, the cock that sprang free was bigger than she'd expected. She'd only seen him semiaroused, not fully hard and ready.

"Oh wow," she said, pulling his shorts off and dropping them before taking him in her hands. "I don't know whether to lick it like an ice cream cone or ride it like a cowgirl."

His eyes were burning when she looked into them. "You can do both, honey. I've got enough stamina for more than one round."

Thank God for that!

Bailey dropped her head and licked around the tip. Alexei made a noise of approval. "It's so beautiful," she said before licking the tip again. She opened her mouth and took him inside, working him with her hands while she sucked as much of him as she could. He fisted his hands in her hair, pushing the lavender curtain aside so he could see her face. She met his gaze, kept her eyes fixed on his as she sucked. It was erotic as hell.

She felt powerful doing this to him, watching his eyes dilate, his nostrils flare, the muscles in his impressive abs clench. Bailey slipped a hand down, cupping his balls, and those eyes shot green sparks at her. He groaned and she sucked harder, bobbing faster, wanting him to come. Wanting to make him feel as good as he'd made her feel.

But he sat up and reached for her, pulling her up his body, breaking that contact.

"I want to be inside you."

She pouted. "I thought you said you had enough stamina for twice?"

He grinned. "Oh, I do—but I gotta get inside you."

He reached over and pulled open a drawer, dragging out a strip of condoms. He tore one from the strip, ripped it open, and rolled it down his beautiful cock. Bailey straddled him, ran her hands up his chest as she lifted her hips so he could position himself beneath her.

She felt him nudging into her wetness, shuddered as his thumb flicked over her clit. She sank down on him slowly, allowing herself time to adjust.

"Oh," she gasped as her body stretched for him. "Oh wow."

He held still and let her do the work of joining them. She appreciated his restraint since it had been so long for her. When she was full of him, she stopped and sat still. Little sparks zinged from her head to her toes as every minuscule movement of their bodies created waves of sensation.

"You good?" he asked, his hands on her thighs. Broad hands. Sexy hands.

"Yeah. You?"

He snorted, and the movement sent a shock wave through her. "Oh yeah. You're sexy beautiful, Bailey." He slid his fingers up one leg, over her clit, rubbing so that she groaned. "You ready for me, gorgeous?"

"Ready?" she gasped. "You're already in me, Alexei. Or did you forget?"

"Forget? Fuck no. I'm restraining myself... because what I really want is to flip you over and fuck you until you can't remember your name."

He plucked at her clit and she shuddered, both at what her body was feeling and at what her mind conjured up at the thought of this man dominating her with his size and power.

"Move, Bailey. Ride me now," he told her, "Or I'm taking control."

———

SHE WAS SO HOT, so wet and beautiful, and he wanted to drive himself into her body until he blew two months' worth of deprivation into this fucking condom. Right now he'd kill to be bareback inside her—but that wasn't a chance he could take with his family history.

She started to move, sliding up his cock and sinking back down again, her palms braced on his chest. He continued to stroke her clit while she rode him.

Her pace quickened, her breathing shortened, and he knew she was close. Damn, she was beautiful, her tits bouncing with her movements, her nipples budding into tight pink peaks that he was torn between sucking and watching bounce.

"Alexei," she cried out, shuddering hard as she came. He reached up and dragged her down for a kiss, wanting to taste her passion. She moaned into his mouth and he thrust his hips upward, filling her, dragging her pleasure out for as long as he could.

He could feel the moment she melted completely. Her body went limp, her muscles sagging with relief. He hugged her to him, pushed her hair from her face, and kissed her tenderly instead of hotly. He was still hard inside her, still ready to burst, but right now it was her pleasure he cared most about.

Poor Bailey, always taking care of others, always working and trying to survive. Never having her own needs fulfilled. Never having a man to fuck her into forgetfulness for a few hours.

He stroked his hands down the silky curve of her back, over her ass. He could feel her juices dripping onto his balls. Carefully, he turned them onto their sides, continued the move until she was on her back and he was deep inside her. She spread her legs, wrapped them around him.

"I want you to fuck me," she whispered. "I need to come again."

His balls tightened, the words digging into his brain and making his cock ache more than it already did. Which he hadn't thought possible, really.

Alexei levered himself up, pumped his hips into her slowly, watched their bodies joining. "That's so fucking sexy," he told her. "Watching myself disappear inside you. Seeing the way your pussy lips stretch open for me. God, I love that you're bare. It looks incredible."

She bit her lip, her big eyes meeting his as he began to move faster. Her tits bounced—and then she put her hands on them, hefted their weight in her palms, tweaked her own nipples while he sank into her. That fucking did it for him. He drove into her, dropped his mouth to hers, and shoved his tongue into her mouth. She took him all. His tongue, his cock, his intensity.

When his balls tightened, he pleaded with himself for a little longer. He needed this release. Needed it so badly. But he wasn't the kind of guy to come alone if at all possible. He needed her to catch fire again...

"Alexei," she gasped, her fingers digging into his arms, her hips thrusting up to meet his. He pumped into her, found the angle he needed—and she splintered apart, her body quivering beneath him as her eyes closed and her mouth dropped open.

"Bailey," he groaned as he poured everything he had into her, thrusting until he was spent. He didn't realize for long moments that he'd broken one of his own rules.

He hadn't pulled out. *Oh holy shit...*

But the condom was intact, and he went to the bathroom to get rid of it. When he came back, Bailey was sprawled on her stomach, arms wrapped around his pillow, gazing up at him languidly. As if she couldn't remember her name. She smiled. Yawned.

He went and lay down beside her, propping himself on an elbow so he could see the tattoo on her ass. He traced it with his fingers. It was a butterfly and a ribbon of words: *Never give up.*

"What's this about?" he asked softly.

"Strength and beauty," she said.

It was obvious now that she'd said it. A pretty butterfly and strong words. A helluva combination. Like Bailey. She was strong and beautiful, a graceful butterfly who never quit.

"I didn't pull out, Bailey. Please tell me you're on birth control."

She blinked. Then she smiled. "Ah yes, the magic sperm. It's okay, I have an implant. If your sperm can get past a condom and that, they truly are magic."

He lay down and pulled her against him. She threw a leg over his and snuggled in close. He told himself he should send her back to the guest room, not engage in this postsexual haze together. But what if he wanted to fuck her one more time?

Yeah, that was the reason he let her stay. He heard her breathing even out and knew she was asleep. Bailey was still in his arms when he fell asleep a few minutes later. Right where he wanted her to be.

Chapter 18

Bailey woke to a hand between her legs, a finger skating over her clit, sending lightning bolts shivering through her entire body. She opened her legs immediately, seeking more. Behind her, Alexei put his mouth on her shoulder, laughed against her skin before nipping it lightly.

"I was gonna ask if you like wake-up sex, but I think I know the answer now."

If the sex was with him, she thought she might like it whenever he wanted to do it. But she didn't say that. Instead, she reached behind her, grasped his cock. He was hot and hard and her core flooded with liquid desire.

"Can we stay here all day and do this?" She gasped as his fingers moved expertly against her clit.

He bit her shoulder. "What about food?"

"Delivery."

"I like the way you think, baby."

She shivered at the endearment. She'd told him not to call her things like baby or honey or sweetie because it made her think of the men at the club and the way they treated the girls like something less than human. But coming from Alexei, it didn't feel wrong. It didn't feel like he couldn't remember her name or like it was just easier to call all women baby. It felt personal somehow, even if it was a common enough term.

He stopped the wonderful thing he was doing and glided a hand up her thigh, pushing it high enough to give him access from behind. She heard the condom wrapper open, and then he pulled her hand away from him. A moment later, the thick head of his cock nudged into her wet entrance.

"Fuck," he groaned as he slid all the way inside.

Bailey groaned too, both from the pleasurable soreness last night had created and from the way he stretched her, causing friction on all her sensitive parts.

He cupped a breast in his hand. The other hand slipped into her folds. "So wet," he breathed against her neck. "So ready for me."

"Please, Alexei—I can't wait any longer."

He pulled out and then thrust deep, filling her, his fingers working her clit as he settled into a rhythm. It felt amazing, so incredibly hot and sexy as he slammed into her over and over. She could feel her orgasm building, feel the tension growing stronger in every cell of her body.

She was close—and he pulled out. "Alexei!"

He rolled her over, toward him, hooking an arm behind her knee and spreading her wide before slamming back inside her at a new angle. She wrapped her other leg around his hip, moaning.

"Need to kiss you," he groaned, letting her leg go and dropping his mouth to hers. Their tongues met, tangling as he fucked her harder, hearts pounding, breaths mingling, bodies frantically straining toward that perfect peak, that moment when the tension exploded and euphoria overcame them.

It happened for Bailey first. Her body stiffened as the fire took hold of her, rippling out across her limbs and making her dig her fingers into his back as she shattered. She was still coming when Alexei tore his mouth from hers and groaned into her neck, coming deep inside her. His cock pulsed as he poured himself into the condom.

They lay entwined for several moments before he lifted himself off her. She rolled over and sprawled on the bed, spent, the aftershocks of her orgasm still zinging through her. He swatted her ass as he got out of bed and left her there. She heard the water running in the bathroom, first the sink and then the shower.

She managed to talk herself into sitting up. She reached for her phone and then remembered it was with her bag in her room. Bailey padded across the hallway and into the guest room. The blinds were down, so she wasn't worried about being seen. Plucking the phone from the charger, her stomach dropped as the text message indicator lit up. She swiped it open and tapped the app.

Kayla: *Yes, I lied. I didn't know what else to do. Alex was nice to me. He went after a guy who stiffed me on a bill once. Made him pay up. I never slept with him, but I wanted him to be Ana's father because she deserves that kind of a dad. Not like our dad, you know?*

Bailey swallowed the knot in her throat. She did know.

Ana is safer with you and Alex. I'm no good for her. And her

175

father definitely isn't. Dunn is her father—and he doesn't care about her. He wanted to sell her to an adoption agency. I couldn't let that happen. He won't ever let me leave him. He'll come for me—but he can't have Ana too. That's why I left her. I thought you'd take her to Alex and he'd keep her safe. He's that kind of man.

Bailey's eyes pricked with tears as she squeezed the phone in her fist. Dammit, he *was* that kind of man. But Ana wasn't his responsibility. Neither was she. In spite of the night they'd shared, she knew this wasn't permanent. Alexei wasn't going to magically fall for her and ask her to stay just because they'd had sex. It didn't work that way.

She tapped out a reply, sniffling as she did so. *Call me, Kayla. Alex is a good guy and he knows people. He can protect you. And Ana. She's safe, but she needs her mother. I know you care. If you didn't, if you really didn't want to be a mom, you'd have let Dunn sell her to the agency. But you didn't do that. So you care and you want your baby. Come home and let me help. Love you, B.*

"Bailey?" Alexei stood in the door, a towel wrapped around his torso, his gaze questioning. "You okay?"

She dragged in a breath and tried to smile. It probably didn't look like much of a smile. "Kayla answered." She lifted the phone. "You'll be pleased to know you never slept with her. She lied because you made a guy pay his bill after he tried to stiff her. She thought you were nice."

He frowned. "I remember that incident. But I didn't realize it was her. Some guy spent hours there, eating wings and pizza, drinking beer—bought a few rounds for the bar too. But then he walked out on a three-hundred-plus bill. Unfortunately for him, he spent a little too much time in the parking lot trying to get into some girl's pants. I walked him back inside and made him pull out his credit card."

"Well, it earned you the coveted spot as her pretend baby daddy when she needed one."

Bailey bit the inside of her lip. She wasn't mad because her sister thought Alexei was a good guy and would be a good dad for Ana. She was mad because Kayla had thought nothing of implicating an innocent man in the first place. Even if she had done it for what she thought was a good reason. Bailey was also mad because Kayla hadn't told her any of this in the first place, hadn't trusted Bailey to help keep her and Ana safe. Maybe Bailey wouldn't be here with Alexei now, but she'd have thought of something. They could have left town. Called the police. Something.

"What aren't you telling me?" Alexei asked.

Bailey pulled in a breath. "Dunn is Ana's father. He wanted to sell her to an adoption agency. That's why Kayla said she left. She thought that I would bring Ana to you, which I did, and you'd keep her safe. She clearly didn't think the whole thing out in any depth."

"You sound pissed." He walked into the room, his gaze straying down her form. She'd forgotten she was naked until then. Her nipples tightened at his perusal. *Sexy beast.*

"A little. She didn't think about how it would affect you to be accused. The way it might disrupt your life. Or mine. Or how being left with her clueless aunt might affect Ana. And what if there were no drugstore paternity tests? What then?"

"We'd have found another way." His towel was beginning to move. He ran his hands softly over her arms. "I know this is important, but I can't fucking think

177

right now," he told her. "You're naked and your mouth is red and swollen. All I can think about is getting inside you again—but first I need your pussy in my face."

Her breath hitched. "You just showered."

"I'll shower again. With you. After I make you come a few more times."

The towel was a tent now. She reached for it, slipped it free, and let it fall. Because he was the only thing making her feel good right now. Her one indulgence.

"Okay… but only if I get to suck you off first."

"No deal, babe. But I'll let you suck me if you straddle my face while you do it."

Bailey shivered at the thought. "Now that sounds like a deal I can wrap my lips around…"

"THANK GOD YOU'RE HERE," Cowboy muttered as Alexei walked into the house behind Bailey. He tried not to laugh at the wide-eyed crazy look his teammate sported.

"Yeah, thanks for taking care of the squirt."

Cowboy put a hand on his shoulder, stopped him from proceeding. "Camel, man, I love you like a brother, but if my wife starts telling me she wants to begin a family, I'm going to kill you in your sleep."

Alexei snorted. "Aw, come on, dude. That little pip-squeak scared you that much? She's cute and pretty easy right now. It gets more difficult later."

"More difficult? Like how? I'm going to have night-mares about changing diapers as it is."

"Miranda made you learn, huh?"

Cowboy grumbled. "Probably wouldn't have

happened if I hadn't told her I was glad it wasn't me having to do it. Even then, I might have gotten away with it if I hadn't said I'd probably never change a diaper in my life because it'd make me gag. I was trying to prepare her, you know, in case…" He cleared his throat. "Anyway, I learned. Right then and there. No matter how much I gagged."

Alexei couldn't stop the laugh this time.

Cowboy frowned. "Seriously. You. Dead. Fragged somewhere. I'll get the guys to back me up. They will when I tell them."

Alexei wrapped an arm around his teammate and smacked a kiss on his cheek before Cowboy could stop him. "Dream on, buddy. You love me too much."

"Eww, don't do that you crazy motherfucker," Cowboy said, pushing him away and wiping his cheek while Alexei laughed harder.

"Then don't threaten me and make me prove that you harbor mad unrequited love for me."

"Jesus. Hell no, not in this lifetime," Cowboy growled. "Not unless you develop tits and a pussy—and not even then because Miranda's the only one for me."

Alexei slugged Cowboy in the arm. Not hard. "I know. Just ribbing you, man. It's funny as hell to watch you freak out." He gazed into the living room where Miranda and Bailey were gathered, Ana cradled in her aunt's arms, Bailey making funny faces and talking in a high-pitched voice. His heart did a little stumble thing in his chest and he rubbed his hand over it. What the hell was that shit?

"I know," Cowboy said, voice pitched low. "It's terrifying as hell to watch women with babies, right? I mean it gets you thinking maybe, if she really wanted to have

one…" He shook his head. "Nope, nope, nope. Not going there."

"Hey, Cowboy," Alexei began, and his friend turned from where he'd been all starry-eyed over Miranda.

"Yeah?"

"How did you know? About Miranda, I mean?"

Cowboy arched an eyebrow. "You asking for a reason?"

"Yeah," he admitted. "I just don't know how people know. I mean maybe fucking the same person is great and all that, and knowing there'll be someone there when you get home instead of having to call a hookup —that has to be a nice thing. But what makes it different? What makes it real? How do you know it's not just infatuation because you're enjoying the pussy too much?"

Cowboy looked far more serious than Alexei would have thought in a moment like this. He'd have expected jokes and innuendo about his life and, yeah, even insinuations about his relationship with Bailey. It was probably obvious they'd had sex by now. Hot sex. Found-a-new-religion sex.

Well, maybe that part wasn't obvious, though he expected the sex part was. He'd spent far too much time alone with Bailey, not to mention she was as hot as a Playboy bunny, for Cowboy not to think he'd gone there with her.

"I'm not going to say the skies parted and a light shone down and I knew," Cowboy said. "But I knew that I felt different with her. And I knew, when I wasn't with her, that I wanted to be. Nothing felt right without her. And everything did when I was with her. The thought of ever being with another woman? Not even remotely appealing. Miranda is the best part of me. I can't be who I am without her. Not anymore."

Alexei couldn't fathom that part. Not be who he was without a woman? Someone else be the best part of him? It didn't seem possible. He liked who he was, liked his life. Well, most of it anyway. Sometimes coming home to an empty house, especially after a mission, was a little lonely. Not that he minded it too much. He was a loner. Always had liked his solitude, probably from growing up surrounded by so much chaos.

"Thanks," he said. "Just wondering."

"You'll know," Cowboy told him. "Maybe not right away, maybe not when you should—but there'll come a moment when it's all clear as rain. And you'll pray to God you didn't fuck it up too badly and she'll still want you."

"Yeah, pretty sure this miraculous woman doesn't exist, so I'm not too worried about it. I'll just keep fucking my way through the greater DC area and feeling sorry for you bozos who've decided to settle down. Especially when the babies start coming," he added.

Cowboy shook himself. "Asshole."

"What, you don't want any little pieces of you and Miranda running around? Being adorable and shit?"

"Not saying that. Just not yet. I want more time with her alone before I start to share."

"Yeah, I hear you." That had been his parents' problem from the beginning. They'd married because she'd been pregnant with him. And then she'd stayed pregnant for years. They'd never had time alone together. Time to learn each other and let their relationship strengthen.

Alexei and Cowboy went to join the women. Bailey

looked up when he approached, her eyes sparkling with happiness. Something inside him twisted, like a key inserting into a lock. It just clicked, and he stood there wondering what the fuck it was. What had just happened to him. He didn't feel any different, so he went to her side and put his hand on Ana's head.

"Hey, pip-squeak," he said. "Did you behave yourself for Auntie Miranda and Uncle Cowboy?"

"Oh, she's just a little angel," Miranda said excitedly. "So precious. Sleeps pretty good too. I was surprised."

"Thank you so much for keeping her," Bailey said. "I know two nights is a lot with a baby who's not yours, and I really appreciate it."

Miranda squeezed Bailey's arm. "Sweetie," she said, her Alabama accent lilting and syrupy, "You don't have to keep saying it. I really did enjoy her." She eyed Cowboy. "I learned a few things about my man too. We're going to have to work on some stuff around here."

Bailey smiled softly at Cowboy. Alexei tried not to feel a pinprick of annoyance at that soft smile that wasn't for him.

"Sorry about that, Cody," she said.

"Eh, she'd have figured it out sooner or later," he replied. "Not to mention, taught me a few things about babies that I didn't know… like how much of a commitment it is to have one. I knew, but I didn't *know.*"

Bailey laughed. "You and me both. It's trial by fire—but you figure it out. Especially when you have help," she finished, glancing at Alexei.

"So hey, y'all want to grab something to eat?" Miranda asked. "We were thinking of going out for Italian. Or Korean. I can't decide."

Alexei wanted to say no. He wanted to take Bailey back to his place, get Ana settled into her crib, and then nail her aunt again while the baby took a nap. Bailey didn't have to work for two more nights, so he'd been busy thinking about all the ways he was going to fuck her. But Bailey was looking at him like she'd enjoy the outing, so he nodded. "Yeah, sounds great. Bailey?"

"I'm hungry. Sure."

"Awesome," Miranda said. "So which do y'all prefer?"

"Pasta sounds great to me," Bailey said, "so long as everyone else agrees."

Everyone did. Miranda turned to Cowboy. "Babe, can you call the restaurant and see if we can get a table?"

He pulled his phone out and walked away to make the call.

Miranda turned to them. "I know it's only midafternoon, but they're pretty popular," she explained.

He came back a few moments later and gave a thumbs-up. "We're good."

Bailey took Ana's carrier while Alexei carried her things to his truck and put them in. Then he took the carrier from Bailey and buckled it into the back seat. It wasn't the first time he'd put Ana in his truck and taken her and Bailey with him somewhere, but it felt different this time. Almost like a preview of some strange future where he had a woman and a kid, the very things he wasn't ready for.

"Something wrong?" Bailey asked when he got into the driver's seat and started the vehicle. He glanced at her, at her pretty face and purple hair, and thought,

Wow. Then he thought, *What the hell have I gotten myself into?*

"What color is your hair really?"

She blinked. "You're just now asking that?"

He shrugged. "I thought I'd know when I stripped you naked, but I didn't realize you'd shaved your pussy. By the time I knew that, your hair color was the last thing on my mind."

Her mouth quirked. "And your mind hasn't been working since?"

"Not really, no. In fact, I'm not sure what made me wonder now, except that I was thinking of your pussy and figuring out how long it's going to be before I get to lick it again."

"Alexei," she breathed, her voice sounding strained. "I don't know why you have such a fixation with doing that, but I'm pretty happy you do."

"Baby doll, pussy is one of my five favorite things."

She snorted. "What are the other four?"

"Tits. Ass. Guns. And pancakes. Love pancakes."

She burst out laughing. "Oh my God, not what I expected."

"So what color is it, baby? You gonna tell me or what?"

"It's boring. Blond, but not sunny blond like Miranda's. More like a sandy blond that wishes it was more exciting."

He glanced at her as he turned onto the main road, right behind Cowboy and Miranda. "Bailey, if you got any more exciting, I'd probably lose consciousness."

She blinked. "Why's that?"

"All that blood draining from my brain to my dick would happen much too fast for me to handle."

Bailey burst into giggles. Alexei couldn't help but laugh too. Damn, she was fun. He liked hearing her laugh. Liked hearing her moan too. Tonight he planned to make that happen as much as possible. Before this was all over and he had to give her up for good.

Chapter 19

Bailey liked Alexei's friends. She got used to him and Cody calling each other by their call signs, which is what they said their nicknames were. Cowboy and Camel. Names for missions. Names that somehow fit them even if they weren't really their actual names.

"So what are the other guys called?" she asked, twirling pasta on her fork.

"Let's see," Cody said, ticking off his fingers. "Viking, Money, Cage, Blade, Neo, and Dirty Harry, though we call him Dirty for short. That's our team. There are others though."

"Yeah," Alexei said. "We've got all kinds."

"How do you get these names?" she asked.

Miranda took a drink of her wine and grinned while Alexei explained. "A variety of ways. Mine comes from my last name, like I said. Cowboy here—well, he grew up on a ranch and liked to ride mechanical bulls when I met him. Money's first name is Cash. Cage is a Cajun from south Louisiana. Viking looks like a Norse god." He shrugged. "It's a play on your name or maybe something you said or did once that follows you around. They can be cool, but they can also be funny."

The waiter came by and asked if they needed anything. Alexei asked for a refill on his water. Miranda wanted more bread for the table.

"What about you, Miranda?" Bailey asked once the waiter was gone. "What do you do?"

They'd been talking about Alexei and Cody's work, but Bailey still didn't know what Miranda did. There were swift glances exchanged between all three of them that had her wondering if she'd crossed a line somehow.

"I'm a government employee," Miranda said smoothly. "I travel a lot, but right now I'm on a break. Like Cody. We try to schedule those together if at all possible. More bread?" she asked, picking up the basket with the remaining bread and offering it to Bailey.

"Thanks," Bailey replied, taking a slice and dipping her knife in the butter. She waited for someone else to pick up the conversation. It soon shifted to other topics, and they ended up staying in the restaurant for a long time, finally ending with dessert and coffee. When Ana got fussy, Bailey reached for her, but Alexei was there first.

"I got it," he said, taking the baby to the bathroom where he'd probably change her diaper or feed her, depending on the issue.

Cody watched him go with wide eyes that made Bailey stifle a laugh. He caught her looking and shrugged. "It's weird, okay? I'm used to a different Camel, not one that cuddles babies."

She thought about the version of Alexei he must be accustomed to. It made her shiver to imagine Alexei in camouflage, weapons strapped across his torso, sweat streaming down his face, fighting for his life in a hot and dusty desert somewhere. She glanced at Miranda, who had to deal with the same knowledge and thoughts about Cody.

But Miranda didn't look worried about anything. She touched Cody's arm. "Let's talk about something else, sweetie. Bailey has enough to worry about."

"It's okay," Bailey said. "I don't really know what y'all do, but I've seen enough movies to have an idea. I think. And we're all complicated, right? What Alexei does at work isn't the entire picture of who he is."

Both of them were looking at her with interest. "Alexei. I don't think I knew that was his name," Miranda murmured.

"Oh. Well." Bailey started to blush. "His family emigrated from Russia. It's what they call him."

"And you," Miranda said.

The blush was spreading. "Well, er, that's what he said his name was. It kind of stuck in my mind that way."

Alexei returned with Ana then. Bailey bit the inside of her lip, wondering if they'd say anything to him about his name, but neither of them did. They finished their dessert and when the bill came, the waiter had divided it into two bills, one for each couple. Bailey reached for her wallet in the diaper bag, but Alexei took out a credit card and handed it to the waiter while Cody did the same.

Once they said their goodbyes and got into the truck, with promises to get together again sometime—promises that Bailey found sort of awkward considering she wasn't Alexei's girlfriend and wasn't going to be around forever—Bailey turned to Alexei.

"I can pay for my food. You don't have to get everything."

"It's okay, babe. You get the next one."

Babe. She liked that. Too much, if she was honest with herself. Everything just felt right with Alexei. Hanging out, taking care of Ana. Having sex.

"I just don't want you to think I expect you to pay for my stuff. You've already done so much."

"I only do what I want to, Bailey. Nobody forced me into this."

"I hope you find Dunn and Kayla soon."

"So you can go home?"

He didn't look at her. Her heart skipped. She didn't want to go home. But she couldn't say that to him. He'd made it clear that he wasn't a relationship kind of guy, and even though she was afraid she was falling for him, she wasn't going to tell him. Hell no. He'd have her shuffled off to a new location in an hour, one of his friends taking her in while they searched for Dunn.

"Yes, of course. I'm ready to go," she said, not looking at him.

Did she imagine his hands tightening on the wheel out of the corner of her eye? Probably.

"We'll get him. Then you can move on with your life."

SHE'D SAID she wanted to go home, but as Alexei stroked into her later that night, hands entwined with hers, fists held above their heads, mouths fused and frantically pulling at each other, he had a burning need to make her want to stay.

Why?

He had no idea, but being inside her like this was heaven. His dick was on fire, his balls throbbing with impending release, every nerve ending in his body primed and ready to go. He held on as long as he could, waiting for her to come—and then she did, her body stiffening beneath his as he drank in her moans, her legs tightening around his waist, her hips arching up to meet him, her pussy grinding on his dick in short, sharp movements that he knew intensified the feeling for her.

That was his moment to let go. He should probably pull out and jerk off in the condom, but it felt too good to stay inside her, to feel the rippling muscles of her vagina enhancing his own release. So he let go, trusting that her implant was up to the job. Praying it was. He tore his mouth from hers and did his own version of a silent scream into the pillow beside her head. They had to be quiet for the baby, who lay in her bassinet nearby.

When he was done, he kissed her softly, sucked a nipple, then got up and went to dispose of the condom. If he wasn't wearing it, he could have stayed inside her, stayed in bed with her wrapped around him. Maybe fucked her again without ever having to withdraw. How nice would that be?

When he came back, she curled into him, arm and leg thrown across his body, soft breath against his neck. He drifted a hand down to her ass, played with her cheek as his other hand caressed her arm. He liked this. Liked it a lot. He imagined himself coming home from his next mission to find Bailey waiting for him. Naked. Wet and ready.

Or not even that. Maybe just kissing him and holding him tight until he collapsed for some much-needed sleep. When he woke, she'd be there, happy to see him.

"This is nice," she said softly, so as not to wake Ana.

He turned his head to her ear. "If you ask me, being quiet was sexy as hell. You wanted to scream."

"God yes. That was amazing. But Alexei…?"

"Yeah, baby?"

"I thought it was supposed to be one night."

He frowned. Yeah, he'd thought that too. His dick had other plans. "Is that what you want?"

"Don't you?"

He heard the hesitation in her voice and knew it was because of him. Because of what he'd said. "I didn't want to promise you anything I couldn't deliver. And I still don't. But I like what we're doing. It feels good. *You* feel good."

Her fingers drifted across his chest, spread over his side. He liked her touch. His dick did too if the mild tingling in that region was any indication.

"You feel good too."

"So we'll keep doing it then. So long as it feels good and we're both having fun."

"Yes, but…"

"But what, baby?"

"You're the first guy I've been with in over a year. I know I work in a sketchy profession, but I'm not promiscuous or easy. I won't be with anyone else while I'm with you. I'd appreciate the same consideration."

Exclusivity. It wasn't usually a conversation that came up. It wasn't anything he'd ever participated in because he didn't stick around long enough for it to happen. But now, lying here with Bailey, a sleeping baby in a bassinet beside the bed, his life felt very surreal. But not terrifying. Maybe because the baby wasn't his and he had the power to get out of the situation when he liked.

But the thought of doing that, of walking away and leaving Bailey and Ana to go about life on their own—well, there was an uncomfortable feeling in the pit of his stomach at the idea. He didn't like it.

So promising her to be exclusive, so long as this lasted, was easy.

"I won't be with anybody else, babe. I promise."

She sighed. "Thank you."

"You said it's been over a year. Was the last guy a relationship?"

"I thought so. I was wrong. He was a guy I knew back home and we dated off and on. But he was dating someone else at the same time. Sleeping with us both. I had to get tested when I found out, but I'm clean. We all were. The other girl… she was someone I knew. Someone I thought was a friend." She hesitated. "That's kind of what finally spurred me to make the move up here. I'd been thinking about it for a while. I knew someone who'd gone to work at the Pink Palace, and she kept calling me about it. So after I found out about Dave and had to get tested and everything, I packed up and moved. Kayla wanted to come too. I let her with the understanding she would not dance. She went to work at Buddy's, thanks to some friends who helped her get the job."

"You must have come to Buddy's sometimes," he said, thinking that she might have been there at the same time he'd been. But they hadn't met.

"I did. I ate there sometimes when she was working."

"And our paths never crossed."

"I think I'd have remembered you if I'd seen you."

"I might have been on a mission when you were there." He frowned. "I probably should tell you this just in case—my life is unpredictable as hell, Bailey. I can get called in tomorrow and be gone for weeks. When I'm gone, I can't call. I can't text or email. Sometimes we can, but not on any regular schedule. I need you to know that can happen, okay?"

"Okay." She nuzzled his neck. "Alexei, you're talking like we might be dating. And I'm not saying we are, so don't panic, but I want to be sure I understand you."

He squeezed her to him. Yeah, he was losing his goddamn mind, that's for sure. He *was* talking like they were dating. And why not? He could date. It wasn't a proposal. He prepared to fumble his way through an explanation.

"I know this whole thing has been kinda fast, but we've spent a lot of time together before we got naked. I like you. Not just your body, which is banging, but your personality. I know life is crazy for you with a baby to take care of, but I like her too. I think I want to be there to help you for a while. So, yeah, I want to keep seeing you. If that's cool with you."

"I want that too…"

"But?" Because he heard it in her voice. Wasn't he supposed to be the one with doubts?

"I think my life is pretty unpredictable right now too. I don't know what's going to happen with Kayla and Ana. I know Kayla wants her baby. I know that she only left her to protect her—but what's going to happen when she comes back? What happens if Dunn is still in the picture? Will we always be running away, trying to stay a step ahead of him?"

Fresh anger surged through his veins. "Baby, trust me when I tell you that Dunn is not going to be an issue. I'm not going to let it happen."

He'd been on the phone with his guys daily, seeking news about Dunn. They still had nothing, mostly because the dude wasn't using credit cards or a registered cell phone. He knew how to move around undetected, but it was the kind of hiding a criminal did, not a trained military operator. He'd slip up eventually. They all did.

Alexei's phone lit up where it lay on the nightstand. It was early in the evening, just a little past nine, but he'd turned off the ringer because of Ana. He snatched it up, saw that it was Blade calling, and slid the button to answer.

"Yeah, man, what's up?"

"I'm at the Pink Palace with Neo and Dirty. Dunn just walked in."

Chapter 20

"What the fuck happened?" Alexei asked his teammates as he stepped from his truck in the parking lot of the Pink Palace. Blade, Neo, and Dirty stood with hands shoved in pockets, watching the blue lights of two police cars whirling steadily beside the building.

"Someone called the cops when Dunn arrived. We didn't know they were coming until it was too late. They busted in and took him into custody," Blade said.

"Fuck." He would have liked for HOT to get the dude first. They could have gotten information on the Kings of Doom's criminal operations and put a stop to the trafficking before they turned him over. The police weren't going to get that done, at least not on a national scale. They didn't have the resources for an operation like that. They'd get Dunn off the street for a bit, maybe a year or two if the charges were really good and the trial went their way, but he'd be back.

"The good news is, he won't be bothering Bailey or Ana for a while," Neo said. "No judge is going to let him post bail. She can go home again, and you can get back to being a grumpy bastard all by yourself."

"Ha ha," he said dryly. "Fuck you."

Neo laughed. "See? Grumpy as hell."

"It's not me, it's you," Alexei said. "We need some time apart, man."

"You got it, homey. You tell that cute babe that when she gets tired of your shit, she can come stay with me. I'll treat her like a princess."

"Not happening, dude. Bailey is mine."

That perked his teammates up. "Really? Yours, huh?" Blade asked. "You're banging her already. You don't waste any time, dude."

Alexei held up a hand in the universal *shut your trap* signal. "No way. No talking about my personal life. Bailey is off-limits to you jerks, got it?"

They shot each other a look. "I think Camel has it bad," Neo said. "Maybe we need to lay off."

"Yep, looks that way," Blade replied, still grinning.

Dirty was grinning like an idiot too.

Alexei wanted to punch them all. And bear-hug them. Being part of a SEAL team was a lot like having brothers. You punched and hugged and teased and laughed on a regular basis. He wouldn't trade that kind of camaraderie for anything. Even if he sometimes wanted to knock their heads together.

"Thanks for keeping an eye out," he said. "I really appreciate the help."

Blade shrugged. "You've saved my ass on more than one occasion. Think you have the right to ask for help."

"Yep," Neo said. "That sniper in Kabul would've taken my head off if not for you."

"Don't forget the insurgents in Damascus," Dirty added. "That coulda been ugly for us all."

"I'm still checking phone records and stuff, looking for Kayla Jones," Blade said. "I'll call you if I have anything. I'll also call my buddy at the PD and find out what's going on with Dunn."

They talked a little while more, then Alexei climbed back in his truck and headed for home. He'd told Bailey not to open the door to anyone and to call him if she needed anything. He hadn't told her he was going after Dunn because he hadn't wanted her to worry.

But now Dunn was in custody, unlikely to be freed anytime soon considering the charges against him, and there was no real reason for Bailey and Ana to stay. They could go home, settle into a routine. Maybe Kayla would come out of hiding now. That would make Bailey happy.

But Alexei didn't like the thought of Bailey and Ana leaving. He wasn't ready for it. Even with the pip-squeak creating havoc in his life these days, he wasn't prepared for that level of quiet just yet. He also needed more of Bailey in his bed. Beneath him, over him, surrounding him.

For a guy who didn't want to commit, he sure was thinking an awful lot about one particular woman. But spending time together wasn't the same as getting married and having a shitload of kids right away. There was time to get to know each other, find out if they wanted to date for a while or if a few days of sex was enough.

Except, hell, he knew it wasn't going to be enough. Not a few days. Maybe not even a few weeks. He liked Bailey more than he'd liked anyone in a long time. He wasn't sure why, considering they hadn't known each other for very long. There was just something about her, something that made him feel good when he was with her. He liked that feeling.

When he reached his house, the lights were blazing inside. He wasn't used to that because he didn't typically leave them on. But it made him feel warm. Happy. She was in there, waiting for him. He liked it.

He turned the key in the lock, opened the door. Bailey looked up from where she sat on the couch with Ana, feeding her a bottle. She had a leg propped on the coffee table and an infant cradled in her arms. She smiled at him, and his world shifted on its axis again.

"Everything okay?" she asked as he shut the door behind him and locked it.

"Yeah, everything's fine." He walked over and sat down beside her, leaning back and sighing as he stared up at the ceiling. "I didn't go to my HQ," he said. "My guys were at the Pink Palace. Dunn was there."

"What? And you didn't tell me?"

He looked at her. "Nope. You'd have wanted to go with me, and I didn't want to take you."

She looked militant. "Damn straight. I'd have wanted to ask him what the hell he did to my sister to scare her so badly. Then I'd have wanted to kick him in the balls. What happened? Where is he now?"

"The police picked him up before we could get him. Outstanding warrants. He'll be arraigned and held without bond most likely."

Her amber gaze searched his. "So he's not getting out anytime soon."

"No. We'll know more in a couple of days."

"I can go home then?"

"Yeah, you can go home."

She blew out a breath and turned her attention to the baby in her arms. Alexei skimmed his gaze over her purple hair, the curve of her cheek, her pretty pink mouth. She was a lovely sight with Ana in her arms. He could imagine her with a baby of her own someday. Maybe.

But who would be the father? That thought opened a hole in his gut.

"I need to text Kayla," she said. "Maybe she'll come home if she knows he's been arrested."

"I hope she does."

"I hope so too." She looked down at the baby in her arms. "I'm getting better at doing this baby stuff thanks to you, but Ana needs her mother. I know what it's like to grow up without a mom and so does Kayla. I don't think she wants to do that to Ana."

"I'm still trying to find her for you. She can't hide forever."

"I appreciate that, though part of me really wants her to come back on her own. Because she *wants* to. Because she wants her baby."

"Here, give me the pip-squeak. You text your sister and tell her Dunn's in custody. Maybe she'll reply."

He took Ana very carefully, arranging her in his arms. Bailey picked up her phone and started typing. A few seconds later, she sent the text.

By the time they got Ana down for the night and fell into bed together, there was still no reply.

———

BAILEY WOKE from a restless sleep to the sound of a

ding. It took her a minute to blink herself awake and process what she'd heard. Beside her, Alexei lay with an arm over his head, his eyes closed. She shifted away from him so she could grab her phone. He felt her move and reached for her, his hand sliding over her waist, her hip.

The phone dinged again and she snatched it. Alexei came awake almost immediately, sitting up with a suddenness that made her squeak.

"What's going on?" he whispered.

She held up the phone. "Text."

Kayla: *He's in jail? Are you sure?*

Bailey: *Yes, I'm sure. He's in jail and he's going to stay there for a while. Where are you?*

Kayla: *Virginia.*

Bailey sucked in a breath. She could be anywhere in Virginia, or she could be within a couple of hours' drive.

Bailey: *Why are we doing this through text? Call me.*

Kayla: *I don't want to. You'll yell at me.*

Bailey: *I won't yell.*

Kayla: *You will. You're always trying to run my life, Bale. Always scolding me. I just can't handle it right now.*

Bailey blinked as a shard of pain pricked her heart. Did she try to run Kayla's life? Yeah, probably. But she was older. She had more experience. She started to type that but stopped. Shame flooded her. Was that a good enough excuse? Could she have tried harder to let Kayla make her own decisions?

She looked up at Alexei. He was watching her silently.

"Did you read the conversation?"

"Yeah."

"She's right. I do run her life. But I'm trying to

protect her. Isn't that a good reason?" She was asking him because of what he did for a living. His job was all about protecting people. Saving people.

"Bailey. Baby." He shook his head. "You're gonna get pissed at me, but here's the deal. When I told you I wasn't going to let you go to work because it was dangerous, what did you do? You got pissed. And you did what you wanted to do."

"It was the right thing to do. It wasn't immediately dangerous. I wouldn't have gone if it had been."

"I wouldn't have *let* you if it'd really been dangerous. But that's not the point. The point is you got pissed that I tried to stop you. Your sister is a woman with a baby. If she can't make her own decisions by now, how will she ever?"

Bailey blinked as tears pricked her eyes. She was the oldest, the one who had to keep them both safe. She'd been in that role for so long. She'd watched her little sister suffer from the loss of their mother and the neglect of her father, and she'd wanted to protect her as much as she could. But maybe she'd done too much. Maybe she'd been too hard on Kayla. Clearly, Kayla hadn't trusted her with some pretty big moments in her life. And some ordinary ones too, like the fact she'd had a boyfriend—even if the boyfriend had turned out to be a creep.

Bailey had tried to protect Kayla, but she'd ended up getting shut out of her sister's life in the process. Instead of being a friend and a confidante, she'd been a judgy bitch who thought she knew everything. Who would share their secrets with that kind of person?

She took a deep breath and started typing. *I'm sorry. I should listen more, shouldn't I? I'm listening now. I'm trying,*

Kayla. Come home. Or let Alex come get you. I won't even go with him if you don't want me to. If you don't want to talk to me, you can talk to him.

She made sure to type Alex instead of Alexei because that's what her sister knew. She glanced up at him. "Is this okay with you?"

"Yeah. Send it, baby."

She did. Nothing happened for several minutes. Then her phone buzzed with an incoming call. She handed it to Alexei, even though it hurt to do so.

"Hey, Kayla," he said softly, getting out of bed and walking into the hall so as not to wake Ana. "How you doing, girl?"

Bailey didn't follow him. She brought her knees up to her chest and wrapped her arms around them, shivering as hot emotion rolled through her. She'd raised Kayla and given her everything she could—but she'd failed where it counted most. She'd failed to be someone her sister could trust.

Chapter 21

"How did you get involved with him?" Bailey asked her sister, being careful to sound nonjudgmental and supportive. Kayla sat at the counter in Alexei's kitchen, a warm cup of tea in her hands. It was nearly five in the morning, and she'd been here an hour now. Alexei had gone to get her while Bailey waited with Ana.

When the door finally opened again and Kayla walked inside, she'd stopped and folded her arms over her body. She was wearing an oversized sweatshirt and jeans with the knees ripped out. Her blond hair was piled on her head in a messy knot. She looked small and vulnerable and lonely, and Bailey had nearly sobbed with relief at seeing her.

She'd rushed over and wrapped her sister in a hug. Kayla had stood for a long moment without moving, then she'd hugged back. She'd also started to cry. Bailey had steered her to the couch and held her while she sobbed. Bailey mouthed *thank you* to Alexei over the top of Kayla's head. He'd tipped his chin at her, acknowledging the sentiment.

After a while, Kayla stopped crying and asked to see Ana. Bailey led her to the room where the bassinet was. Ana was sound asleep, so Kayla didn't touch her, though she stood and watched her for a long while.

Bailey had led her back out to the living room and then into the kitchen and plopped her down. Now she'd made tea and handed her sister a cup. They'd been talking haltingly about James Dunn and Kayla's relationship with him.

"He came up to me in the grocery store and told me I was the most beautiful woman he'd ever seen. I know that's lame, and I didn't fall for it at the time, but then he turned up at Buddy's one night." She shrugged. "He's very charming when he wants to be. He kept coming in, kept ordering from me. He never pushed me into anything, was never inappropriate. He was just so nice and sweet, not like some of the other guys there. Plus he was interested in me."

She shot a glance toward the back rooms where Alexei had gone. Bailey knew it was to give them privacy, though Kayla probably thought he could come back at any moment. "Alex was nice to me too, but he was never interested."

Bailey felt a tingle of uneasiness. "Were you interested in him?"

Kayla's expression was solemn. "At first. But he never looked at me twice, like I said—and then there was James. He treated me like I was precious and rare. So I started going out with him. He's not as crazy good-looking as Alex, but he's rough and rugged—and I just sort of fell for him."

"You didn't tell me you had a boyfriend."

She sighed. "I didn't think you'd like him. He was in

a motorcycle club, and they were all kind of rough and tough, you know? He took me to their clubhouse on the Eastern Shore. There were drugs and alcohol. I knew you'd never approve." She took a sip of the tea. "It was illicit and exciting. He never pushed me to do anything though. He seemed to respect that I didn't want to drink or smoke pot. He found it cute, I guess."

"When did you find out you were pregnant?"

"I was feeling super tired and I realized I hadn't had my period at all. I looked it up online and decided to take a pregnancy test. When I told James, he gave me this story about how we'd get married and raise our baby together and be a family."

"So you went to California?"

Kayla's gaze dropped. She didn't say anything for a long while. Then she met Bailey's eyes again, tears sparkling in hers. "I didn't go anywhere, Bale. I went to the Eastern Shore and stayed with James in the compound. He didn't want me working, didn't want me doing anything but resting and preparing to have our baby."

Bailey's heart throbbed. Kayla had been in the same state the whole time. Across the Chesapeake Bay, so close she could have come to visit at any time.

"Why didn't you ever come see me?" Bailey asked, throat tight. "I worried about you."

"I know. I'm sorry. And I'm sorry I told you I was in California. It was James's idea so you wouldn't come looking for me. And he wouldn't have let me visit you anyway. He didn't let me leave the compound without an escort."

Bailey wanted to put a bullet between James Dunn's

eyes right about now. But she told herself to remain cool or Kayla would clam up.

"He was afraid that you'd convince me to leave him." Kayla shook her head. "I know it's crazy, but he had me believing that you were looking for me so you could break us up and force me to have an abortion."

Bailey's jaw dropped. This asshole she'd never even known about until this week had spent a lot of time maligning her. And all so he could control Kayla.

"I would have never done such a thing," Bailey protested. "That kind of choice wasn't up to me, and I would never presume it was."

Kayla reached out and squeezed her hand. "I know, Bale. I let myself believe him because he cared so much. Loved me so much. He put me on a pedestal and I believed him. I didn't realize what was going on until after Anastasia was born. I was such an idiot; I know that now. I knew the club did things, had their fingers in illegal activities, but James told me he wasn't involved in any of that. And then I found a suitcase with condoms and weed in the closet and I confronted him about it. He had an explanation, of course. But then I read an article in the *Post* about sex trafficking—and it explained what the condoms and weed were for. James would take trips, just a few days at a time, and always driving. I knew then that he was pimping out girls. Keeping them stoned and selling their bodies to as many men per day as he could. Several of the guys do that with the younger girls. But the club also runs a prostitution ring with willing girls."

Bailey wanted to go and burn this club down. Right damn now. But she remained calm, cool. Soothing for her sister. "You decided to leave."

She nodded. "I did, but I wasn't sure how to get away. He kept my phone, only letting me message you sometimes so you wouldn't report me missing. I had no license, no phone, no car. I relied on the club for food and medicine for Ana." She sucked in a breath and it came out in a sob. "Sorry," she choked out. "Dammit!"

"It's okay, honey. You don't have to keep talking about it. You're here now. And James Dunn isn't getting to you."

"He tried to take Ana away. He wouldn't let me breastfeed her, so we bottle-fed her—it was so he could sell her for adoption. I told you my milk didn't come in, but it did. My God, it was so painful to have it and not be able to feed her." She closed her eyes. Shuddered. "Anyway, he got a call from the agency, and he didn't even bother to hide it from me. That's when I knew I had to go no matter what."

Bailey hated James Dunn with the fire of a thousand suns. If he were here right now, she'd kill him with her bare hands. And if she felt that way, what must Kayla be feeling right now? Bailey put her arms around her sister and hugged her tight.

"It's going to be all right, Kay-Kay," she said, using the name she'd called Kayla growing up. "You're safe with us. Alexei and his friends won't let anything happen to you or Ana. Nobody is taking that little girl away from you."

Kayla hugged her tight. "Thank you, Bale. I know you love me. I know it."

"I love you and Ana both. And hey, I didn't fuck her up while you were gone," Bailey said brightly. "I learned to change diapers and everything!"

Kayla laughed through her tears. "I was so scared to

leave her—but he called me. He told me he was coming for me. And I knew I had to leave her or risk him finding us both. I called one of the girls I knew who had successfully left the club. It was risky, but she really does hate them and had no interest in letting James know where I was. But I wasn't sure at first, and I couldn't take the chance. If she turned me over, at least he wouldn't get Ana too."

A wail came from the bedrooms. "Well, I guess someone is awake," Bailey said. "I bet she'd love to have her mama instead of silly Auntie Bale for a change. Though I have to tell you, she does kind of love Alexei. He's amazing with her."

"Alexei. You said that before. I didn't know that was his name."

Bailey flushed. "Family name. He mostly goes by Alex. Speaking of the devil," she said as Alexei emerged from the hall with a fussing baby in his arms.

He looked up at them and smiled—and Bailey's heart stuttered to a stop before racing into overdrive. God, she loved his smile. Loved his body. Loved being with him. Loved that he was so competent and protective.

It hit her then what all those things meant when added together. She loved Alexei Kamarov. Somewhere in the past few days, she'd taken a leap—and fallen head over heels for the man striding toward them with a tiny baby cradled tenderly in his grasp. My God, it was an ovary explosion looking at him like that.

"I changed her, but she'd probably like a bottle."

Kayla rushed over and took Ana in her arms, cooing and talking as tears rolled down her cheeks. "Did you miss Mama, little Anastasia-belle? Did you? Mama missed you. Oh my God, sooo much!"

Alexei met Bailey's gaze. Her heart throbbed and her eyes filled with tears. But were they for Kayla and Ana, or for herself and the realization she'd fallen for a Navy SEAL who'd told her he didn't do commitment?

"I'll get the bottle," he said to her as he passed. But then he stopped and bent down to give her a quick kiss. It took everything she had not to throw herself into his arms. "You did good," he said softly. "Way to listen and be supportive."

"Thank you." She stood on tiptoe to kiss him again when he would have walked away. "I owe you."

His eyes blazed hot. "You don't—but there are some things I can't turn down. Just so you know."

"What did you have in mind?"

He grinned. "I'll tell you later."

"THE KINGS OF DOOM," Lieutenant Colonel Alex "Ghost" Bishop, HOT's second-in-command, announced as they sat in the SEAL team's ready room and stared at the projection on the screen. "They've been on the Eastern Shore for about two years, expanding their operations slowly. They've been running guns, drugs, and women—and they're looking to expand operations even further. When James Dunn went to West Virginia with nineteen-year-old Megan Root, it was a test. He drove her around the state, kept her high, and pimped her out—up to twenty guys a day. When the police pulled them over for speeding, Megan wouldn't say she was being held against her will. The only thing the police had the two of them on was possession. But of course Dunn left as soon as he was freed and came back here."

"Jesus," Colonel John "Viper" Mendez said. He'd walked into the room right after the briefing started. Every last one of them, including Ghost, had snapped to attention when the main man came through the door. He'd told them to go at ease and then taken a seat and told Ghost to continue. "Sick fucks."

"Understatement, sir," Ghost said.

Alexei had called his team commander, Dane "Viking" Erikson, and given him the story about Kayla. Viking called the team together for a meeting. They'd informed Ghost, who'd gone to work—set subordinates to work, actually—digging up all the intel that could be found about the Kings of Doom. Which was significant, apparently. Dunn had spent time in Buddy's a few months ago, but he'd been the only member of the club there, and they'd had no reason to suspect him of anything. He'd just been a guy in leathers hanging out and waiting for a girl.

"This is outside our scope of operations," Mendez said, frowning hard. "We're active-duty military. We don't enforce laws inside the borders of the United States by an act of Congress."

Alexei had known that, but he couldn't sit by and do nothing. If HOT knew, maybe something would happen. Even if it wasn't by direct order or acknowledged by the command. One of the downsides of HOT was their inability to do what they did best within the borders of the US. But that's what other organizations were for.

Mendez looked thoughtful. Then he snorted. "I think I know just who to call."

Alexei thought the man would disappear at that moment. He'd get up, go make his call, and they'd find out later if he'd managed to do something about the Kings of Doom. But no, Mendez made the call right there on the secure phone in the ready room. He set it to speaker so everyone could hear.

"What's up, sweetie?" a male voice on the other end said. "You taking care of my girl?"

Ian Black. It took Alexei a moment to recognize the voice, but once he did, he knew what Mendez was going for. Black was deep cover CIA. He had resources, not to mention a fluid interpretation of what he could and could not do. The man employed mercenaries around the globe. He was precisely the guy to get the job done.

Mendez shook his head and rolled his eyes at the same time. "Kat is pregnant and demanding. I'll survive, but barely. I think."

"Aww, well, you should have been more careful with your loaded weapon, Johnny. Hi, boys," he added, letting them know he was aware they had him on speaker.

"Everyone says hi," Mendez deadpanned. "And as much as I'm enjoying the girl chat about my private life, I've got a problem I need you to look into."

"What kind of problem?"

"Sex trafficking." Mendez laid it out for the man.

When he was done, they all heard Black growl. "Motherfuckers."

Alexei shot a look at his teammates. They all wore some variation of surprised expressions. Ian Black was typically irreverent as hell and unflappable. He was the kind of guy who'd tell jokes at a funeral if asked to speak. Nothing seemed to bother the man.

Except this, apparently. Alexei wasn't a fan after that incident in Qu'rim where his team had nearly gotten killed by a tribe of nomads that Black had negotiated to sell their women and weapons to, but the man rose a notch in his opinion with that single word.

"So, you got an idea about it?" Mendez asked.

"I'll see what I can do. I know some people."

"Appreciate it, Ian. Let me know what I can do for you."

"There is something, now that you mention it."

Mendez lifted an eyebrow. "Care to enlighten me?"

"Not at the moment. I'll be in touch. Over and out."

"Over and out. Take care of yourself, you crazy fucker," Mendez added.

They heard Ian laugh. And then the connection went dead.

Chapter 22

"So," Kayla said, eyebrows lifting. "You and Alex, huh?"

Bailey looked up from where she was washing the dishes that she'd used to fix breakfast for her and Kayla. It had been a strange morning after a sleepless night. They'd been awake most of the night, so sleep was done in snatches that morning. After Kayla and Ana went to the guest room and lay down, Bailey and Alexei collapsed together for a few hours. There'd been no sex because they were both tired, but he'd wrapped his arms around her and held on while they slept.

At some point, he'd stirred, kissing her neck and cheek. "I have to go in to work, babe. Be back as soon as I can."

She'd stretched and arched her body against his, making appreciative noises at the erection pressing into her abdomen.

"Got time for a quickie?" she'd whispered.

"Fuck yeah," he'd said. He'd entered her without the condom this time, and they'd both groaned with the perfection of it. "I shouldn't do this," he'd whispered. "But damn, it feels good."

"Pull out when you come. If it makes you feel better."

He'd stroked into her hard and fast until she caught fire and came with a cry that she muffled against his shoulder. When he came, he withdrew and pumped semen onto her belly. It was sexy as hell to watch him come. She spread it over her skin, painted her nipples with it.

"Jesus, Bailey," he'd said fiercely. "I just fucked you, and you still manage to make me feel like I need to do it again."

He'd left her in bed and gone to shower, then stopped to kiss her before leaving. "Stay here today, okay? At least until I come back. Dunn's in jail, but that doesn't mean some of his cronies aren't looking for Kayla too."

"Okay."

She'd gotten up to shower, gotten dressed, and gone to fix coffee. Kayla emerged a short time later, and that's when Bailey made breakfast. Now her sister was looking at her with that questioning gaze, and Bailey's stomach flipped.

But she wasn't going to lie.

"Yeah, me and Alex." She shrugged. "It just kinda happened."

Kayla made a face. "Be careful, Bailey. He's sexy as hell, but those guys…" She shook her head. "They had more women after them than you can imagine whenever they were hanging out at Buddy's. Women find out those guys are SEALs and throw themselves at them. And the guys, well, they're guys. They don't turn the women away."

Bailey frowned. "I know that, but I didn't throw myself at him. It just happened. In fact, neither of us wanted it to. But it did."

"I'm certainly not anyone to give advice, believe me. I just thought you should know what it's like for them. They cycle through women pretty quickly. I watched it happen for months."

Bailey's heart ached at the thought. But she'd known what she was signing up for. The scratching of an itch. Hot sex with a hot guy. Except she'd fallen for him, which had definitely not been part of the plan. So what now? Stick around and take as much as she could get— or cut him loose now and move on with her life?

"We aren't getting married," she said. "I don't expect anything out of him."

"That's good." Kayla grinned. "So, is he good in bed?"

Bailey felt herself blushing. "Kay-Kay, why are you asking me that?"

Kayla laughed. "Look at you turn red! Oh my God, he is good, isn't he?"

Bailey shook herself and laughed. "All right, fine. Yes, he's amazing. He knows how to find all the right places, and he doesn't get tired. It's the best sex I've ever had."

"Well that's not hard to do. Your last man wasn't exactly a winner by any stretch of the imagination."

Kayla had never liked Bailey's old boyfriend. "Just because Dave was a douchebag doesn't mean he was bad in bed."

"True. So was he?"

Bailey frowned. "Not bad necessarily. But nothing like Alexei."

Kayla grinned again. "And there you go with the special name. Careful, Bale, or I'll think you're falling for this guy."

Oh, you have no idea.

Bailey scoffed. "It's just sex. Hot, dirty, amazing sex. His dick is magic. His tongue—you don't even want to know."

"Uh, yeah I do," Kayla said with a laugh. "I'm your sister—I want all the dirty details."

So Bailey spilled some of the particulars, but she kept the more private things to herself. The way Alexei made her feel when he touched her, the way her heart nearly burst from her chest. She didn't get specific about anything, but she told Kayla enough that her sister was watching her raptly.

"Wow. Okay, now I want one. A SEAL, that is." She laughed, and Bailey laughed with her. But then she sighed and shook her head. "I'm afraid there'll be no more guys for me for a long time though. Nobody's going to want a woman with an infant whose father's in the big house, you know?"

"The right man will come along, Kayla. And he won't care about any of those things." She smiled brightly. "And hey, Alexei and I aren't going to fall in love and live happily ever after or any of that romance-novel shit. It's just a fling."

Kayla sobered. "I want to leave here, Bale. Go somewhere new and start all over again. Somewhere that James won't come looking for me when he gets out of prison."

Bailey's heart skipped. She didn't like Kayla talking

of leaving, but then again, it was the most logical thing to do. Why shouldn't they both go? They could find a new state, a new place to live, somewhere with a cheaper cost of living. Maybe Bailey could enroll in community college, find a job, start building that new life she wanted. Or if not that, at least she could find work that wasn't in a strip club. Then again, the whole reason she stripped was because of the money. But she was tired of it. Tired of the numbness that went along with it and the walls she had to put up to survive.

There was no real reason to stay. None but her desire to be with a man who'd warned her up front that he wasn't going to commit to her. If they moved, Alexei would be sleeping with someone new in no time.

"Maybe it's time," she said, even though her heart cracked at the idea.

Kayla frowned. "You'd go with me?"

Bailey took her sister's hands in hers. "Of course I'd go with you. You're my sister. And you've got my cute little niece to take care of. You need me."

Kayla pulled her hands away and threw her arms around Bailey's neck, hugging her tight. "I've been such a jerk, Bale. I'm sorry. You're the best sister—best friend —I could ever have."

Bailey tightened her arms around Kayla. But her soul ached at the thought of leaving, even if it was the right thing to do.

———

ALEXEI DIDN'T WANT Bailey going back to the Pink Palace, but he didn't know how to tell her that without her getting pissed. Because it was illogical and possessive and a whole lot of things he shouldn't be feeling. But tonight was the night she was scheduled to return, and he'd thought of little else for the past two days.

She'd seemed a bit distant, but then she'd fallen into his arms every chance they got. She was hot and beautiful, and he couldn't seem to get enough of her. He'd been going in bare the past couple of nights, and it felt divine. He pulled out every time, but he really wanted to stay inside her when he blew. There was something about being in her that felt like the best thing he'd ever experienced. He told himself that couldn't possibly be true, but every time he went in with nothing between them, he felt a profound shift in his psyche. In his soul. It was the oddest feeling.

One thing was different about her lately though. She was increasingly distracted by her sister's presence. He'd returned home after meeting with his team to find her and Kayla hugging and crying about something. She wouldn't tell him what it was other than to say she thought maybe she and her sister were on the right track again.

Having Kayla around took a little getting used to, but she was quiet most of the time. She took care of her baby, and it was clear she loved the kid, which was a bit of a relief for Bailey, he was sure. Kayla apologized to him for saying he was the father and sending Bailey after him. He'd told her he wasn't mad about it.

And he wasn't. Because he wouldn't have met Bailey otherwise. But now Bailey was going back to the club, and it was driving him crazy. She'd be taking her clothes off onstage in a few hours, shaking her cute little ass and baring her tits while men hooted and made indecent suggestions. He could barely stand the idea. It drove him crazy to imagine it.

Crazy enough that when Kayla got caught up watching television, he dragged Bailey to the bedroom and pushed her back on the bed, sliding her jeans and panties off and burying his face between her legs. She moaned and thrashed as he licked her pussy relentlessly, driving her toward a shattering climax. Then he turned her over and fucked her from behind while she buried her face in the pillow and tried to cover her moans.

After it was over, after he'd come off the high of an orgasm so intense it sizzled down into his toes, he lay beside her and sucked in air.

"Wow," she said breathlessly. And then she rolled over and laid her head on his chest. "I'll miss this."

Alexei frowned, hand stilling where it was busy tracing the groove of her spine. "We'll still see each other," he said, assuming she was talking about going back to her own place. "You can sleep over here, I'll sleep over there. It'll work out." He swallowed as he thought of something else. And then he said it because what the hell? "Or you and Kayla and Ana can stay here. Until you find a better place to live."

He felt her stiffen. And then she relaxed again, her fingers tracing circles on his chest. "I want to stay. So much," she said, her voice barely audible. "But I think I have to get Kayla settled. She needs me."

I need you.

But he didn't say it because it was too foreign. Too shocking. He'd never said such a thing before, much less thought it. Yet here he was, thinking it. And thinking about how he didn't want other men looking at her banging bod and dreaming of fucking her. That was *his* territory.

His?

"She's a grown woman, Bailey. She needs your support, but not your twenty-four-seven presence."

She stiffened again. This time she pushed herself up until she could gaze down into his eyes. "She's my sister. She's been through hell. And where else would I be, huh?"

He didn't hesitate. "With me."

"You want me to stay? Why?"

He searched his brain. "Because I like you. I like being with you."

She frowned down at him. "I appreciate that. I really do. But it's not a reason. You don't need me for anything but scratching an itch. Kayla needs my support, like you said. I can do that better if I'm in the same house with her and Ana."

Her words stung. "I can scratch my itch with anyone. I'm choosing you."

"But for how long?" She shook her head when he didn't reply. "It's not enough, Alexei. I need more than that."

"More?"

"Yes. Is that so surprising? I dream of finding the perfect person for me just like everybody else does. I want love and marriage and yes, babies—but not right away on the babies. One day. I want those things, and I know you aren't the man who's going to give them to me. Because you told me so when this whole thing started."

"Jesus, Bailey—I know what I said. But I also know I can't lie and tell you I've changed my mind. I might—

hell, I don't know. But I need more time before I go thinking that way."

She sighed and dropped a kiss onto his shoulder. "Time is something I don't have. I have to make decisions now."

"What kind of fucking decisions?"

She searched his gaze. He didn't like the feeling gnawing into his belly. "Kayla wants to move to another state. Start over. She doesn't feel safe here anymore. I'm planning to go with her."

All he could do was stare at her while his chest tightened as if there were a boulder sitting on it and squeezing all the air away. "And you didn't think to mention this to me before now?"

Her lashes dropped over her eyes, hiding their amber fire from his gaze. His heart felt like a dead weight in his chest. *What the fuck?*

"I didn't think I needed to discuss it with you, no."

He didn't know what to say. What to think. Was it crushing him to imagine her leaving? Hell yeah. But was that enough to try to stop her? What was he supposed to say to her?

"I thought we were friends, Bailey."

"Friends with benefits? Because that's all we seem to have going here. Unless you have something else to say to me."

He didn't speak. He was too busy trying to process it. Her mouth flattened as she spread her palm over his pectoral muscle and then patted him. "Okay then. That's what I needed to know."

She pushed herself upright and swung her legs over the side of the bed. Then she grabbed her clothes and started tugging them on. Panties, bra.

"Bailey. It doesn't need to be like this."

She whirled on him. "Like what, Alexei? You mean the part where I stop spreading my legs whenever and wherever you want, because you can't give me a good reason to stay?"

She tugged her T-shirt over her head. Then she started shoving her legs into her jeans.

"What do you want from me?" he demanded, shoving his way out of the bed to face her.

Her eyes narrowed. He didn't miss that she let her gaze fall to his cock, then back up to his face.

She put her hand over her eyes and stood there shaking her head. "I'm such an idiot. Such a damned idiot."

He thought that was what he wanted to hear—but then he thought maybe it wasn't. Because she didn't seem to mean she was an idiot for wanting to leave. She meant something else, but he didn't know what.

He crossed the distance between them and put his hands on her arms, smoothed them up and down soothingly. "Bailey, baby. We can figure this out. You don't have to leave."

She jerked away from him. He was so surprised by the move that he didn't try to stop her. He stood there with his hands in midair for a long moment while she turned her back and sucked in deep breaths.

"What's wrong?" he asked. Because this was territory he'd never ventured into before. He was lost as hell.

She whirled back, gaze sparkling with tears. "I let myself like you, Alexei. Too much. I *want* to stay—don't you get that? But I can't stay for a sexual relationship that could end tomorrow. It has to be more than that." She shook her head. "But you don't want more, and I'm not trying to force you into it. So I just need to go while it doesn't hurt so much."

He swallowed. What the fuck could he say? She was right. He didn't want more. He couldn't. His job, his life, wasn't conducive to more than this right here. He'd be gone on another mission in a couple weeks, and she'd be alone again. Was it fair to ask her to stay when she had her sister back again and the two of them could start over somewhere else? Somewhere better for raising a baby. Because she couldn't stay here and strip and live in that crappy apartment anymore. It was time for something better.

"When?" he asked.

She blinked. "When are we going? Is that what you're asking?"

He nodded.

Her eyes just kinda went dead. "Soon. I have to give notice, pack up our apartment. Figure out where we should go next. A couple of weeks probably. At least."

"Okay. I'll help any way I can." He jerked his pants on, grabbed his T-shirt and tugged it over his head. He pointed at her suddenly, emotion welling up inside him like a fucking pot boiling over. "If this is about the Kings of Doom—they're done, Bailey. Your sister isn't going to have to worry about those motherfuckers ever again. Did you really think I'd let them continue to exist after what Kayla told you?"

Her eyes widened. "What did you do?"

His jaw snapped shut. He couldn't tell her that. Couldn't mention Ian Black, or HOT, or any of it. She wasn't authorized. If they were together, there was a point at which she'd be briefed on HOT—not the real mission, but the sanitized version of it—but it wasn't the kind of thing he could tell her now. She was leaving. They were finished. Whatever this was, it wasn't going to keep happening.

"What I had to do. Trust me, they won't last much longer. A few weeks at most."

"Alexei…" She shook her head. "I can never thank you for all you've done for us. So much more than you ever had to do. I hope…" She sniffed. "I hope we'll stay in touch."

"Yeah. Sure. We can do that," he said, even though it felt like someone was dragging a dull knife through his guts.

"I should get ready for work."

The knife twisted. And he suddenly had to get out. Just get out and think for a while. "Yeah, I need to head to the base. Training."

He grabbed his keys and shoved them in his pocket. Then he walked out without another word.

Chapter 23

Alexei walked into the indoor shooting range at HOT and set down his range bag. He unzipped his rifle case and took out an MK12 light sniper rifle. He laid it on the table in front of him, dug out a thirty-round magazine, and snapped it into place. He already wore his ear protection and shooting glasses. He didn't always have the luxury of this stuff in the field, but when you practiced, you wore protection.

He picked up the rifle, sighted it in, and fired. It wasn't difficult to hit the target at these distances. Indoor ranges had limitations, even if this one was built for long-range practice. Just not the kind of long-range practice he liked to get in from time to time. Fifteen hundred yards. Two thousand yards. Those were more challenging, and there was another military range nearby for that, currently closed. But since he needed something to blow off the steam currently building inside him, he'd come to HOT.

He needed to shoot the hell out of a poor innocent target or ten. He'd also like to go a few rounds with the punching bag in the gym. That was next. Because he was pissed and hurt and, yeah, somewhat confused about his reaction to the whole thing.

So Bailey was moving out of state. He'd known her for a little over a week now. Why should it matter if she left town? Sure, she had a body he loved to explore. She was tough and decisive and brave, and she worked her ass off.

He thought of her getting ready to step out on that stage at the Pink Palace and his stomach twisted. He couldn't stand the idea of those assholes in the audience looking at her as anything less than the funny, sweet, gorgeous woman she was. But they wouldn't see that. All they'd see were tits and ass and their own dirty thoughts.

Alexei fired again and again, trying to erase that image from his head. He spent about an hour firing everything in the bag—the rifle, his Glock, a sweet Ruger SR1911 he'd picked up recently, a Colt 1911, a Sig Sauer P239, and an HK45CT. When he'd depleted his ammo, he packed everything up and returned the bag to the armory, minus his personal weapons, which had to be unloaded and stored separately from the ammo while transporting them on a military facility.

Alexei headed for the gym where he changed into workout gear and hit the treadmill. Maybe he could sweat Bailey out.

Or maybe not, because by the time he got off the treadmill half an hour later, she was still in his head. He'd been punching the shit out of the bag for about twenty minutes or so when he saw movement in his periphery.

He glanced up. Blade was watching him. Neo and Dirty were setting up the bench press with weights.

"You okay, dude?"

"Yeah, why?"

"You seem a little stressed."

"Nope."

"You have your house back yet?"

"No."

"Shit, man. It's your turn to host poker this weekend."

Alexei stopped punching the bag and glared at his teammate. "Seriously, that's what's on your mind right now? Poker?"

"Yeah. Cage scammed me at pool the last time we were at Buddy's. I want to win my money back."

Alexei felt like he'd stepped into an alternate dimension. One where life unfolded the way it always did while his own life was somehow falling apart.

"They'll be gone by then," he said numbly and then hit the bag again.

"Excellent," Blade replied. "So you and Bailey… there's nothing going on there?"

Alexei stopped again. Stared at Blade. "Why would there be?"

Blade held up both hands, palms out. "Man, I hear you. But Cowboy bet Cage you were falling for her. Viking took Cowboy's side. I took Cage's."

They were betting on him? Him and Bailey? Shit.

"What about the others?" he asked.

"Even split, dude. I say you're too much of a loner to ever let a woman get you by the balls. Cowboy and Money think nobody's immune. Just because they're pussy-whipped doesn't mean the rest of us have to be, right?"

"Right." But were they pussy-whipped or were they

happy? Alexei thought of Cowboy and Miranda at the restaurant the other day. The camaraderie they had. The easy laughter, the shared jokes, the significant looks.

Had his parents ever had that? All he remembered were two stressed-out people trying to raise six kids. They never had enough money or enough time. His mother's English hadn't been very good to begin with—though it had gotten better over time—and she'd been isolated. Had that contributed to their breakdown?

He suddenly needed to know. Alexei walked away from the punching bag and toward the locker room. Blade called out something behind him, but he didn't pay attention. He went to his locker and took out his cell phone. He wasn't in a restricted part of the facility, and phones were allowed. He sat down on the bench, wiping sweat from his brow, and scrolled through his contacts until he found his mother's number.

She answered on the second ring. "Alexei. Is everything okay?"

She spoke in Russian, so he answered her in the same language. But first he pulled the phone from his ear and frowned at it. Did he really not call her that often? Did something have to be wrong for him to call?

"Everything's fine, Mom. But I wanted to ask you something…"

"Well then. I have my book club coming over soon, so I can't talk very long, but what did you want to know?"

He stared at the wall opposite. How to ask her these things? Maybe he should call his father instead. But his dad was a big personality, a man with a healthy sense of ego who rarely accepted fault for anything. *And isn't that a partial answer, dumbass?*

"Why did you marry Dad? Did you think it was forever?"

She was quiet for a minute. "What kind of question is that, Alexei? Of course I thought it was forever. But I was very young and naive. Your father... Well, he was incredibly dynamic and intelligent. I was dazzled by him. We should have waited, perhaps. But there was urgency. He wanted to apply for a position in the US, and he didn't want to leave me behind. Why do you want to know this?"

Alexei drew in a deep breath. "I met someone. But I don't think I know how to be in a relationship..."

"Oh, baby, of course you do. You and this lady are not your father and me. We were young—and I had no sense of who I was for many years. When I figured it out, we had grown apart. So does this lady challenge you, or does she agree with all you want?"

Alexei wanted to laugh at the mere idea of Bailey agreeing with all he wanted. "She definitely challenges me. And I like her. A lot. But I'm not sure if it means anything or if it's just..."

Well, he wasn't going to say what he thought it could be. Not to his mother. She surprised him, however.

"Lust?" She must have felt his surprise through the phone because she made a noise. "I know what lust is, Alyosha," she said, using her pet name for him that she hadn't used since he was probably about twelve and told her it was a baby name and not American enough. "I know how young people are. I used to be one."

She laughed at that, and Alexei pinched the bridge of his nose. He was telling his mother about a woman? Asking her advice? Crazy. He was crazy. Bailey was making him that way.

"Listen to me, Alyosha," she said. "The point is that you don't always know. Sometimes you think you can't live without a person. And sometimes you don't know what it is you want. But if you can't stop thinking about her. If she has you twisted up inside—if you're calling and asking me about her, a thing you've never done with a girl in your whole life—then maybe there's something worth exploring there."

She had a point. "Maybe."

"Your father and I grew apart. It was both our faults really. We were very passionate for each other in the beginning, but we didn't nurture it. Passion is like a flower. You must tend it, or it can wither and die. We didn't tend it. That's what happened. We ceased to be compatible, though we are still friends. Yes, it was painful when it ended—but I wouldn't change my relationship with your father. It gave me you and your brothers and sisters. Every moment was worth the ride."

Worth the ride.

"Thanks, Mom."

"You're welcome, honey. Now, before you go, when will you come visit me again? It's been too long."

"Soon," he said and meant it. It had been too long. Too many deployments, too much work. And the urge to be alone with his thoughts when he returned from a mission.

"Bring your lady. I wish to meet her."

"I don't know if she is my lady," he admitted. "She's a little pissed at me right now."

"Alexei, language." She made a noise that sounded like scoffing. "You are a handsome and charming boy. You'll win her over if you want to."

Alexei snorted. Only his mother would call him a

boy and get away with it. "Thanks, Mom. I really have to go. Love you."

"Love you too, Alyosha. Come visit!"

Alexei promised he would before she would let him go. He put the phone down and sat on the bench, thinking about what he needed to do now. Go to Bailey and tell her he was an idiot? Yeah, she'd appreciate that. She'd probably lift an eyebrow and ask him what was new about that revelation.

Oddly enough, he couldn't wait to see her reaction. He jumped up and headed for the shower. He was just toweling off when Blade came into the locker room, frowning hard. Alexei recognized that look. His heart skipped a beat. Were they about to get orders again? Was he going to lose his chance to tell Bailey he was a fool? When they returned, would he be able to find her again?

But it was something much worse than an impending mission.

"James Dunn was set free an hour ago."

BAILEY'S HEART wasn't in it tonight. She didn't want to work, but she had to. If she and Kayla were leaving, she needed as much money as she could earn to get them somewhere new, especially since Kayla hadn't been working in months and had no income at all.

It seemed strange to have to drive herself to the Pink Palace instead of Alexei driving her. But he wasn't back by the time she was ready to leave, and she knew he wasn't planning on coming back for a while. He was angry with her. Well, she was angry with him too.

If he wanted her to stay, he needed a reason. A damn good reason, not just that he wanted to have sex with her. Though, dammit, she loved the sex. It was hot and earth-shattering and perfect. Just like the man.

She sniffed as she got her crap together for the night. She hadn't intended to push him about his feelings, but once she'd revealed that Kayla wanted to move and Bailey had to go with her sister, she'd needed him to tell her why he didn't want that to happen. She'd needed him to feel *something*. She'd fooled herself into thinking he must, because he couldn't keep his hands off her and he'd trusted her enough to forgo a condom. For a man who swore he'd never done that with anyone, she'd thought it had to mean something.

It didn't. Or not enough anyway. Hell, she'd even told him she would stay if only he'd give her a reason. She'd practically begged him to tell her he cared—but instead he'd asked when she was leaving. That was the moment her heart broke in two. That was the moment when she knew there was nothing between them. She was a body to him, nothing more.

Well, she could go and be a body at work too. At least she got paid for gyrating her hips—and there was no danger of emotional entanglements there.

Bailey fixed her makeup and hair, put on her track-suit, then grabbed her bag with the sequined bra and G-string and her costume. She said goodbye to Kayla, who was rocking Ana on the couch, then went and tossed her bag into the ancient Volkswagen.

The car started up right away, as if being neglected the past few days had given it a chance to rest. It was dark out and a little chilly, so Bailey cranked the heater on. It didn't do much besides move the air around. By the time she pulled into the parking lot, it still hadn't warmed up.

"Stupid car," she grumbled as she shut off the engine. There were a few cars already in the parking lot. Guys who came early to drink and then stayed for the show. She stared at the building, the neon-pink sign flashing on and off, the little gold crown at the top of the word Pink. Was this what her life had come to? Really?

She'd never been ashamed of what she did. It was performance art, albeit without a lot of clothing. But tonight she wanted to walk away and leave it all behind. She wanted to get started on the next phase of her life. Go to college, get a degree in nursing, get a real job with benefits and security.

But this was what she had to do right now. Bailey shoved her car door open and grabbed her gym bag. She'd go to Deke and tell him she was leaving soon. Then she'd get through three sets, try to sell some lap dances, and go back to Alexei's place after work. Tomorrow she'd take Kayla and Ana back to the apartment, and they'd start looking at places to go.

Bailey closed her door and locked it. A hand slapped down over her mouth. She started to scream, but something sharp pierced her arm. A needle? She jerked and tried to fight, but she wasn't as strong as her assailant. He hauled her backward and then shoved her forward quickly, knocking her head into the doorframe. The blow stunned her, and he used the opportunity to wrench her wrists behind her back and bind them with a zip tie.

Then he opened her car door and shoved her inside before getting in beside her and starting it up. He'd taken her keys from her hand. She tried to sit up, tried to shake her hair from her face and see who he was. But she was starting to feel groggy, and movement was harder now.

He jammed the pedal to the floor and her car lurched into gear, throwing her back against the seat. When he took a sharp turn, she fell against the door. Her head throbbed and her stomach roiled.

"Who?" she managed to force out with what felt like a superhuman effort.

There was no answer.

Chapter 24

"What do you fucking mean he was let go?" Alexei growled as he and Blade piled into his truck and headed for the Pink Palace. Neo and Dirty were on the way to his place. Alexei had been dialing Bailey's number, but she wasn't answering. That didn't mean anything since she could be inside the dressing room at the club, getting ready for the performance.

"The judge in the case set bail. He made it. He's out."

Alexei was angry. And scared. Fear wasn't the kind of emotion he was used to feeling, but it was definitely there. A strong, acidic emotion that he didn't like at all.

"Why the fuck would the judge let that motherfucker go? We were told it wasn't going to happen." But there were things that went on behind the scenes sometimes that nobody had an explanation for. Somebody owed somebody else. Somebody had dirt on somebody. Favors, marks, threats—something was called in and a decision was made. Someone, somewhere, had fucked up. On purpose or not, it didn't matter. The result was that Dunn was out—and he was pissed.

"No idea, dude. But I bet some heads are gonna roll over that one."

Not soon enough for Alexei. They reached the Pink Palace, and Alexei searched the parking lot for Bailey's Volkswagen as they careened through. He didn't see it, but that didn't mean it wasn't there. He and Blade jumped out of his truck and stormed the club. Brian the bouncer was at the door. His gaze flickered with recognition.

"Is Honey with you?"

Alexei's heart dropped. His stomach flipped. "No. She didn't come to work?"

Brian shook his head. "It happens. The broads don't show up sometimes. But Honey never did that before. She's always been reliable."

Alexei clenched his fists at his sides. "You see James Dunn in here tonight?"

"Dunn? No. Cops arrested him last night."

"Yeah, and today he posted bail."

"Fuck."

"Right. You got cameras in the parking lot?" Alexei asked.

"On the building, but they cover most of the parking lot. Come on, let me take you to Deke. He'll pull up the footage."

SHE WAS CHAINED TO A BED. That much she knew. Bailey moved her aching head, grogginess clouding her mind, making the room spin. She wanted to hurl, but there was nothing in her stomach. She knew that because she'd already hurled everything she had. She remembered that each time she woke. Remembered stepping out of her car to walk into work and someone putting a hand over her mouth and a needle into her arm before throwing her into her car. She hadn't passed out right away, but it seemed to happen within minutes.

Now she was in a room, on a squeaky bed with a musty mattress, and she had no idea where she was. There was laughter coming from somewhere. Male? Female? She wasn't sure.

"She's awake," someone with a rough voice said. Raspy, like they smoked a lot.

"Oh? Good. Nobody likes fucking a cold fish."

Fucking a…?

Panic settled into her brain, rolled through her in waves, stirred up the nausea in her belly again. She started to retch.

"Goddammit," the same voice said. "She's gonna be useless if she can't stop that shit."

"She'll stop," the rough voice said.

"How much did you give her?"

"Enough to knock her out and get her here. I've never had anyone hurl from it though."

"Get her in a shower. Clean her up."

"Fucking hell," Rough Voice grumbled.

"You got a problem with doing your job?"

"No."

"Good. Do it and shut the fuck up."

The chains clanged and then Bailey was levered up, blanket and all, and carried somewhere. Cold water sluiced over her and she yelped, fighting the weight of the wet blanket. She managed to get free of it, but every effort she made to leave the shower was met with a shove back into it.

Then the water was turned off and rough hands stripped her of her clothing while she slapped at them and fought ineffectually. Her gaze eventually focused on the man stripping her naked. He was big and mean-looking, with tattoos and a long beard that was divided into braids. He wore a leather vest with patches. One patch stood out from the others. It was big and consisted of a skull with coffins on either side that had a K and a D in them. A banner over the skull said KINGS OF. Below the skull, the banner said DOOM.

Oh shit. Alexei had said the Kings of Doom were going down, but apparently they weren't done yet. Her heart dropped into her toes.

"Nice set of tits, girlie," the man said as he tossed her sodden clothes onto the shower floor and left them. "I enjoy a shaved pussy too."

"No," she said, that one word dragging from her. She could form the words in her head, but nothing wanted to come out. What the hell had they given her?

The man laughed. "You say that now, but pretty soon you won't say a damned thing except *yes, please.* If you want your next fix."

Bailey's heart pounded. What? She dragged the recesses of her brain for what Kayla had said. A suit-case. Condoms. Drugs. Sex trafficking.

Anger filled her. She would fight. She *had* to fight.

He tossed a towel at her and she barely caught it. Her fingers didn't want to work right, but she somehow managed to get the towel around her body before she sank onto the floor and tried to force the breath in and out of her lungs.

"Come on, girlie," the man said, reaching for her again. He didn't pick her up this time. He just dragged her back down a hallway and into another room with another musty mattress. She heard music thumping through the walls, and laughter. She could smell cigarette smoke—and marijuana smoke—and whiskey. There was also the smell of sex. Panic filled her lungs, expanded the throbbing in her head. She remembered hitting the side of the car, the exploding pain in her skull.

"Well, there's our lovely Bailey Jones," a man said, standing up from where he'd been waiting in a chair.

James Dunn.

His was the voice she'd heard earlier. The one saying she needed to be ready. He was loosening his belt. Unsnapping his jeans.

"I'm going to enjoy fucking you good, Bailey. When I'm done, you're gonna tell me where Kayla and the baby are. And if you don't, I'm gonna let Dirk here fuck you. And if you still don't talk, I'm gonna haul your ass into the common room and let every single mother-fucker in there have a go at you at once. Pussy, ass, and mouth, all getting used. How many dicks can you take at the same time, Bailey?"

"No," she forced out again. Nausea rolled. Her head pounded.

Dunn advanced on her, caught the edge of the towel, and ripped it from her body. His gaze traveled over her as she scrambled backward, hitting the edge of the bed, falling back onto the mattress. He reached out to shove her down when she tried to spring back up.

"I'm going to enjoy this. More than you realize."

"No!"

"Hold her down, Dirk," he said to the man standing by and watching. "Hold this bitch while I fuck her into submission."

Chapter 25

The security footage from the Pink Palace showed a bearded man wearing a do-rag and a motorcycle jacket with patches on it hanging out in the parking lot. When Bailey drove up, he started toward her car. He didn't travel in a straight line. He snuck around behind parked cars, getting closer each time until the moment she got out of the car and he attacked.

Alexei's gut twisted with anger and desperation. Blade snapped photos of the dude at regular intervals so Alexei didn't have to. He just watched. And seethed. When the man hauled her back and then slammed her head into the door pillar, Alexei vowed he'd find the motherfucker and make him pay. It looked like the guy jabbed Bailey with a needle, but they couldn't really tell. Then he shoved her in the car, climbed in after her, and drove off.

"Fuck," Deke Mitchell said.

"Any idea who that guy is?" Blade asked. Because Alexei couldn't untangle his emotions enough to use his voice just yet.

"No, man. Never seen him before."

"Kayla," Alexei finally managed. "She'll know." Because the dude was with the Kings of Doom. Alexei was certain of that. And since Kayla had lived with the fuckers, she'd probably know who he was. James Dunn hadn't come for her himself. He'd sent someone. So he could keep clean of the crime.

"Right. Let's go. Thanks, Deke," Blade said.

The old SEAL looked pissed. "You boys get that fucker, you hear me? Fuck him up good."

"We're gonna," Alexei said as he stalked out the door.

They sprinted for the truck. Blade called Neo as they were en route, telling him what had happened. By the time they got to Alexei's house, Kayla Jones was pacing the floor. When Alexei opened the door and walked in, she launched herself at him, grabbing his arms, pleading with him.

"Please save her. You have to save her! He'll hurt her, Alex. I told Bailey he would kill her, but he won't. Not really. He'll just make her wish she was dead."

Alexei removed her hands from him, gently, and walked her over to the kitchen table where he could sit her down. Neo was standing by, frowning. Alexei met his gaze, wondered at the way he looked at Kayla, then dismissed it as unimportant.

"I need you to look at a picture," Alexei said, using his calmest tone. He had to switch into operator mode, had to treat this like any mission to save hostages. Had to pretend he didn't care about Bailey while inside he was dying.

Blade took out his phone and gave it to her. She scrolled through the pictures. "It's Dirk. He's one of the enforcers for the Kings. He does the dirty work for the boss and some of the higher-placed lieutenants."

"Why would he take her?"

Kayla wrapped her arms around her body and started to rock in place. She was a slight little thing. Pretty. No wonder Neo put a hand on her shoulder and squeezed. Kayla stopped rocking then. Sat up straighter. Her brows drew together and her jaw firmed.

"James probably sent him. Because he believes Bailey knows where I am. He wants me back to punish me—and he wants to sell Ana to the adoption agency. They'll pay a lot for an infant, especially a clean one. He'll try to force Bailey to reveal where I am. When she does, he won't let her go. They'll pimp her out, Alex. They'll keep her high and they'll sell her body. At first, it'll be the club that has a go at her. When she's sufficiently broken enough, someone will take her on the road and pimp her out all day every day. Truck stops, bars, pool halls. Wherever they find guys willing to pay."

"I thought you weren't aware of this shit, Kayla? You told Bailey you didn't know about it until you found a suitcase with condoms. What gives?"

She sucked in a breath, her eyes sparkling with tears. "I didn't know, I swear. I pieced it together after—and while I was staying with Joanne, the girl who left the club. She clarified some things for me."

Alexei didn't have much sympathy for her at the moment. "You didn't want to know, Kayla. But if you spent the past several months in that place, you had an idea of what was going on. You just didn't want to admit it to yourself."

A sob burst from her.

Neo didn't take his hand off her shoulder. "Lay off, Camel. She's upset enough, don't you think?"

"No, he's right," she said. "I rationalized everything. James explained so many things away, and I believed him. I shouldn't have."

"Would Dirk take her to the club's compound or somewhere else?"

"The compound. Absolutely. It's set on forty acres, and there's a mobile home park there as well as the main club."

A fucking nightmare. "How many buildings?"

"Three main buildings and fifteen trailers."

Fifteen fucking trailers. Jesus. "Where are they most likely to have her?"

Kayla shook her head as tears flowed down her cheeks. "I don't know. James and I lived in one of the trailers—it's a blue-and-white one, fifth trailer on the right when you enter the park. He might take her there first. But I don't know for sure."

"How the hell did you get out of there, Kayla?"

She swallowed, her face pale. "Ana had a well-baby appointment. One of the women took me. I told the nurse I was afraid for my life and I needed to get away. She wanted to call the police, but I convinced her not to. She stalled Neesa—that's who took me to the appointment—while I went out the back. The nurse gave me money and called a taxi for me, and I took it to Annapolis and then took another to the apartment complex."

"How did you know Dunn wouldn't find you there?"

"I never told him where I lived before I ran away with him. I didn't want Bailey to see him, so I always met him somewhere. My license had our old address on it, so he wouldn't have gotten it off there even if he tried. Once I moved in with him, it didn't matter anymore."

"Where is the compound? Do you know exactly?"

She nodded. "Yes. I can take you right to it."

"Just give us directions. Write it down if you have to."

"Sure. Yes. Of course."

"I'll get Viking on the phone," Blade said as Alexei grabbed a pen and paper from the table by the door and shoved them at Kayla. "See if we can't get Black on the line."

"I'm not waiting for a team to assemble," Alexei said. "We don't have that kind of time."

"No, I don't think we do either. But they need to know what's happening. And if Black has assets in place, he can help."

"That's fine," Alexei said. "But Dunn and this Dirk asshole are mine."

"Copy that," Blade said as Alexei stalked over to his gun safe and rolled the combo. The doors opened to reveal his own personal arsenal. He reached in and started to load weapons. Time to hunt some fucking bikers.

WHATEVER THEY'D GIVEN her was starting to wear off, but not quickly enough. Bailey felt drunk and high and sick, or what she assumed drunk and high felt like since she'd never been either of those things in her life. There was a decided loopiness to the whole thing, but not so loopy that she wasn't aware of what was happening.

She was naked, on a bed in a dark and dingy room, and two men were advancing on her. One grabbed her wrists while she kicked at him. But her kicks were ineffectual and he soon subdued her, wrenching her arms high above her head and holding them there. He positioned himself above her head as well, trapping her arms between his body and his tree-trunk limbs. Her legs were still free, and she kicked out at the other man —James Dunn—as he shoved his pants down and tried to lie on top of her.

"No," she cried out as his rubbery dick pressed into her thigh. It wasn't quite hard yet, which was a bonus for her. The more she twisted and fought, the limper his dick became.

A fist landed in her belly, and she started to retch as the air whooshed from her. At the first touch of the fist, she managed to tighten her core muscles, but it wasn't quite enough. The pain radiated out into her chest, her limbs. She couldn't breathe.

"Fucking bitch," Dunn growled as he stood over her and jerked on his dick. "You aren't making this any better for yourself. Be nice to me and I might reconsider letting Dirk here fuck you."

"Hey, man. No fair," Dirk said. "I grabbed her for you."

Something shook the bed as the room grew much brighter. A second later, a thundering boom reached inside and knocked them over the head.

"What the fuck was that?" Dunn said, stumbling back from the bed and over to a window. A window?

She hadn't realized there was one, but that was the source of the light that had made the room brighter.

There was another explosion. Fire whooshed into a column in the sky. Were those screams? She wasn't sure because her blood pounded so loud in her temples and ears that she couldn't really hear much of anything.

"Goddammit, what the hell?" Dunn said as he stuffed his dick back inside his pants and zipped them up. "We gotta get to the armory!"

He grabbed the chains from the floor, and he and Dirk wrapped them around her and locked them tight before sprinting from the room. Bailey lay there for a full minute, trying to clear her mind of the remaining grogginess before she started twisting to get out of the chains. They'd wrapped them around the bed and her body like a straitjacket, and she couldn't move much. The little distance she did move dug the chains into her naked flesh. The links bit into her skin, and she could feel them grow slippery in spots. She knew she'd cut herself, but she didn't care if it meant she could somehow get out of these things.

"Help!" she screamed, though her voice was weak and not quite a scream. "Help!"

Another fireball lit the night sky, closer this time. Bailey fought harder to break free. She didn't want to die. She wanted to live—and she wanted to tell Alexei she loved him. It might not make a difference at all, but it didn't matter. When you loved someone, you told them. Just in case you never got to see them again.

Chapter 26

Ian Black arranged a helicopter. Alexei, Blade, Neo, Dirty, Viking, Cage, Cowboy, and Money, all suited up and ready to kick some serious ass, boarded at a private airstrip. It hadn't taken the team long to get themselves to the rendezvous point. They'd been on their way the moment they'd gotten word that Dunn had walked out of custody.

This was a private mission without the sanction of HOT. But somebody somewhere had worked their magic, and the SEALs were currently assigned to some shadowy organization that didn't have to play by the same rules as the United States military. Alexei didn't know how it had happened. He didn't care either.

All he cared about was getting to Bailey and getting her out before the Kings of Doom abused her. She was there. They knew it for a fact now. Black had people watching the compound, and they'd reported the arrival of an ancient Volkswagen Bug. A man had been driving. What appeared to be a woman with pale hair slumped in the passenger seat. It was too dark to verify the exact hair color, but the woman had to be Bailey.

The helicopter zoomed straight to a drop zone within the forty acres. The SEALs rappelled down a line onto the ground. A man came out of the shadows. Their contact from Black's team. After a few quick introductions, they were off and running through the woods.

"Got an extraction team waiting with SUVs," Jace Kaiser, Black's man, said as they ran. "We've set charges near their fuel-storage facility. They've also got an armory and an ammo-storage facility—that's regrettably not hardened," Jace added with a grin. "Charges set there too. It'll be a helluva show."

They all knew that the blame for the explosions was going to rest squarely on the Kings of Doom. Black's men—and the HOT SEALs—were never here. The whole thing would be set up in such a way it would point to some sort of faulty decision made by the club.

"Do you know where they took the woman they just brought in?" Alexei asked.

"There's a group of trailers a little distant from the others. They use them as a brothel. They took her there about an hour ago. I'll show you which one."

Alexei told himself to get prepared for what they might find. What if it was too late to save Bailey from Dunn's plans to use her body? What if she'd already been violated and hurt?

He gripped his weapon against his chest a little harder and focused on the run through the woods. If she'd been violated, if they'd taken her sweetness and fire away, made her frightened and mistrustful instead— well, he'd do whatever he had to do to bring her back.

He'd fight for her. He'd slay dragons for her, and he'd prove to her that he had her back. Always.

They reached the outskirts of the compound. Alexei scanned the area with his night vision goggles. There were motorcycles parked in the yard, men and women inside one of the buildings and on the porch to that building. It was an old structure, probably been there for fifty years, with weathered wood and a multitude of old gas and oil signs hammered onto its face. In any other setting, it'd be charming.

But not here. Here, it was a sick parody of a normal bar setting in a country town. Because what they were doing here—doing to women and girls against their will —was illegal and immoral and unconscionable.

"Which trailer?" Alexei asked as they observed the buildings from a safe distance.

"See that cluster over there? Five of them. They took her into the second one."

"All right," Viking said. "Let's get into place so we can blow this puppy and get to work."

"Copy that," everyone said. Then they split up and went for their designated target. It had been understood from the beginning that Alexei was going after Bailey. Blade was at his side as they ghosted through the night toward the trailer. He wanted, more than anything, to kill Dunn—and Dirk—but that was not what they were here for. Their orders were simple.

Get Bailey. Raid the operation and get the goods on how it functioned. Don't kill anyone unless absolutely necessary. He hated that last part, but he understood it. A military operation with casualties in a quiet Maryland town wouldn't go over well if it made the front page of the *Washington Post*. Not that it was technically a military operation, but anyone with any knowledge of how Spec Ops worked would see through the smoke screen.

"Delta Echo is in place," Viking said into their earpieces, using the military alphabet to identify himself. "Leaders, report."

"Alpha Kilo in place," Alexei said. The rest of the team reported in.

Jace Kaiser came over the comm. "Prepare for fireworks, my friends. Juliet Kilo, over and out."

A moment later, the night sky exploded into light. Alexei and Blade waited to see who would appear outside the trailer they were watching. After the second explosion, James Dunn ran out the front door. Dirk was right behind him.

Alexei lifted his weapon. Blade's hand came down on his arm, gripping it hard. "Not what we're here for, buddy. Not tonight. Let's get your girl."

Alexei pulled against Blade's hold for a second. Then he growled and dropped his arm. He could have taken the motherfuckers out with a tap to their heads and never missed a beat. But that's not what they'd been ordered to do.

He broke into a run, heading for the trailer. Praying Bailey was in there and that she was okay. If God would only let her be okay, he'd never ask for another thing in this life.

BAILEY STRUGGLED AGAINST THE CHAINS, uncaring that they cut her, and screamed as loud as she could. She feared it wasn't very loud. The building shook and someone else screamed nearby. Another woman?

"Help me! Please!"

Bailey couldn't stop the sobs that welled up in her chest and broke free. She wanted out of here so badly. She was angry and scared and the tears were coming whether she wanted them to or not. No matter that she told herself to stop, they wouldn't.

Suddenly there was a commotion in the building. Booted feet pounding against the floor. The entire building shook. Why did it shake? Dark shapes burst into the room where she was trapped, and she screamed again. One of the shapes rushed toward her, and she tried to shrink away.

Gentle hands landed on her skin. Tender hands. "Bailey. Baby. Oh God, baby."

She blinked and tried to gulp back a sob of relief. "Alexei?"

"Yeah, honey. It's me."

Yeah, so she cried harder at that revelation. Way to impress him with her strength. And then she just didn't care anymore. Who needed to be strong when you had someone else to do it for you? Sometimes it was okay to hand over the reins to someone else and let them carry you. There was plenty of time to be tough later.

Tender hands slipped over her, assessing the chains while he tried to soothe her at the same time. "Don't cry, baby. I got you. I'm getting you out of here. Promise."

If not for his voice and his hands, she wouldn't know it was him. He was dressed in black, with a helmet and what looked like a binocular thing on top that he'd shoved back when he'd rushed over to her side. His face was dark, and he carried a gun slung over his shoulder and an ammo belt that contained bullets and other things she didn't even know.

"Alexei. You found me. Thank God you found me," she blubbered. Was she even making sense? She didn't know. Her head hurt. Her body hurt. And she was still fuzzy, still not able to focus for very long without feeling nauseated. "Sick," she said. "So sick."

"I know, baby. I'm going to take care of you." He took something from his clothing and then she heard a snap and felt the chains give way. They were thin chains, like dog chains, and he was cutting through them. One by one, they fell away. He pulled them back, then shoved them off the mattress, cussing beneath his breath as he did so. She felt him ripping at the sheets, and then he picked her up wrapped in one. She didn't even care so long as she was getting out of here.

He cradled her close and strode out of the room. Another dark-clad man met him in the hall. He was also holding a woman in his arms.

"Objective acquired," Alexei said. "Copy that. Alpha Kilo out."

"Let's boogie," the other man said.

It was a strange conversation, but she didn't have time to figure it out because they rushed out the door and into the night. Bailey clung to Alexei, arms around his neck, face buried against his chest as he ran. She wanted to stay awake, wanted to enjoy every moment she had with him, but the pain in her body wouldn't let her.

"Love you," she muttered. And then a curtain dropped over her eyes and everything went silent.

Chapter 27

She woke to a strange beeping sound. And she was cold. Bailey tried to shift, but her body refused to move. Panic welled inside her and her eyes snapped open.

The room was white. She had an impression of machines and tubes before a face hovered over hers. A face she recognized.

Kayla.

"Bailey, oh my God—you're awake. It's okay, sissy. You're safe. You're in the hospital. They just have to check some things out, but you're okay. Can you hear me?"

Bailey managed to nod. She felt so sleepy. "Can't... move."

"It's the medication. It'll wear off and you'll be fine. But it's keeping you from feeling the cuts and bruises right now." Kayla smiled, but the smile shook at the corners. Bailey tried to frown, but it hurt to frown. Her entire head hurt.

"Alexei..." His name was a whisper. A cracked whisper.

Kayla jumped up and grabbed a cup with a straw. "Sip some water, sissy."

Bailey sucked on the straw. The cool water felt good on her throat. She wanted to smile to reassure Kayla—if her sister had reverted to calling her sissy, something she'd only ever called her when she was small and scared, then Bailey figured that Kayla must be worried sick.

"Alexei," she said again.

"He was here. He's been here the whole time, but you've been out for a while and I told him to go home and change and I'd stay with you. Figures you'd wake up while he was gone." Kayla smiled brightly. "He really does care about you. He didn't want to go, but he needed to eat and shave and get some rest. He looked like hell—handsome hell, but still rough."

Bailey closed her eyes. Alexei was here. He cared.

He cared?

"Ana?" she asked.

"She's with Miranda while I stay here with you. I swear she grew an inch overnight, Bale! You just wait until you see her again."

Bailey squeezed her sister's hand. Then she fell back asleep. The next time she woke, it was darker in the room. The machines still whirred, but she felt more alert. And she wasn't scared this time. She felt safe. And when she tried to shift this time, her body obeyed. Joy flooded her at that small movement.

She turned her head—and Alexei was there. His head was on her mattress. He sat in a chair beside the bed, bent over, forehead on his arms where they were crossed beneath him. His fingers were near hers. She stretched hers out, touched his.

He sat up so fast she squeaked. But then his fingers closed over hers and his other arm went around her head as he stood and leaned down to look at her. "Bailey? How do you feel? Are you in pain? Want me to get the nurse?"

She lifted her arm—it obeyed, thank heaven—and pressed her fingers against his mouth. His delicious mouth. His lips were soft and full, and she wanted to feel them on her body again. One more time before she and Kayla left.

"Alexei." She smiled.

He kissed her fingers, and then she traced them over his mouth and along his jaw. So beautiful. So strong.

"You scared me," he said, and she frowned.

"Scared you? Why?" Her voice sounded cracked again, and he picked up her cup of water, fed her the straw. She sipped until her throat was somewhat soothed.

"You had a bad reaction, baby. They injected you— Jesus, I hate to tell you this, but you'll hear it soon enough—they injected you with heroin. It should have made you high and euphoric, but you had a different reaction."

Bailey's blood turned cold. Heroin? Her entire life, she'd vowed never to try drugs. Never to drink. Never to be what her parents had been. And James Dunn had injected her with heroin. She assumed it had been James Dunn, though in truth she didn't know which of the two men she recalled seeing in the room had done it.

"You're okay," Alexei rushed on to explain. "You've been in the hospital for a couple of days. They've flushed it out of your system and taken care of your cuts and bruises. You had a bad blow to the head, but there was no internal bleeding or other damage. A slight concussion, but you're doing fine."

Bailey tried to remember everything that happened, but parts of it were fuzzy. She remembered cold water, being naked, James Dunn trying to rape her. But it hadn't happened because there'd been an explosion. Or she didn't think it had happened. Had it?

"I was naked. He was going to rape me…" She pulled in a breath. "Did he?"

Alexei's face showed more emotion than she expected. He closed his eyes, his jaw flexing as he gritted his teeth. Then he shook his head. "No. The doctors used a rape kit on you. The only, um, DNA inside you was mine. Which my command knows, by the way. My bosses," he clarified when she frowned.

"Are you in trouble?"

"No, not yet."

He smiled down at her. She could drown in that smile. But then she remembered that she was leaving and he wasn't planning to stop her. She dropped her gaze and tried to hide her broken heart. But he gently tipped her head up until they were looking at each other again.

"You need to know some things, Bailey," he said very seriously. "Are you ready to hear them?"

She didn't know where this was going, but she nodded anyway. When you had to pull off a bandage, it was best to rip it all at once, not peel it slowly.

"I have an unpredictable and demanding job. You got a taste of it the other night. There will be times when I tell you I have to go and I don't know when I'll be back. It could be days. It could be weeks. I'll call when I can, but it won't always be on a schedule. And then there's the possibility I won't come back at all. It happens, though not too often. We're well trained and well equipped. Best motherfucking military in the world. But I promise I will always come back to you so long as I have breath in my body."

Bailey tried to process everything he'd said. It hadn't been what she'd expected. But what did it mean? "Are you saying… are you telling me you want to date me?"

He frowned. "Date you? No. I don't want to date you, Bailey."

Her heart deflated as if he'd pierced it with a dagger. She tried to pull away, but he wouldn't let her. He forced her to look at him. So she did. She glared at him, angry that he would say all this shit—and then it hit her. The patience in his gaze. The determination. There was more here, and she needed to listen.

"I don't want to date you," he said, his voice soft. "I want to *be* with you. Right now. Always. I don't want you to leave. I want you to stay. I want you to move in with me, and hell, I want you to marry me someday, when you're ready. I want you to wake up with me and go to sleep with me, and I want to come home to you every night. And when I can't come home to you every night, I want to come home to you at the end of the mission."

Hot tears slipped down her cheeks as she stared up at him. He was blurry, damn him.

"I love you, Bailey Jones. I've never felt that way about anyone, and I don't know how to do this whole relationship thing at all, but shit, it's love. It's what I see when I look at the way Cowboy looks at Miranda or Money looks at Ella—hell, half my team is married or engaged, and every one of them is an idiot over the woman they love. So, yeah, I feel like a fucking idiot over you—and maybe this is too much right now, but dammit, I've been sitting here for two days praying you'd survive and planning to tell you how I feel the moment you were awake enough to listen."

His speech finally trailed off, and she kept on crying. Damn him. Damn the drugs they'd given her. That had to be the reason.

She turned her head away and pulled herself together as best she could. Then she glared at him. He looked taken aback. And crushed, which she hadn't intended at all. She gripped his arm. It was like wrapping her hand around solid iron.

"You idiot," she said, her throat still aching. "First of all, I love you. Second of all, why did you have to tell me all this right now when I feel like shit and look like death warmed over? A girl wants to be dazzling when a man tells her he loves her for the first time. You've ruined the fantasy."

"Jesus H. Christ, Bailey," he said in a whoosh of breath. "You scared the shit out of me. I thought you were going to tell me to go to hell."

She smacked him lightly. "Hardly. I knew I loved you the second you cradled Ana and took care of her when I had no clue how—"

"You did not," he interrupted. "You thought I was a man whore who'd knocked up your sister."

Bailey couldn't help but laugh. God, it sounded rusty. "Okay, fine. I thought you *were* a man whore. But when Kayla and I were talking that night that you went and got her from Virginia, and you came out of the bedroom carrying Ana—you smiled at me, and I knew."

He grumbled. "Well, I was a fucking idiot. I had to call my mother and ask her about her relationship with my dad. I told her about you and she pointed out that I'd never mentioned a woman before. So, yeah, I was trying to figure it out. But when I heard that Dunn was free? I lost it. When I knew you were gone? I fucking went crazy."

Bailey could still picture James Dunn tugging on his dick. Trying to make it hard. She shuddered with the memory. "What happened to him?"

Alexei's expression clouded. "Not enough for my liking. The Feds took control of the compound. Dunn and his fellow gang members are being held—*without* bond this time. It's a federal case now. The Kings of Doom are finished for good, like I promised. I just wish it had happened before they grabbed you."

Bailey closed her eyes as a wave of tiredness descended. "Stay with me," she whispered.

His lips feathered over her brow. "Always. Go to sleep. I'll be here when you wake."

Chapter 28

Three months later…

ALEXEI TOSSED his duffel into his truck and jumped inside, eager to get home and wrap his arms around his woman. The SEALs had just returned from a mission, been debriefed, and now they'd been dismissed. It was nearly two in the morning, and he couldn't wait to see Bailey. He was tired, dirty from the desert, still wearing some smears of greasepaint he hadn't gotten completely off, and he needed about six days' worth of sleep.

When he pulled into the drive, her car was there and his heart leaped. He hadn't called her because of the time. Kayla and Ana were there too, and he didn't want to wake any of them. Well, he wanted to wake Bailey. With kisses and caresses and, if he was lucky, some sweet lovemaking.

He paused before climbing out of the truck and texted her. Might not be a good idea to sneak up on her now that he thought about it. He'd been teaching her how to defend herself. Her and Kayla both. He didn't need to find himself on the floor clutching his balls while they smashed his head in with a baseball bat.

Her answering text was swift. *What? You're here? Now?*

Yeah. Coming inside in two seconds. Don't knock me over the head with a frying pan.

He hadn't even closed the truck door when the front door of the house was yanked open. Bailey came running outside and jumped into his arms as he dropped the duffel and opened them for her.

She wrapped her arms and legs around him and kissed him as he spun her around, holding her tightly. She wasn't wearing much. A tank top. No bra. Tiny panties that he planned to drag off with his teeth.

"Baby, I'm dirty," he said when she let him come up for breath.

She growled. "Oh, I sure hope so. I've missed you so much. I'm ready for you to be as dirty as you want."

He snorted. "Not what I meant, but yeah, I'm planning to be dirty, baby doll." He squeezed her ass, let a finger skate over her hot center. "I want to be in here so bad."

"Oh, you are getting in there. Immediately." She kissed him again, her tongue plunging between his lips, tangling with his. His heart hammered, euphoria soared in his veins. Love, sharp and hungry, filled him. If they weren't outside in the middle of the night, he'd unbuckle his belt and fill her right now.

"I missed you, Bailey," he said. "So much. You were all I thought about."

"Take me inside and make love to me," she gasped as he dropped his mouth over her throat, tasting her, needing her. Loving her.

He reached down and hooked the duffel onto one arm, slung it over his shoulder, and carried both her and the bag inside the house. He didn't want to put her down, but he did so she could quietly shut and lock the door. He left the duffel on the floor and let her drag him to the bathroom where she flicked on the shower and turned to start dragging his clothes off. She knew he wanted to shower first, bless her. He helped her and then ripped her top off and, remembering his plans to remove her panties with his teeth, dropped to his knees and pressed a kiss to her pubic bone through her silky panties. Then he dragged them down until they fell before spreading her with his thumbs and curling his tongue around her clit.

Her fingers dug into his hair. "Alexei—oh my God, I missed this so much. My fingers just aren't the same."

The thought of her rubbing herself into orgasm made his dick ache. He licked her into a shuddering orgasm and then rose, lifting her until she'd wrapped her legs around him again. He stepped into the shower, pressed her to the wall, and drove into her. They both groaned with the rightness of it.

"I love you," she gasped as he pulled out and thrust into her again.

"I love you too. So fucking much. I live for this, Bailey. For coming home to you."

Everything was right with her. So right. He hadn't known what was missing in his life until her. So he showed her as best he could with his body, and then he took her to bed and did it again before falling into a deep sleep that was filled with dreams of her.

When he woke, the sun was streaming into the bedroom and Bailey was fully dressed in jeans and a silky top with low heels that made her look so fucking sexy his dick started to tingle with interest before he was even fully awake.

"Hi, baby," she said, coming over and setting down a cup of coffee on the nightstand.

He pushed up on an elbow. "Is that for me?"

"It is. You want breakfast?"

"What time is it?"

"About eleven. I have class at one thirty, so there's still time to whip up some pancakes for my baby."

"Mmm, pancakes. One of my five favorite things," he said with a grin. "Any chance of getting my other favorite things this morning?"

She laughed. "Guns? Sure, I'll put one on your breakfast tray. You can clean it while you eat."

"Tease."

"Oh," she said exaggeratedly. "You mean the other things? Tits, ass, and pussy?" Her fingers went to the buttons of her silky top. "I might manage to provide those. Would you like a strip tease?"

"Does it end with your pussy in my face?"

"If you want it to." She laughed.

"Fuck yeah."

"You know," she said as her hands ran down her body and back up again, emphasizing the sexiness of her form. "I've retired my G-string and Velcro. But for you, I'll make an exception."

His dick was stone. He threw the covers off and let her see it as he wrapped his hand around its length. Her jaw went slack. "Oh," she breathed. "And there's one of my favorite things."

"You want this?" he asked, stroking himself.

"Desperately."

When it was over, when they lay beside each other naked, sweaty, and panting a little bit, Alexei reached for her fingers, grasping them. "Damn, you make waking up fun."

She rolled and threw her arm over his chest. "You still want those pancakes?"

"Hell yeah."

She kissed him and then got up to dress. He followed her lead, yawning as he shuffled into the kitchen. The sunlight was on her hair, highlighting the pale pink strands as she moved around the kitchen, grabbing a mixing bowl and the ingredients she needed. No boxed mix for Bailey. She made them from scratch, and he sat to watch her.

"Where's your sister and the pip-squeak?"

"Kayla's been taking Ana to a mother's-morning-out program while she works answering phones in a real estate office. She's getting on her feet, slowly but surely."

She no longer worried about James Dunn coming after her. Dunn and many of the Kings of Doom were behind bars. The club was disbanded, the compound seized by the Feds, and the girls who'd been trafficked were now free. It wasn't much more than a tiny dent in a huge problem, but it was something.

"Let's move," Alexei said, and Bailey stopped what she was doing to look at him.

"Move?"

"To a bigger house. Maybe one with an in-law apartment for Kayla. So she can have her own space but still be near."

Bailey looked hopeful. "I think that's a good idea. You don't mind moving?"

He shook his head. "Nah. Besides, I want a master

suite with a shower so I don't have to worry about accidentally walking in on your sister—or her walking in on us. Last night… Hell, I wanted to make a lot more noise than we did."

He liked that she could still manage to blush when he talked about the things they did to each other. "I did too."

"I like coming inside you," he said, just to see that blush deepen.

"On that subject, the implant is holding up," she told him. "In case you were worried."

"I wasn't. But I'm glad. I think a little pip-squeak of our own would be great. But maybe not yet."

"No, not yet. I need to finish nursing school first." She poured baking soda into the flour and started to mix in milk. "I got an A on the first exam in both my classes," she added.

"That's awesome, baby. I'm proud of you."

She smiled at him, and he felt almost unbearably happy. It was that simple. She smiled, his world felt right. Anything he could do to keep that smile there, he was doing it.

It was crazy how different his life was from just a couple of months ago. He'd avoided relationships. Run from any hint of emotion. He'd shut people out and kept them at a distance. Even his teammates didn't know who he really was. They only knew what he gave them, and that was only as much as he had to. Oh, he trusted them implicitly and they him—it had to be that way for them to survive—but that didn't mean they *knew* him. Because he didn't let anyone know him.

Until now. Until Bailey.

He stood, went to her. Slipped his arms around her

waist while she poured pancake batter in the hot pan. She made a soft sound in her throat and kept on working. He wanted to make love to her again—he always wanted that—but right now he was content to stand here and watch her fix pancakes. To simply be with her. Because that's what love was. Being.

"So while we're looking for this new house," he said as he breathed in her sweet scent, "why don't we make it official?"

"Official?"

"Marry me, Bailey."

She went utterly still. And then she turned in his arms, her eyes shining. "Alexei, I want that so much— but are you sure? It's only been a few months and—"

He pressed a finger to her lips to cut off the stream of words he knew was coming. Bailey was adorable. And practical as hell.

"I'm sure. Without you, I'm no good, Bailey. I didn't know I needed you until you showed up on my doorstep and accused me of fathering Ana. But ever since then— Hell, I can't live without you. You've ruined the single life for me."

Her eyes searched his. Then she smiled again, that smile he loved so much. "Yes," she said simply. "Yes."

Just like that, the rest of the pieces fell into place. This was real. This was love. And it was fucking amazing.

Epilogue

_____

Camel and Bailey's housewarming party was in full swing. It was late afternoon and the grill was smoking with meat. They'd just moved into a cute three-bedroom house with an in-law apartment in the suburbs, and today was the day they'd invited the team over to celebrate.

Blade sat in a chair by the outdoor fireplace and watched the dynamics of all the couples present. Viking and Ivy. Cage and Christina. Cowboy and Miranda. Money and Ella. And now Camel and Bailey. Not to mention that Neo was giving off a weird vibe around Kayla.

It was interesting even if completely foreign to Blade.

Bailey had a huge smile on her face as she walked up to Camel with an empty platter for the steaks. He took the plate and set it down, then wrapped an arm around her and kissed her as if his life depended on it.

Man, Blade would have never in a million years bet that Camel would fall for anyone. The dude was like a block of ice on missions. Nothing rattled him. Nothing until Bailey, that is. Blade would never forget the moment he'd squeezed Camel's arm and stopped him from killing those two bikers. Oh, they'd deserved it, no doubt. But it would have created more problems for HOT than they needed. Ghost had taken a chance sending them on that op in the first place, so they had to stick to the letter of their task.

But man, seeing Camel like that—it shook Blade up a little bit. Because his teammate had never been anything but logical and cool and utterly precise in all he did. Until Bailey.

Guess love did that to a man. Because Camel Kamarov was totally in love with the gorgeous woman clinging to his side. She even called him Alexei, which Blade hadn't known was his name until he'd heard her say it. Blade shook his head as he took a pull from his beer. Never woulda thought his stoic teammate would fall so damn hard.

But, yeah, if the woman he'd loved were chained to a bed in a bikers' brothel, Blade probably would have lost his shit too. It was bad enough that Blade had found another woman chained up like that. He'd been sick over it, but it had been strictly duty for him. He'd gotten her out and turned her over to the medics, and though he still thought about the sheer evil of it sometimes, he didn't know the woman and wouldn't even recognize her if he saw her again.

That's how it was supposed to be.

"Man, what're you thinking about so seriously over here?" Neo said as he ambled over and sank down, beer in hand.

"Nothing really. Stuff."

"Yeah, I hear you." Neo took a long drink of his beer.

"So what's up with you and Kayla Jones?" Blade said, going in for the kill. Because why not?

Neo jerked his head around. "What are you talking about?"

"You keep looking at her. She looks at you sometimes." Blade shrugged. "Just wondering."

Neo let out a breath and shook his head. "It's nothing. Just being friendly."

"Ah, okay." Friendly. *Riiight.* "So you want to get out of here in a little bit, head for Buddy's or maybe that new place down by the water? Maybe we'll find a couple of SEAL groupies, get laid—"

"Not really feeling it tonight," Neo cut in. Blade wanted to laugh but didn't. "I got things to do at home when this is over."

"Yeah, I hear you. Just a thought." He waited a couple of beats before speaking again. "Man, sure is a cute baby."

Kayla sat in a chair with little Ana cradled in her arms, feeding her a bottle and making faces at her. She was a gorgeous woman with a pretty face and lots of blond hair piled on her head in a messy knot. No wonder Neo was intrigued. But she was also a woman with a little baby, and Blade was pretty sure Neo wasn't ready for that kind of complication.

"She is a cute baby. Not too fussy, you know? My sister's kids cried all the time at that age."

Blade wouldn't know. He didn't have siblings. Didn't have any friends with babies. All his friends were right here. Well, some of the other HOT team members had babies, and he considered them his friends, but he didn't hang out with them very often.

"Hey, y'all ready for steaks?" Bailey said as she walked by with a steaming platter.

"Hell yes," Blade said as he stood and followed her to the big picnic table.

Everyone fixed a plate and they all ate and talked and laughed for a good couple of hours. There was a game of beanbag toss, some horseshoes, and a lot of laughter. When it was time to go, Blade thanked Bailey, congratulated Camel on his excellent taste in women, and headed for his Jeep.

He was halfway home and feeling weirdly out of sorts when his phone rang. He answered. "Yeah?"

"How was the party, Blade?"

He recognized that voice. His heart kinda squeezed in his rib cage at the sound of his commanding officer on the other end of the line. What the fuck had he done wrong to warrant a personal call?

"It was great, sir."

"Excellent," Mendez said. "Need you to come in, Blade. Ghost and I want to talk to you about something."

Holy shit. He'd fucked up now. Was it the fighting? Must be the fighting. But sometimes he had to blow off steam, and a good match could do that. He wasn't supposed to risk his body that way since he was a government asset, but sometimes... Hell, sometimes it was necessary.

"Yes, sir. I can be there in fifteen minutes, sir."

"We'll be waiting... And Blade?"

"Yes, sir?"

"Don't mention this to your teammates just yet."

"I, uh, of course not." Not telling his teammates implied he'd still be around to talk to them. Which was a relief. "I'm not in trouble, sir?"

"Not yet," Mendez said with a chuckle. "But you haven't heard the assignment. Or seen the woman."

"The woman?"

"We'll talk when you get here."

"Yes, sir. On my way, sir."

The line went dead. Blade floored the Jeep. An assignment. A woman. It didn't make a damned bit of sense. He laughed suddenly, exhilaration flooding his veins.

No, it didn't make sense. But that's what made it a challenge.

Bring. It. On.

About time things got interesting…

Who's HOT?

Alpha Squad
Matt "Richie Rich" Girard (Book 0 & 1)
Sam "Knight Rider" McKnight (Book 2)
Billy "the Kid" Blake (Book 3)
Kev "Big Mac" MacDonald (Book 4)
Jack "Hawk" Hunter (Book 5)
Nick "Brandy" Brandon (Book 6)
Garrett "Iceman" Spencer (Book 7)
Ryan "Flash" Gordon (Book 8)
Chase "Fiddler" Daniels (Book 9)
Dex "Double Dee" Davidson (Book 10)

Commander
John "Viper" Mendez (Book 11)

Deputy Commander
Alex "Ghost" Bishop

Echo Squad
Cade "Saint" Rodgers (Book 12)

Sky "Hacker" Kelley (Book 13)
Malcom "Mal" McCoy
Jake "Harley" Ryan (HOT WITNESS)
Jax "Gem" Stone
Noah "Easy" Cross
Ryder "Muffin" Hanson
Dean "Wolf" Garner

SEAL Team
Dane "Viking" Erikson (Book 1)
Remy "Cage" Marchand (Book 2)
Cody "Cowboy" McCormick (Book 3)
Cash "Money" McQuaid (Book 4)
Alexei "Camel" Kamarov (Book 5)
Adam "Blade" Garrison (Book 6)
Ryan "Dirty Harry" Callahan
Zach "Neo" Anderson

Black's Bandits
Ian Black
Brett Wheeler
Jace Kaiser
Rascal
? Unnamed Team Members

Freelance Contractors
Lucinda "Lucky" San Ramos, now MacDonald (Book 4)
Victoria "Vee" Royal, now Brandon (Book 6)
Emily Royal, now Gordon (Book 8)

Also by Lynn Raye Harris

To be kept up to date about all of Lynn's new books, sign up for her newsletter by clicking here.

The Hostile Operations Team Books

(Click on link for more info)

Book 0: RECKLESS HEAT

Book 1: HOT PURSUIT - Matt & Evie

Book 2: HOT MESS - Sam & Georgie

Book 3: HOT PACKAGE - Billy & Olivia

Book 4: DANGEROUSLY HOT - Kev & Lucky

Book 5: HOT SHOT - Jack & Gina

Book 6: HOT REBEL - Nick & Victoria

Book 7: HOT ICE - Garrett & Grace

Book 8: HOT & BOTHERED - Ryan & Emily

Book 9: HOT PROTECTOR - Chase & Sophie

Book 10: HOT ADDICTION - Dex & Annabelle

Book 11: HOT VALOR - Mendez & Kat

Book 12: HOT ANGEL - Cade & Brooke

Book 13: HOT SECRETS - Sky & Bliss

Sign up for my newsletter to be notified about all future releases!

The HOT SEAL Team Books

(Click on link for more info)

Book 1: HOT SEAL - Dane & Ivy

Book 2: HOT SEAL Lover - Remy & Christina

Book 3: HOT SEAL Rescue - Cody & Miranda

Book 4: HOT SEAL BRIDE - Cash & Ella

Book 5: HOT SEAL REDEMPTION - Alex & Bailey

Book 6: HOT SEAL TARGET - **Coming August 2018!**

Sign up for my newsletter to be notified about all future releases!

The HOT Novella in Liliana Hart's MacKenzie Family Series

HOT WITNESS - Jake & Eva

7 Brides for 7 Brothers

MAX (Book 5) - Max & Ellie

7 Brides for 7 Soldiers

WYATT (Book 4) - Wyatt & Paige

About the Author

Lynn Raye Harris is the *New York Times* and *USA Today* bestselling author of the HOSTILE OPERATIONS TEAM SERIES of military romances as well as twenty books for Harlequin Presents. A former finalist for the Romance Writers of America's Golden Heart Award and the National Readers Choice Award, Lynn lives in Alabama with her handsome former-military husband, two crazy cats, and one spoiled American Saddlebred horse. Lynn's books have been called "exceptional and emotional," "intense," and "sizzling." Lynn's books have sold over three million copies worldwide.

To connect with Lynn online:
www.LynnRayeHarris.com
Lynn@LynnRayeHarris.com

Made in the USA
Columbia, SC
13 May 2018